OTHER NOVELS BY YVES NAVARRE IN ENGLISH

Sweet Tooth
Chronos' Children

Our Share of Time

Yves Navarre

Our Share of Time

Translated from the French by Dominic Di Bernardi
and Noëlle Domke

The Dalkey Archive Press, 1987

Cover photograph by Harold Chapman

ISBN: 0-916583-17-1
Library of Congress Catalog Card Number: 86-72136

Publication partially supported by grants from The National Endowment for the Arts, a federal agency, and The Illinois Arts Council, a state agency.

First Edition

*A novel is not told. It is lived.
To each his own feelings, footfalls upon a bed of pine needles.*

1

When it happens you don't expect it. You don't expect anything
anymore. You lose your head for just a second and someone walks into
your life, turns it upside down, tenderly, brutally, making a place for
himself. Even before anything has happened it's already too late. You
can't tell who is choosing whom, when, how, why. You only know these
things later when everything is over and each person holds the other
accountable for what has gone on. And if I tell you about what
happened last summer with a young man, it's not to tear him apart.
What we lived through together for such a short time tore us apart; it
was vibrant, exhilarating, violent—and pathetic. But I must tell the
whole story through to the very end. Not to shirk it off, but to bear up
under it, something new to wear for the days ahead.

Nothing can make sense of how senseless unhappiness is. Grown used
to this need we have to understand everything we too quickly forget—
because of all the breaking up, breaking down, breaking hearts when
things come to an end—that there were moments of sharing and
selflessness, moments of—for want of a better word—happiness. These
moments are irreplaceable.

I'm forty years old. I live in Paris. I'm gay. I teach French literature.
And I am all too familiar with literary tricks not to be on guard, from the

word go, against a too self-conscious virtuosity: all I want is to tell what happened in the plainest, most straightforward way, to head straight for my goal—this boy. Because I loved him. Too much, too perfectly, too imperfectly, you'll see for yourself. And because I still love him. But did I ever really know him?

And if I speak to you directly as if you were here, listening to me, I have a reason: within the mystery of these pages, the silence of these signs, the twists and turns of these lines, I am hoping that you will love as I have loved, that you will live as I have lived, that you will examine your life the way I am still examining mine. Literature has produced too much literature for itself and by itself, defining its own structures and styles, its objectives, fashioning and refining its arcane rhetoric. Matters for literary cliques. Literature has forgotten how to live. This is my first novel.

Of course, this is autobiographical. But I'm not dictating it into a tape recorder and I won't make it smell sweet like a bar of soap. Where does the story end, where does the novel begin? This is the tale of my outburst. Had we forgotten how good the struggle felt, how rough it was? How senseless. How happy I am: I am not alone anymore. And everything is beginning again.

I have an apartment in the Batignolles section of Paris, on the third floor, no elevator, with an unblocked view of the courtyard on one side, and of the open trench of the Gare Saint-Lazare train yards on the other. Yes, I did say trench because when I first visited the place seventeen years ago (I had just passed my examination and been appointed to the high school of the Butte, where I'm still teaching)— when I leaned out of the window of my room-to-be and looked down, my head began to spin. Suddenly, the ground dropped away twice the height of the building; and then there were those rails in perfect rows. Those days there were still a few steam engines, and streams of smoke crawling along, tattering and fading away, passing obstructions: the lines of the tracks reappeared all the more straight and gleaming. Sometimes I saw the slanting rays of the noonday sun strike the bottom of this trench and make the metal sing like a sword's.

In this neighborhood there's a church where once a year you can still see girls making their first communion in white lace dresses. The church stands on a square where men used to pick each other up at night by a pissoir. There were police raids. Roving thugs and muggings. You really couldn't tell after a while who was defending whom, and from whom. Those were times when tender nights could end up in tragedy. Toward the end of the sixties, a body was found one morning, stabbed to death, completely disfigured. Without any pants on. The pissoir was torn down. Like all the pissoirs in Paris. They planted trees in their place. During the day on the square around the church mothers gather with their children, baby carriages, babies, and there are old people on the benches who don't say a word, to anyone. In this neighborhood pastry shops are open with a passion on Sundays, the bread is as crusty as the bakers themselves. The grocery stores belong to Algerians and are as cluttered as open markets. Home delivery. Across from my building, there is a bar, The Lizard. The owner has a white Ford Capri convertible. My name is Pierre. I almost forgot about the shoemaker. In the window of his shop he put up a sign: "Only Real Leather."

The facade of the building was cleaned. The staircase is spotless. You have to wipe off your feet twice. Once before going through the lobby, so you don't leave footprints on the tile floor. And again, after crossing the courtyard, because every step of the staircase is waxed. I never put up my name on my apartment door. Courtyard staircase, third floor, that says all you need. I rent the place.

Four small rooms. A dining room and a living room on the courtyard side, a bedroom and my study on the train-yard side, and a hallway in between. Off to the side, near the front door, there's a bathroom where you can easily get black and blue, and a kitchen where you have no choice but to stand up straight and without really moving turn your whole body around to fix meals. A year and a half ago I had the wall between the dining room and the living room torn down: this new room became my study. And my former study, a spare bedroom. Why, for whom? I was hoping someone would arrive. At last. To stay a while. I'm formally declaring my identity, or at least, the identity of the story to come. A year and a half ago, for my thirty-ninth birthday, I realized that I did not fit into my apartment very well. To work in, I presented myself with the largest room. For the days ahead, I created a guest room. For my friends. Although I was making ready only for one. Quite a chance to take. The same chance I would take at night heading for the square. Not knowing what to expect. That time of my life when encounters were abrupt, abrasive.

A year and a half ago, before the renovations, I sorted out my possessions. I filed away, threw away, put away—good riddance. I said good-bye to cheap souvenirs, to the unavoidable odds and ends, to clothes I had stopped wearing long ago. Haphazardly I crammed everything that might remind me of the years gone by into large plastic bags—meetings on the sly, short-lived expectations, Roger, Antoine, Loïc, Jean-Pierre, friends, lovers, companions, postcards, snapshots, address books, gifts that I held onto because you must never throw away a gift from a friend. What friends? What faces? In the name of what feeling, long gone, gone away?

The apartment is painted white. The wall-to-wall carpet is dark blue. I had the living-room chimney cleaned and ever since, in the evening, I light a fire. For sixteen years the fireplace screen had not been lifted. In my library I was quite content to keep only the books I had loved, more or less in the order I had read them. So there is my desk, and across the room, the fireplace. A sofa, a round table with four chairs, houseplants, music, and two bedrooms. Mine. And someone else's, longed for, soon to arrive. He arrived. His name was Duck, a nickname. His name is Duck. He passed through. He is still here: I am writing.

My parents live in Saint-Mandé, in a bungalow with a French-style gravel lawn around it. My father, a retired engineer, diligently watches his television programs. As for my mother, she has once and for all given up making the fourth at bridge when they have friends over. She knits baby clothes for my elder sister's younger children, whose older children have already entered college and voted for the first time last year to the Right or rather to the Center like their parents. And so on and so forth.

Jeanne, my elder sister, lives in Le Havre. Her husband went to the Naval Academy. She just had her fifth child. Françoise, my other sister, lives in Saint-Cloud in a high rise. Her husband went to the National Institute of Technology. She has six children. I'm the godfather of one of Jeanne's daughters and one of Françoise's boys. I don't see much of my family. They don't ask me anymore, "When are you going to get married?"

In the summer they all get together at La Baule on the Boulevard des Pins in a house called Blue Skies. I still remember a few sailors at Saint-Nazaire, the year I got my first motorbike. And I would go to the Bois Poulinguen to let myself be fondled. Or sucked behind the old city walls of Guérande. I was sixteen. I thought I was leading a totally authentic life. I had nothing to confess to my family. Nothing worth mentioning. And now I don't see my relatives much anymore. Or rarely. When they call me up they ask, "I'm not interrupting anything?" And so I've created a life for myself off to the side. But I'm not removed. They are still there. Saint-Mandé, Le Havre, Saint-Cloud, La Baule. I have to write these lines with them in mind. You can never really change. And even as I talk about them, a tenderness grips me in the pit of my stomach, a hollowness, a hunger. I am one of them. They are still making the decisions. All the more so because their lips are sealed.

And Duck will hold this silence against me.

In my building, courtyard stairway, second floor on the right, I have a good friend, Marie. We live one floor apart. We go to the movies together. She is a layout designer. She's my age. She's the one who comes to water my plants when I'm out of town. On the ground floor in the main building, on the left, there's Mariette. She makes fancy hats for theater productions. She is eighty-two. Marie does Mariette's shopping. Every day I drop by to say hello.

Mariette, Marie, and Pierre. I don't think the other tenants know each other. If I tell my own story, it will also be the story of my two friends, and of the others, all the others, everybody, who knows? Even if the details of my family background establish that I am not just anybody—

Naval Academy, Institute of Technology, beautiful suburbs, conventional marriages, votes fluctuating from Right to Center, and the intellectuals on the Left burrowing into the soil, proliferating and depleting themselves, castes, cliques, clans. Mariette makes hats. Not one actress or set designer has ever invited her to see her creations on stage during a performance. They've always forgotten about complimentary tickets. And the hats are beautiful. As for Marie, she does the layout for brochures and industrial journals. Sometimes when I talk a little too late into the evening with her, at her place or mine, she utters, as a way of saying goodnight, the same short statement: "The elder stem is medullary." From the Latin *medula*, for *marrow*. A botanical term. Used to describe stems having a thick pith. And so time goes by. Mariette's hats, Marie's layouts, Pierre's classes, from Ronsard to Baudelaire, from Montesquieu to Camus, the last three years at the lycée, I am a well-respected teacher. Every morning I exercise for twenty minutes before going to school. You only notice you are growing old by the way other people look at you. And having young men you love see you grow old is unacceptable because as the years go by you are less and less accepted. In the very beginning with Duck, I thought we were only as old as the time we spent together, a few minutes, a few days, nothing at all.

I took out a mortgage on a tiny house in the heart of a village along the Rhône, opposite Mont Ventoux. Three cramped rooms, no garden, and women for neighbors. I have been spending my summers there for the past ten years. Alone. The name of the village is Peyroc.

Quick, quick, the story. It's at the tip of my fingers, I don't want to waste time in introductions, setting the scene with too much detail, telling everything about my life beforehand. And what if the story exposes me the way Duck might have exposed me if he had stayed, a little while longer, if we had won each other, from each other, for a little longer while? When trains go by, bound for the suburbs, the building shakes a little. But I want to live in the heart of Paris. In the heart of my story. When it happens you don't expect it. You don't expect anything anymore. You lose your head for just a second and someone walks into your life, turns it upside down, tenderly, brutally, making a place for himself. Even before anything has happened it's already too late. You can't tell who is choosing whom, when, how, why. You only know these things later. When everything is over. And the same thing happens all over again. Always. End of the warning. The very beginning of everything. To be continued. Chapter two. The Nikko Hotel. A few days before meeting the young man, Duck.

2

I don't know what got into me that morning. A Saturday morning. It was a long weekend with Monday off and a hint of something in the air which was invigorating and made the chestnut trees break into blossom. I had not gone south to Peyroc for these three hollow days, partly out of laziness and of being afraid to find out I'd be even lonelier there than in Paris, but even more because I had papers to correct. And then again, there was something in the renovated apartment that was unfinished. I hadn't put back the paintings and lithographs and drawings or even the posters in the bathroom. This absence of images bothered me as if everything about the white walls brought me back to myself, cloudy mirror, glossy pages upon which I cast no shadow. A feeling rose up and took hold of me. I was not written. Nor even being written. I did not exist. I had lived a whole stretch of time, the first thirty-nine years of my life, letting myself be diverted by my surroundings, my family's values, the rigors of my profession, the secret rites of my nights, encounters coming out of nowhere and leading nowhere, and by the joys of reading, listening, seeing, going out. In fact, I was averting myself.

And all around me the bourgeois mentality, as dynamic as it is deadening, generating a shadowy sensuality during those nights on the prowl, was so organized that it was able to conceive of nothing that might break the numbing rhythm of an uneventful life. Or nothing more than trivial events, bumps, bruises, scratches, not anything you could call a real wound, if you think about it, unless it's the wound of loneliness when it becomes more and more a matter of solitary confinement. Growing old doesn't help. And age, for the men who share my darkness and my night, is all-important. The way you look determines the way they look at you. Chance meetings are also diversions.

I had taken down the paintings. And I missed them. The sudden bare space of the walls made me uneasy. I had just spent the night correcting a whole pile of papers. It was dawn. So dangerous to get a whiff of a Saturday dawn in the springtime. Marie had gone to visit friends in Chantilly. Mariette was staying with her sister in Chateauroux. I had the double duty of watering Marie's flowers on the windowsill and of feeding Boubou, Mariette's cat, who is deaf, blind, old, so old that he has to be placed in his litter to pee. These things tied me down. But I made no plans to see anyone and something told me the phone wouldn't ring.

The two bedroom doors were open. The morning sunlight was shining through the hallway. On the courtyard side it was cool and dark. Children were playing with a ball. The woman on the first floor, main building, was cleaning her four windows with meticulous care. From my study, I could see the guest room with its brand new bed and brand new sheets. Nobody had slept there. Three months had gone by. In the mail, there was only a letter from the First National Mutual Insurance of Paris with a four-page form for their records and all kinds of requests for the exact dates due for my payments and if there had been any changes in my financial situation. Questions about my private life, including the exact nature of my supplementary income. But I don't have any. To find out the dates I had to wade through batches of administrative nonsense. And my head began to spin as on that first day, leaning from my open window above the trench of the railway yard, gash of the long-distance trains. I don't like being forced to organize my life by using codes, registration numbers, notarized documents, summonses, last notices and bills.

And I know I am taking a very big risk, for all this is quite ordinary. But the prelude to a meeting is sometimes as important as the meeting itself. And heroes are not necessarily heroic. If there is anything glorious in this story it will only be found in plain everyday happenings. And that's how, on that Saturday morning, I decided to go away, once and for all, far far away, as anonymously as possible. I was neither depressed nor particularly tired. It has occurred to me, since then, that one does not necessarily decide to commit suicide while under emotional duress or in the midst of a crisis. The decision comes simply, almost spontaneously, hardly a decision at all, triggered by nothing more than realizing that all these years have gone by which have never quite measured up to the years you have yearned for. You want to step boldly into the life of your dreams, a dream of a beautiful selflessness, yet you never manage to cross the threshold. Until you stumble upon a hotel door. For me it was the Nikko Hotel.

And it's a funny story. It makes me smile. Let the smile it brings to my lips show that there is nothing remarkable about my case.

I carried the idea of suicide around with me, a little like a game. For three years now, whenever I had a chance during my visits to Saint-Mandé, to Havre for a baptism or dinners with friends, I would steal all kinds of dreadful drugs, of the "Do-Not-Exceed-Prescribed-Dosage" variety, from their medicine cabinets after locking the bathroom door— supposedly, to wash my hands. I concocted my "Satan's Brew." As Marie would say, "A romantal and sentimentic idea." The poison of classical tragedies. But it was only a game. A child's memory? At seven, they took me to see the Cocteau film *L'aigle à deux têtes*, a matinee showing at a movie theater near the Madeleine. Because I had made the honor roll that term: it was my reward; and my mother wanted to buy coats for Jeanne and Françoise at the Trois Quartiers. The Empress in the film had poison concealed in her rings.

At about nine in the morning I left the bare-walled apartment. I was carrying a shoulder bag, which had at the bottom the bottle with all the pills. I stopped by Marie's to water the plants and Mariette's, to pet Boubou, put him in his litter box, wait a bit, and leave him enough food for two days. When I came out of the building, the owner of The Lizard was spraying his Ford Capri with a hose. It's illegal on this street. But it just wasn't any Saturday. It was a long weekend, the first of the year. I even kicked a ball and the children playing with it laughed because I had joined in their game, awkwardly. My mind was elsewhere. I had the self-confident gait of those who don't know where they are going. Or know only too well.

I walked down toward Saint-Lazare, the Opera, the Grands Boulevards. I was telling myself things such as, "I was not born where I wanted to be," "When all is said and done, I've had some wonderful times," "I used to like my job in the beginning, but now, you see, they don't listen to me," "No one ever really cared about me. Marie and Mariette won't hold it against me. Françoise and Jeanne are going to inherit what I have." I was speaking out loud to myself as I walked along. I am sure that passersby thought I was eccentric. But I wasn't really looking at who was going by. I had no particular destination and I wasn't wandering aimlessly.

I headed for the Molière fountain and the Comédie Française, which Marie calls the "Tragédie Française." Then I crossed the Louvre gardens. The Pont des Arts was "closed indefinitely, for repairs." I went back to the Pont-Neuf. On the Vert-Galant, the tip of the Ile de la Cité, there were bare-chested young men stretched in the sun on the banks and a girl who was playing the guitar. I had lunch on the rue des Canettes. I decided to go to the Bon Marché. I saw trucks carrying away rubble in front of the Lutetia swimming pool. The sign was half torn down. In the showers of this pool, those days when I had mandatory physical education and on the Thursday afternoons of my childhood, I saw naked bodies, immense, magnificent, under the water and through the steam, hands lathering skillfully, and stiff penises. I can't remember clearly if I was lured or if I did the luring, who seduced whom, but in the stalls I let myself be taken and I also did the taking. It was long before Saint-Nazaire, Le Pouliguen or Guérande. Long before Blue Skies. The swimming pool smelled of chlorine, tiles, and the underground dampness. I went back home drained, white, scoured, expertly moulded. No one suspected that the well-behaved, perfect child that I was could escape watchful eyes and surrender himself more completely than he ever would again in his life.

I stayed a long while, contemplating the Lutetia swimming pool. They were draining it completely like a deep abscess. A sign announced the forthcoming construction of a shopping center containing sixty stores. I stood there, fascinated by the trucks loading and unloading. I went to a nearby café to drink a cup of tea. They served it in tea bags and it was tasteless. After that, I got lost on the rue de Babylone, behind the Invalides. The Rodin Museum had just closed. I walked toward the Military Academy. I passed under the Eiffel Tower. Seeing it from underneath, its four paws spread wide, almost made me smile. There were tour buses around the Trocadero fountains. I decided to head for the high rises along the Seine; I wanted to get a closer look. And then I found myself on the doorstep of the Nikko Hotel. With my shoulder bag. The bottle at the bottom of the bag. My mind made up. The sun had just set. The idea to end it all, there, in an ultra-modern Japanese hotel, tickled my fancy. "Do you have any luggage, sir?" and "That'll be how many nights?" I answered evasively with a smile, with a slight touch of boldness and gave my address in Peyroc. No one showed me to my room. The elevator was like all elevators and the hallway carpet like the ones in the Hilton hotels. On the doorknob, I hung up a "Do Not Disturb" sign, which was written in English and Japanese, the only distinctive feature of the hotel. I latched the door from the inside. I turned on the television, the picture without sound. And I gave the room the once-over. Except for an engraving depicting a pagoda in the spring, nothing really stood out. There was nothing special about the room. A comfortable place. Indifferent.

I stayed in the bathroom and in the bath a long time. The suds overflowed. I wet all the towels drying myself. I wanted to be clean and neat. Since my body was not necessarily what it had been, I had to treat it with special care. I am neither handsome nor ugly, my hair is neither short nor long, my eyes neither blue nor green, they take on the hue of the pullover, I am neither tall nor short, my chin is a touch determined, I have a scar on the shin of my left leg (I bumped into a low table in Saint-Mandé some ten, twelve years ago), I am neither blond nor dark, no distinguishing features, nothing exciting about all this. You take a last look at yourself. Smiling vaguely, without bitterness in the mirror above the sink. You turn off the bathroom light and walk into the bedroom.

Just then I got hungry. I ordered dinner and a bottle of good wine. I waited forty minutes. They wheeled it in on a cart. I signed for it and gave an extravagant tip. Completely out of line for someone earning a teacher's salary. The waiter said "Enjoy your dinner" with a heavy Spanish accent. I checked to see that the sign was still in place. And once again I latched the door from the inside.

Curtains drawn wide open. It was dark outside. From the twenty-third floor, it wasn't Paris anymore but a city constellated with lights, absorbed in the task of above all not caring about other people and other things. And so much the better. It was someplace and nowhere. I turned off the television and the bedroom lights. It was nine in the evening. The meal was sitting there. I wasn't hungry anymore.

I was thirsty. So I drank the wine with the pills. Three by three, like the stairway steps when I am rushing home. In fact I wasn't hungry anymore because I was afraid of throwing up the poison from Saint-Mandé, Havre, and from so many homes belonging to those I thought were my friends. I couldn't afford to botch my last act. I blamed no one. I had planned everything to the last detail. Then the thought that someone might knock at the door to take back the cart prompted me to throw the food into the toilet, to crumple the tablecloth slightly, to stain the napkin and to shove everything into the hallway; checking the hanging "Do Not Disturb" sign one last time, I latched the door from the inside once and for all. I was unsteady on my feet. The pills were taking effect. I collapsed onto the bed, naked, arms spread out like a cross. I was laughing. This was it. I would never have suspected it would be like this, the day before, when I left school.

White, like the white of walls. In a blur, a pagoda in the springtime, a picture, and a smell of chlorine on the skin, and rubble, all jumbled together. Children singing as they stroll along, behind pinewoods, fragrance of classrooms, the sound of turning pages, the rustling of leather jackets in gay night clubs, streams of smoke, Marie's laughter, my mother's knitting needles clinking together—I saw white, everything horribly white. I heard sounds, melodies, I breathed in the air and the wind, I sniffed at sweet scents, odors, stenches, like a blind man I touched bodies, hips, chests, skins, but I saw nothing. The only rational thought I had that night was when I told myself I wasn't seeing anything, that I was seeing white because no one had ever really opened his eyes to see me. White. I saw white. Everything was swaying. The Nikko Hotel rocked back and forth, a metronome. And soon, the rhythm was broken. Nothing left. I won. So long. Farewell.

When I opened my eyes again, I was still lying flat on my stomach, my right cheek against the sheet, between two pillows. I moved the fingers of my left hand. I was cold. I was "tuckered out" as Madame Vérini in Peyroc would say, deliciously numb. It was light outside. The pale light of the earliest hours of a morning. I laughed, just like that, in my head. My lips were cold, as if frozen, motionless. I couldn't feel my feet anymore. My knees hurt. My stomach was hard as a rock. Then I coughed and I really woke up. I didn't move. I couldn't. My head started to spin, bursting with questions. What day was it? A day later? And the school, classes, I had classes. How long had I slept? The Satan's brew was too strong, the poisons from Saint-Mandé or Havre ineffective. Here I was. Back. Nobody would ever know. I blew it. No fuss. And it's funny.

Gradually I caught my breath. I moved one arm, then another. I pushed the pillows out of my way and lay on my side, looking out on the city, rubbing my arms for warmth. Quite near the hotel, down below, was the elevated train; I watched for the approaching cars but none came. So it wasn't yet five in the morning. I had plenty of time to pull myself together. And everything seemed predictable. Predictable aposteriori. The papers were corrected. Marie's flowers were watered. Mariette would come back from Chateauroux and would simply find that Boubou had peed a little everywhere. Or else she has come back already, and so has Marie. Tuesday night, I have a date with Bernard. He is coming for dinner. He is a nurse in a suburban hospital. He has broken up with a man he had lived with for six years and he has had it with all the big questions. We have been seeing each other for two months regularly every Tuesday, that's all. "That's all and that's a lot," another of Marie's expressions. I was saying all this to myself that morning after that Saturday at the Nikko Hotel.

Around six o'clock, the clock built into the night table ticking away, I was able to get up. I took a shower, then a bath. I didn't dare look at myself in the mirror above the bathroom sink. I didn't have anything to shave with. I ordered breakfast. I couldn't swallow anything solid but I drank some scorching hot tea. And I got dressed.

It was only when I paid the hotel bill, for three nights, that I realized it was Tuesday morning and that I had slept the whole time. The cashier jotted down my identity card number on the back of my check, as a safety measure. I looked a mess. But I was happy. It was seven o'clock in the morning. I had time. All the time in the world. Ahead of me. All the time I needed, once again?

In the cab, I looked at Paris, the streets, boulevards, the avenues when life starts up again after a long weekend, this notorious first long weekend of the year. There were leaves on all the chestnut trees. A soft green. And this blue sky rising, beckoning. Now and then the driver glanced at me in the rearview mirror. "So, the Nikko Hotel is really something?" I shook my head no. "Should I drop you off at the corner of the rue de Rome or should I go around by the city hall of the seventeenth arrondissement?" I answered "Rue de Rome" with a smile. All I'd have to do is cross the bridge, enclosed by a rusty railing bristling with barbed wire at the top, overlooking the railway yards and the packed morning trains passing by, disappearing, one after another. People don't throw themselves from bridges anymore. At any rate, not from this one. They can't anymore. To get up to my apartment, I tried to take three steps at a time. But I couldn't.

At 9:15, I was at school, clean-shaven, neat, pale. And that Tuesday morning, my students listened to me with their eyes fixed upon me. Wonderingly. And that evening, chapter three, Bernard came to have dinner at my place as usual. I had given back the marked papers and taught every class. Two days before Duck.

3

This is really an unremarkable story, but it's mine. You attribute extraordinary destinies to people, so as to better consign others to silence or oblivion. You only attribute to beings who contribute nothing in return. Don't expect me to sidestep the matter. Don't make accusations too quickly. I will accuse no one. Time casts its own judgment, that's enough. It unites, reunites, separates. Time is working with us, dreadfully. But there is greatness, here, now. The horse-chestnut trees of the square no longer know if they should be expecting girls making their first communion or remembering a man stabbed to death, his nose in piss, guts spilling out, a beautiful job by some punks from the Porte de Clichy. There is one thing that will never be taken into account by theses or political programs such as they are formulated and flaunted, and that is meeting people, meeting someone, bumping into someone, finding happiness without any calculations or plans. Waiting expectantly, as well as coming upon disappointment or an embrace: meeting someone.

The misunderstanding has lasted too long. You miss the point. You're no longer listening. Listen. I can't stand speaking to deaf ears anymore. And neither can you. "I understand it all!" the scholar says, with elation and bitterness. What all of them are after is power, wallowing in the grief and understanding of all things and events. They know everything about everything, there is no room left to chance, and they lend support to each other. They set the poor against the rich, the haves against the have-nots, the innocent against the cunning, the old against the violent, and as for the violent, they strike in a vacuum. They set everything against everything and each person stays in his place. That's what they're after. On the Right as well as on the Left, fanatics, they wear themselves out giving their lives to a faith which has been lost, denied, rejected, forgotten, grown suspect. They continually re-establish the order of dictation. They dictate. Oppression no longer means gagging people but forcing words out of them. And we'll all remain, more or less, with a suburban bungalow instead of a heart, and, all around, gravel which, trampled down underfoot, makes the same sound for everyone. Bernard grabs me by the back of the neck: "I don't understand what you're saying to me." He takes off his jacket, unbuttons his shirt collar: "I'm tired. I just worked an eleven-hour shift. Only ten minutes for an apple at lunchtime. How pale you look. Kiss me." He kisses me.

It's the seventh time that Bernard has come over for dinner. We both know that each successive Tuesday constitutes something close to a feat. We met at the West Side, late, one night, a little before closing time when they turn the lights back on and begin emptying the ashtrays and collecting the beer bottles. That's when you see the real faces. The eyes. You feel a little uneasy about still being there with the others, like the others, the chance meeting not having occurred. The artificial chance of gay bars. You feel as if you're in a costume, jeans and jacket, looking a little on the prowl, or blasé. Bernard, that evening, said to me, "Quick, let's split." We came back to my place. And we made love methodically, skillfully, from foot to head, forgetting nothing in the inventory of recesses, soft spots, hairs, touches, bites, and he only playing one role brutally, sealed, planted on top of me or bent between my arms to give himself more fully. Light-headed, fulfilled, in high spirits, two hours later we decided to see each other again. "Next week?" And so on and so forth. Marie already knows. On Tuesdays, she doesn't come knocking on my door. She waits for Bernard to leave, keeping her ears open for his footsteps on the stairs and calling me up, "You'll introduce him to me?" "Not yet." "He's the one for the guest room?" "Certainly not."

Bernard is a butch, a genuine butch. He accepts his role and plays it without affecting the mannerisms of the opposite sex. He doesn't come—"being taken is enough for me"—and he never closes his eyes—"they all make love behind their eyelids, I'm sick of it." He has an honest, good-natured laugh. "I'm not boring you, I hope, by saying things like this?" And if I keep quiet, he pinches my shoulder and whispers, "What are you thinking about? the eternal question, but that's part of meeting someone. So, what are you thinking about? Tell me!"

It's a simple ritual. He arrives. We don't say much to each other. Work, rain, school, hospital, verbal ping-pong, always the same remarks, and, quickly, we undress to lie down, on a blanket, in front of the fireplace. "And don't forget, tonight, to give me the title of the record that you always put on. I want to have it at home." At home? He lives in Gennevilliers. It's more convenient for the hospital. A two-room apartment in a recent building. "I've a twenty-year mortgage." He smiles. "I'll look like what in twenty years?"

I remember all those remarks of his. I keep them within myself like sweet tokens. I hold them back, then like fresh water, I set them free on this page. Everything must be as clear as water flowing from its source. I don't have to show any affectation either, and following Bernard's example, I want to accept a role, a single role, neither executioner nor victim, neither good nor bad, but only myself embodied in these sentences to receive a caress. "You OK?"

That Tuesday, Bernard takes my face in his hands. He shakes my head. "But what's happened since the last time?" My only answer is a smile. He bites the tip of my nose and it makes me laugh. But suddenly, on our knees, facing each other, a blazing fire in the fireplace, and our shadow thrown upon the ceiling, I have the feeling that Bernard is swaying back and forth dangerously, a metronome, like a tower, in the night, and I with him, inside. Then we stretch out and with an infinite precision we caress each other. He repeats, "You OK?" and gradually we find each other again, one and the other, the body of one, the body of the other, as we look at and touch each other and moisten each other as need be. Deep within, I think there is no greater mystery and no more fundamental discovery within our grasp than that of the other, through the body, his fingers, his arms, his skin, his openings. Nothing more vast nor more tender than the palm of a hand, the sole of a foot or the curve of a knee. How to manage to forget nothing? Folds and hollows, lips, tufts of hair, saliva, the heart pounding, and the body, all stretched out, before you, when you sit up to get a full view of the other. Naturally, I've often thought that. But that Tuesday, Bernard's mouth had a different taste, and his sex, even his chin. Even though for so many years I defended myself against becoming the victim of taboos and interdictions, the slave of this idea of sin linked to the prowess of the body, I had never tasted someone from so close, and so skillfully, my eyes so wide open, my tastebuds so alive, and my grasp so sure. Maybe because I had just screwed up my exit. Maybe also because Bernard wanted me as much as I wanted him. And with him, I felt secure. Seventh time. "And it gets better and better every time, don't you think so? You're not saying a word? Oh, Pierre!"

Fragile, our meeting made no demands. It made its savour all the more powerful. Bernard surprised me because in him I found a place for myself and felt it fit me comfortably, physically. Need I be explicit? The gloomy, haughty mind resents being spoken to about the body, even though everything begins there, the place from which we've come. And the glair is the same, at that moment, as it is later, when we return there, there, and there. So many births for nothing, and these orgasms like a plea. Bernard grows worried: "Tell me what's wrong?" He questions. So, to defend myself, I'm going to make him speak. We sit down at the table. The other meal.

He unfolds the paper he has just bought to "kill time" in the metro. Laughing, he reads to me, without pausing, the main headlines. "Jérôme Would Often Fall, Admits the Mother-torturer of Bar-Le-Duc"; "Chinese Premier's Stupendous Flying Trapeze Act"; "He Had Money, a Job, Friends, and He Murdered without Any Motive"; a pope who declares "Stand Up for the Family and Defend Yourself against Divorce and Abortion"; a president of the Republic who asserts, " 'The Most Significant Phenomenon for Youth Is the Mediocrity of Our Politicians' "; a prime minister who confesses, " 'Too many ministers are vile flatterers. In one party as well as in the other, those in political office are so incompetent that they leave free rein to the government' "; and a communist party which discovers that "the pursuit of pleasure, of sexual fulfillment, the refusal to accept any social inhibitions provided they respect individual freedom, opens up a field of discovery to changing mental habits, to which the present offers landmarks without setting boundaries." On page four, Bernard goes on: "Old Lady from Vitry le François Is Dead, Devoured by Her Fourteen Dogs." The last sentence of the article: "Marguerite Voiron died in total indifference, but also in a solitude she had chosen. With a profound hatred toward human beings. Marguerite Voiron's fourteen dogs have been gassed." Final period. Bernard folds up the paper. He smiles and leans toward me. "I'm hungry, how about you?" He takes my left hand and bites it. "And it kills time. If I buy a paper, it's to find out where they're at, where we're at, what's going on. And more and more I see the insanity of words and facts, from bottom to top, everywhere. He offers me the paper. "You want to keep it?" I saved it. Today it serves as evidence.

Undershorts, T-shirts, bare feet under the table, sitting side by side, a round table, soup, steaks, salad, cheese and fruit, Bernard pours the wine. "Drink, it will put back some color in your cheeks." He sets the bottle down on the table, frowns: "What did you mean when you were talking about continual reestablishment of dictation?" I lean toward him. I grasp the medal he wears around his neck and which never leaves him. "What's written on it?" I read: "Neither compel me nor prevent me." Bernard takes my hand, puts it back on the table. "Eat. Or else everything will get cold, as they say in upper-middle-class houses, middle-class houses and middle-middle-class houses." He laughs. "It's my family's motto. A present from my mother. Neither compel me nor prevent me! After all, that's the answer you didn't give my question. All right?" Two sips of wine. "Are you satisfied?" A smiling pause. "What are you trying to make me say, anyway? It's nice together? Isn't it?"

I ask him why. "Why, what?" "Oh, well, your friend and you, you lived together six years and then you broke up. How long ago?" "Two months." "How?" "One evening I found my suitcases on the landing, I had forgotten that it was not really our place, that it had remained his place." "Any reasons?" Bernard smiles. "Yes, some grievances." "Tell me about it." "His name is André. He is your age. Nine years older than I. I met him in Greece, one summer. On a beach. I was traveling with someone. He too. I decided right away that he was the one. I did say, *decided*. We exchanged addresses. When we got back, I saw him again. I had a room in Paris. He lived on my way to the hospital where I was doing my last year of training. So I got into the habit of sleeping at his place. It was easier, in the morning. And then I moved in, but I don't quite remember when. All I can say is that the first three years were good, for him as well as for me. All we could see was what was pleasant and comfortable. We were really free. We had each other, that was enough. He is personnel director in a factory which manufactures ball bearings. I'm in physical therapy for old people, paralytics and incurables. You wouldn't believe how many cancer patients I see in their terminal stages. But the evenings were nice and weekends and vacations. The first three years. The fourth and fifth, we more or less repeated the first three. I didn't listen to him like before and vice versa. When we went out, he would look around, and me too. Little presents didn't have the same charm. And little gestures, little nothings. Don't make me talk . . ."

Bernard bites into an apple. "The second of the day!" He empties the bottle of wine in my glass and in his, the last drops for me. He laughs. "And so now, you'll be getting married!" He wants to clink glasses. And here we are going tchin tchin. "Put the record back on, will you?"

Music. Bernard spits out a seed, wipes his lips, moves his chair back, legs stretched out, his hands locked behind his neck. "In fact now I must tell you the whole story to the very end. A year ago, everything started to fall apart. Fits of irritability. Of impatience. He is the one who advised me to buy the apartment, near his place. He even took care of everything so that I'd get credit. My parents helped me too. And then André's parents were beginning to have their doubts about the two of us. And doubt for them is like a sedative when they begin to acquire too much evidence. André went out alone, and so did I. Often, in the morning, for breakfast, there was no bread. André had forgotten to buy any, so had I. Multiply this little kind of detail and you'll know the truth, if there is one. Two months ago, he went out. I went out. He came home before I did. And surprise, my luggage on the landing. No choice but to go to my apartment. Since then, he calls me all the time. As a neighbor. But I've decided to let him sweat it out. I did say *decided*."

Bernard gets up, takes off his T-shirt and undershorts. Kneeling in front of the fireplace, he lights the fire. I put away the dishes, the knives, the forks and the glasses. Bernard says loudly, as if I were far away, "And now, I'm settling into my place. I'm buying everything, little by little. There was only one bed, not even sheets. Not like your guest bedroom." I push the chairs in around the table. The music, a little louder. Bernard holds out his hand to me. "Come!" And here I am again, on my knees, before him. And if I speak of Bernard, this evening, two days before Duck, it's because there is no real passion except for subjects which don't look like subjects, apparent flimsiness under which, like a sliver under a nail, pain can arouse the mind. Nothing is dictated. Everything is listened to. "Here!" Bernard places his medal around my neck. "Only for a while. Until I leave." He kisses me. "Get undressed, come on, faster than that." And as we burst out laughing, we roll around on the blanket, in each other's arms, our eyes wide open. The fire is crackling.

"I want to come." "Don't hold back." I saw the Nikko Hotel and Bernard spoke to me. I forced him to expose himself even though he was the one asking me the questions. That's where terrorism begins, the subtle terror of couples when the one who has everything to say keeps quiet and the other, trusting and stubborn, lays himself bare. I came. And it gave me as much pain, Satan's brew, as pleasure, nothing rocked back and forth anymore, everything was in its place. Seated with his legs crossed on top of me, Bernard reaches out with his hand and caresses my lips. I kiss his fingers. He smiles. "So then, you don't want to say anything to me?"

In the shower, he shouts, "Put the record back on! And jot down the title on a scrap of paper, otherwise you're going to forget again!" I execute the order. I fold up the blanket and put a log in the fireplace. Eleven o'clock in the evening. Everything is unfolding very quickly and very pleasantly. While drying himself in the hallway, he drips a little on the carpet. He glances into my room. "We've never made love on your bed." Then the guest room. "I don't get it. When you've someone in your life, you share the same bed. André, he was a real pillow. A genuine featherbed."

Bernard or the others, he among so many others, and myself among so so many in my life. And when I think about our love affairs, I tell myself that nothing really sets them apart from each other. Perhaps that's where my subject lies, my presence in this text. Anyway, seeing everything from the outside, the most narrow-minded people to the most indifferent want to set things apart from each other, point out with their fingers, belittle. They have such a keen sense of humanity and intelligence that they have forgotten what pertains to the human and the senses. No, you won't prevent me from writing this novel to the very end. It will flow from its source for those who like to dive. And bathe. Reading what you praise, judges presiding over confusion, literary hacks, dictators of junk, I tell myself that for people like you, the only order that can exist for you is the established order. And every day, in every class, when I analyze these classic texts which you so often ridicule, disorder, fortunately, is reestablished. The disorder of passing time, or time passing headlong, mystery of the noble feelings which you think you have banished, disgraced, and which irritate you in your present time, in the idea you formed about the present. Only an idea.

Bernard takes the medal back and slips it around his neck. "And who are *you* waiting for, do you know?" I answer, "Someone . . ." "What kind of someone? Why? When I think about it again, I regret nothing and I regret everything. Nothing when everything between André and myself was relaxed, with no problems. And everything when André and I started calculating. Calculations are the beginning of schemes. At that point, everything goes wrong." Bernard falls silent. He gets dressed. He takes the title of the record I have noted down on a piece of paper. "You shouldn't have made me talk." He shrugs. "It was fine between us. It was good enough the way it was."

I put away the blanket. I slip on a pair of pants and a shirt. I am barefoot on the carpet. Bernard looks at the books in the study. "You've read all this?" I nod yes. "I don't read, or very little. But I admit it." He looks embarrassed. He goes over and sits at my desk, in my armchair, his hands flat on my files. "One thing is for sure, it's that you and I will never be unemployed. I with the dying, and you with your students." He laughs.

And I laugh with him. I place myself behind him, my hands on his shoulders. He throws back his head and I kiss him on the forehead. A masculine kiss. A brotherly kiss. Or just a kiss. For his embarrassment and for mine. Then I close my eyes. And I tell myself that it's over. That Tuesday, our last Tuesday.

And it's not sad. It's the way it is. Bernard gets up, walks into my bedroom, then into the guest room, like a tour of inspection, his hands clasped behind his back, it's an act. Then he takes the paper again and, standing in the main room, he reads other titles: "Nationalism for Sheep" . . . "Prevent the Irremediable" . . . "Poignant Appeal from the Amnesty International" . . . "The Cult of Continuity" . . . "The Red Cross, A Sick Old Lady" . . . "Captains of Industry Assess Their Positions within Society" . . . "Unions Demand Participation in the Responsibilities in Industrial Reorganization." Bernard drops the paper on the floor. "Enough." He smiles. "It's crazy, all they can dig up in one day. For nothing." And me, with my hands in my pants pockets, I am cold, the cold of the Nikko Hotel, and I am sleepy, the other kind of sleep. I lower my head and look at my feet, one on top of the other. Bernard draws closer, takes me by the chin and forces me to look at him straight in the eyes. He whispers, "See, we shouldn't have talked."

On the desk, he notes down his phone number. Another scrap of paper. "This time, it's up to you to call me. For another Tuesday. Whenever you want. Whenever you'll feel like talking too." As he leaves, he says to me, "Thanks for dinner." He rushes down the stairs. "And see you soon!" That was two days before Duck. It was a quarter to midnight. Marie came up to see me. Chapter four. The links of the chain.

4

"It's happened." "What?" "He's on the way." "Who?" "Him."
"Who, him?" Marie leans back against the door, places her hands on
her stomach. "I'm expecting a baby." She kisses the forefinger of her
left hand and places it on my nose. "And don't ask me whose it is." She
walks into the kitchen. "You look awful." She runs water into the sink.
"I'm going to do the dishes. It's very good for conversation."

"My flowers? You only came to water them once. You didn't stop by
Mariette's this evening?" A dishtowel around her waist serving as an
apron, Marie rolls up the sleeves of her pullover and pours just what's
needed of detergent into the water, the right amount. She has a theory
about detergents that kill. "Try as you might to rinse three or four times,
there is always a little left that you absorb, afterwards, when you eat."
Marie has theories about everything. As a joke. Speaking about her
now, the story would turn into a romance and become romanticized.
She breaks in, here, with the news of a baby, and that's exactly how it
happened. I had hardly had time to catch my breath when she was
already in the kitchen doing these dishes which she "hates most of all to
do. Worse than vacuuming!" I stand in the doorway. No room for me.
Kitchenette. She says, "Don't move. I'm going to explain everything.
Even if these kinds of things can't be explained. But I am so very happy.
I must tell you everything." She leans over, scrubs the dishes, rinses

them and places them one by one in a dishrack. She laughs. "As though you could tell everything." She turns toward me, winks, smiles ironically, then gets back to work. "You really do look awful. It also strikes me that your young man left more quickly than usual. He went down the stairs four at a time. Is it over with him?"

Marie has very short blond hair. She is small, slight, with a good figure. She has freckles at the base of her throat and on her arms. She placed her three bracelets on the refrigerator. Sam's, Jacques's and Bertrand's. Occasionally her sentences will begin with "nothing to do with Sam, Jacques & Bertrand, but I loved this film because it moved me," or sometimes with "he's a man of the Sam, Jacques & Bertrand type, so I said good-bye and good riddance. Right away." I write *& Bertrand* because on her night table, in Marie's bedroom, there is a cloth-covered notebook on which she has written, very ornately, with beautiful letters, bright red, the title of the novel which she'll write one day when she "has the time" and which will tell the story of these three love affairs. "For the time being, it's too close to reality, the cover is enough." As a layout designer, she confesses, "I like the *&*, like that, *&* is a link. It links all three of them. It binds them to the stake. They'll stay put until the time comes when I'll treat them the way they treated me." I've never met any one of them. Marie moved into her apartment seven years ago, right after Bertrand. Since then, I've seen her have brief affairs. She lives her life. I live mine. We keep track of each other, to a certain extent, and we pretend to tell each other everything. We often get together, for the simple pleasure of being together. Françoise, Jeanne, and especially my brothers-in-law think she is my "hidden mistress" and that one day "who knows, you little sneak." It's their way of speaking and defending this sacrosanct idea of "good family" which "guides and binds" as Marie says. Mariette, on the other hand, and it touches us, is convinced that one day, Marie and I will get married. "Are you listening to me?"

"Good." Marie throws the empty bottle into the trash can and rinses the two glasses with elflike efficiency. A playful voice. She turns her back to me, and this is no doubt what lends her a little of the self-confidence which charms, surprises, and arouses suspicions when a person is caught red-handed in his confession of happiness. "Three months ago, a little after Christmas, I decided that the year would be really new. Like you with your renovation, your brand-new apartment." She turns around, a quick glance. And she leans over again. Another dishtowel to dry the plates. "Only I chose to redo the apartment within and to treat myself to what Sam, Jacques & Bertrand had been unable to give me. Or rather what they ripped off from me. No comment. You know how they rip off babies in cases like that? And every time, kaboom, Prince Charming finds another place for himself."

The plates in the cabinet, the knives and the forks in the drawer. "I gave all the men in the office the once-over at the studio. And I picked him out. His name is Tadzio. It's a ridiculous name, but it's a hunk of man who wears it. He comes down from generations of slaves who rowed for centuries in the Mediterranean. I say this because he has huge hands, grey eyes and black curly hair. He is married. Three children. At the studio he is the big shot of the Publicity Department, billboards, sign boards, displays. But that's all he can ever talk about. On his desk, there are snapshots of his vacations, sand castles, a family portrait. It's touching. Everything you dream of. In short, I picked him out. Nothing easier. No one ever took any notice. Very tactful. Exactly what he'd been waiting for for years. For three years maybe. It all took place at the Modern Hotel, near the Place des Ternes, at lunch time. Never the same room, what do you expect in those kinds of hotels? A small point of honor, I paid the doorman, every other time. And these rooms are as gloomy as cardboard boxes. I didn't say much. And above all, he didn't understand why, suddenly, I gave myself over to him, a little bee. He let himself be plundered. I'll never forget the sound from the boulevard and the drawn curtains, the towel lying on the bed and the light bulbs hanging in the bathrooms. So much for atmosphere." Marie drains the sink and cleans it. "He knew nothing about my plan. He still doesn't." Marie wipes out the sink with the dishtowel, washes her hands and turns around to me, and it seems there's a small tear of joy in the corner of her eye. She smiles. "And he'll never know. But since this evening, five o'clock, in the waiting room of the gynecologist's, browsing through *Jours de France*, it's certain. I have my pregnancy calendar. I set it on the night table, in my bedroom, in place of the Sam, Jacques & Bertrand notebook. Are you happy?"

Marie folds up the dishtowels, puts away the salt shaker, runs the sponge mop over the floor. She washes her hands again. "The dishes are done. And I feel good. I am carrying a stowaway. When you're forty, you have to be careful, it may be the last crossing. So you have to make up your mind. I made up my mind. It's happened!" The kitchen is tidy, spic and span. "Shall I get things ready for breakfast?" She pinches my chin. "Don't look so glum, you're not the daddy." And I kiss her on the forehead, leaning down a little, as I always do when we say good-bye. We go into the main room. She laughs. "The pope's the one who's going to be happy. Did you see, in the newspaper?" Here we are in front of the fireplace, sitting with our legs crossed. "I'll have to let out all my pants." We look at each other, like two children. "Now, tell me about your weekend." Silence. She takes my hands and squeezes them tightly. "Don't you want to?"

It was a sweet moment of complicity. One of Baudelaire's lines came to mind. "My cradle pressed against the bookcase . . ." Marie was here, at my place, with her news, her decision. "By the way, I'll leave my bracelets with you. I've also decided to go bare-armed. Symbolic? Nostalgico-comical? And if you're thinking about giving me any presents, give me books about expectant mothers, precautions and happiness all included." She leans toward me and stretches out on the floor, her head on my lap. "At what time do you work tomorrow morning?" I answer "Eight o'clock" in a very low voice, as if I were afraid. Marie whispers, "When all is said and done, I know nothing about you, you know nothing about me. Or so little. Maybe that's what friendship is all about." She closes her eyes and curls up. "Can I stay another few minutes?"

That brief moment lingers on, short-lived happiness. What strikes me about Marie is the naturalness of what she does, her spontaneity, this good nature constantly flirting with unhappiness without ever drowning in it. Marie is fragile and determined, alone and a loner, carefree and incredibly caring. Now, she's quiet. She presses against me, hugs my knees. I tell myself she's going to cry because so many scripts are imposed upon us. We live them beforehand. Anticipated situations. And once again, I think about the dictation, Bernard's leaving, his phone number on the desk. Another Tuesday? Certainly not next Tuesday. We have "talked." You must silence the Andrés, the Tadzios and the others. Other lives. And focus only on your own. Marie takes a deep breath while staring into the fireplace. "I've turned off the heat at my place. You too?" "Yes . . ." "In Chantilly, there was a smell of spring in the air. A powerful scent. In the old days, when I was little, it would go to my head. This weekend it got me in my womb."

Marie gets up. "Ten after midnight. I'm off. Tomorrow we're having dinner at Mariette's. It's a special occasion. She insists on it. She wants to celebrate what's happened. She is convinced that the baby is yours. Say something to me, anything, at least a glance, a smile?" I didn't know what to say.

In the doorway, Marie turns around. "I don't intend to tell my parents about it. It would cause hysteria in Biarritz. My brothers? I'll let them know as late as possible. They'll pretend to be mad, the way the Landes farmers get mad. Deep down, they think it's very funny. For them, Sam was Jewish, Jacques a communist, and Bertrand, too trendy. This time, they'll have no chance to be jealous of the father, and the father won't have the responsibility of supporting a son. I'll take the responsibility on myself." Marie opens the door. "Yes, it'll be a son!" A giggle. "We'll see about the first name." On the landing, a little wave good-bye. "And if it's a daughter, we'll decide at the last minute. Everything but Marie. It's too much of a burden." Little peck on my forehead. "See you tomorrow?" "See you tomorrow." "What's your first class about?" "*Polyeucte.*" "Poor kids."

Marie goes into her apartment. I go into mine. I see myself again paying the bill at the Nikko Hotel, coming home, classes, students' eyes, suddenly, that day, attentive ears. I see Bernard again, lying down, his head arched, all spread out, and I am astonished by the fragile nature of desire when it cannot outlive speech. I see Marie again, placing her hands on her belly, beaming with the news. I hide the three bracelets under my pullovers. Naked, on my bed, my hands locked behind my neck, I stare at my bedroom ceiling. History, even if it is bloody, even if it is tragic, can be less serious than you think. And everyone's personal history too. Happening in our trite and hazardous present. Duck was drawing near and I didn't know it. Everything was falling into order for the disorder of his arrival. His breaking in. That evening, that Tuesday, Tuesday night into Wednesday, I peered into the night, listened intently to the sound of freight trains, the rumble of the first commuter trains. The first glimmer of daybreak. I felt open and ready, at last. A dizziness. The day would go by, go by, until dinner at Mariette's.

5

Mariette's apartment, ground floor between the street and the courtyard, smells of ostrich feathers, ribbon, dust. Mariette closes the shutters every day at six in the evening, summer or winter. "Too late or too early, that way I see the seasons go by. Before, Boubou would take advantage of it to get away. Now he's too old, like me. He looks around inside. That's all. Isn't that right, Boubou?"

Marie did the shopping for dinner. I brought the wine and a cake. From one room to the other, you have to thread your way between hatboxes, baskets of petersham, skull caps, hat skeletons, bags of braids, tassels. Everything is scattered around on the chairs, on the sofa beds. There is a small, narrow bed in each room. And a clock that ticks differently in each room. Three different times of day. "It's like the three of us," Mariette said one day, "we don't have the same conception of time and will never be set to the same hour. But we love each other."

Mariette has a high-pitched, delicate, brittle voice, a thread about to break. Mariette has a voice full of laughter, a laughter approaching a scream. "My men have always held that against me—my voice. The ultimate insult when they left me. They would say, 'And anyway, with that voice of yours!' " Occasionally, at the movies, at a restaurant, or summers in Peyroc, when she visits me, Marie imitates Mariette and we laugh about it. But that's only because we miss Mariette. Mariette is our ant. She hoards, and holds us close. Looking innocent, she listens to everything and forgets nothing. This evening, as she clears off a table to set the dishes, she rants, "Chateauroux is a ghost town and my sister doesn't have her wits about her anymore. I wonder if she even recognized me. She kept repeating the whole time, yes mamy, yes mamy. It's insane, at seventy-nine! Seventy-nine! She was the youngest of the five of us. Anyway, I did my good deed. That is what you used to say, isn't it, Pierre, when you were a boy scout?" Marie answers for me, "Yes, Mariette. You're right. But Pierre never was a boy scout. Right darling?"

Like a game. A toy doll's dinner. Marie prepares the meal. Mariette takes out the silverware and the fine glasses. I pet Boubou. Here we are around the table, I uncork the wine, I fill the three glasses and we make a toast. Mariette looks at me, and then at the other, and tells us in a clear voice, enunciating, as though sharing a secret, "I know, Pierre, that you are not the daddy. And with good reason. I also know, Marie, that you'll love this baby. I hope so. At any rate, here, tonight, with you, in my home, I feel very good. Even if you're the ones who prepared everything. Even if I've left things in their usual mess. I know all that. Because friendship is not a matter of conscious choice. It's a matter of expression." Mariette raises her glass, takes a sip, then another. "It's a very good wine. Thank you."

"I don't want to embarrass you and above all . . ." Mariette falls silent, looks at us, her eyes full of concern, sets down knife and fork, wipes her lips with a napkin. "But here I am saying sad things to you." She smiles. "Whereas I should be telling you inspiring, cheerful things. Come on, Pierre, you're a bad wine steward!" Once again I pour wine, and we raise our glasses. Mariette glances around, her setting, the boxes, hatboxes, baskets, bags, rolls of tulle and gauze, pin cushions. Clinking her glass, she laughs: "To my family! Straw hats, military caps, turbans, fur hats, sun bonnets, head scarves, sombreros! They even requested fedoras, for a music hall, and they never looked soft enough, from far away. The stage manager always told me everything should be judged as seen from the highest balcony. That only from up there things could be seen as they are. And I never forgot that. Even though I still don't understand it."

"It's just like waiting. I can't believe how both of you expect things to come to you. All the time. And I can tell you, I have sewn enough velvet, plush, silk, straw and felt plush, even cardboard during the war, women had their foreheads sawed in half, I have done enough stiffening, patching, steaming, ironing, smoothing to have the right to give you a small piece of advice: don't wait anymore!" She laughs. "And it's funny. Don't wait for anything, anymore, never again, don't expect things anymore, at any time. Nothing is ever really given. Like your baby, Marie. You have to steal. And you have to hold on. And above all, keep moving, keep moving if there is still time. As for me, from now on, I'm like Boubou, I stay where I'm put. I'll never go back to Chateauroux."

Marie glances at me. Mariette is having a good time. Boubou is sleeping in a box of pompoms. You can hear the juke box from the Lizard bar and from time to time the click of the entrance door to the building. I slice the cake. Marie holds out the plates. Mariette fixes her bun, white hair, then she straightens her brooch, at her neck. She is wearing her finest blouse. Mariette is frightfully thin. When she stops talking, you look at her and you see her such as the years have sculpted her, eroded her. A mere nothing would shatter her. Marie and I anticipate her every last gesture. And yet she leads her life when we're not with her. She gets around. She has visitors. She still gets orders. On the sewing machine and all around, she has work in progress. And, shrill whisper, a thin trickle of sound, hanging in the air, she tells us, "Mariette is not my name. It became my name. We were three friends, three apprentices in a dress shop, in the beginning, in '36, when we took this apartment. The neighborhood was classy and convenient. The building was brand-new. We each had a room, a bed, and we'd work in one room, or the other, everywhere. There was Maria, Henriette and I. My real name is Renée. I am the *r* of Mariette. Maria went back to Sapin in '57. Henriette died in Volvic in '59. I kept on going, all alone with our name. And I think everything always goes in threes. Like us this evening. And I had never told you about that before. You always think you've said everything but you always forget the most important. You even forget what you dreamed about. When I was a little girl, I would have liked to become a lawyer's wife and to live until the first of my great-grandchildren got married. It was the idea *I* formed about *my* life. It was an ordinary sort of dream. I have no regrets. Only I haven't quite succeeded." Mariette smiles at us. "And what about you?" Silence. "What about you, Marie, and you, Pierre?"

Marie starts talking about Biarritz, her parents' wool and baby clothes store, the vacation she spent at her grandparents' in the Landes and about her older brothers who wanted to become farmers and "repossess their lands." Marie stresses the word *repossess*. Everything was due to them. High school, in Bordeaux. She lived at her cousin's house. And Paris, inevitably, afterwards, "to escape from the wool, the baby clothes and the manure. I wanted to become a reporter. And travel. And then, bam, I went to a school of design. Because Sam was in that school. You know the rest . . ." Marie helps herself to more cake. "And you, Pierre? You never speak about your parents. And I know you're going to answer me that you still think about them. As I do."

I'm not recomposing the past. The past proposes, that's all. It listens. All you have to do is listen. Memory discriminates, molds and high-lights. Come forward people, come out from behind your masks! Mariette, Marie and I have doubts about the other: the third one is always isolated. It's our way of paying attention, the very beginning of affection. A precaution so the relationship lasts. And surely this is what is most important, and not the commotion of news reports and life's side-shows, spectacular moments which fill up the chapter of daily life, the grind of fleeting success. Mariette starts humming, "My name was Renée, and I didn't meet any lawyer . . ." We laugh. Marie imitates her. "My name is Marie, I'm expecting a baby and he will be haa-ppy . . ." My turn? I take Boubou in my arms. I hold him in front of me, above the table. Then I place him on my lap and caress him. "Come on, Pierre, sing, it's your turn." Mariette leans toward me and places her hand over mine. Her fingers are like needles. "Please." I think I am blushing. Like the child from Saint-Mandé, long ago, long ago . . . Marie gets up, collects the plates. "Let him be, Mariette. He is like the clocks here, fast or slow compared to the other two? We'll never know!"

At the doorway, Mariette repeats, Mustn't wait. Got it?" She smiles, she'd like to be mischievous. "I have made too many hats not to tell you my truth: there's nothing but hypocrisy. Everybody lies, nobody really loves. People only buy lies. And even then, only when the lies are fun!" Good-bye. Good night. On the third floor landing, I kiss Marie on the forehead, leaning down as usual. She pinches my chin, her favorite gesture. "Isn't it true that you too dreamed of another life and that you're not quite living the life you wished for?"

6

The Nikko Hotel, Bernard, Marie, Mariette, Polyeucte and Boubou. Duck can arrive, the ground is mined. You run after the horizon. A shadow thrown behind, a shadow which carries you forward, carries you away, ahead. The first can be seen, the other can't. It leads, it abducts you. Time is passing by, there is no more time. One day, you count up the years. What's left?

My name is Pierre Forgue. I was born in a bathtub, lathered by my older sister. Jeanne and Françoise were commissioned to take care of me, at the end of the day. I was their doll, the little brother, the baby of the family, their pride and an object of jealousy. I made them into rivals and they quarreled to find out which one would get the washcloth. The other one had to make do with the bar of soap. First they splashed me with water and then they fought, ripping the washcloth from each other's hands, the bar of soap slipping away from them and sliding on the tile floor of the bathroom. They shrieked or giggled, I could never tell the difference. One would have to create the verb *shriggle*, shriek and giggle, for them. And meanwhile, standing, naked, in the bathtub, I shivered. I was three, four years old. It was during the war. The soap smelled like ivy. And I liked being scrubbed by the washcloth, behind, "little pig," and in front, "Don't go pee-pee." I had a penis like a comma. Françoise and Jeanne, laughing, pulled on it. Hard, very hard.

They called it "playing with my little lady." I never cried. I didn't defend myself. One day would come when they wouldn't play with me anymore. A detail. An utterly trivial detail? Yet, every time I lather myself, in the shower, my sisters are there. They tug at me. I do everything possible to silence the memory because theoretically, it's not significant. But there it is, in the washcloth, behind, and in front. The original sensation.

My name is Pierre Forgue. I was born at the table, during a formal dinner. The obligatory soup, summer or winter, neat and fresh vegetables, cheese and salad, pie, fruit and often sweets. You have to sit up straight and never say a word. To ask for something is dangerous, to refuse something is insulting. All sentences must begin with "please." My sisters bubble over with laughter together. There are strange pauses between my parents as they look at each other, or even worse, as they avoid looking at each other. There is an emptiness between which makes my head spin. I suspect they only love each other because we're there, and they're not always happy to have us with them. My sisters amuse them because they're a pair. But as for me, I am just here, sitting in my place. I have a whole side of the table to myself, my father to the left, opposite me, my sisters and my mother to the right. I am the referee who keeps silent and waits for the end of the game to fold up his napkin and retire to his room. A maid, never the same one, there's a new one every six months, will bring the coffee into the living room. When there are guests, we dine in the kitchen. There were trees and lilac bushes in the garden. My father had everything cut down at the end of the war "because of the dampness" and "so sunshine would flood the house." Sunshine in Saint-Mandé? Sometimes I am instructed to rake the gravel and I do it, meticulously, sort of the way my sisters do their hair, relentlessly with mommie's brushes. Duck, you never knew about that. And this is what you met. I reveal it to you today, at the risk of justifying your silences. Tenderness, ambiguous, cannot be explained.

Forgue, Pierre, Henri, Emmanuel. Emmanuel means *Jesus with us*. I discovered the theater at church. And music. And perfumes. I came to know the tediousness of sermons you understand nothing about, and the danger of high-sounding rhetoric. It still holds me prisoner. I live with it. I struggle against it. My father gives us some money for the collection. My mother paints her lips red as well as her fingernails and toenails, a bright red which fascinates me. At mass, she is beautiful. I look at her, but she doesn't see me. I am too small. The baby of the family. I am still there, begging, on tiptoes. The five of us, on our knees for the offertory, nicely skewered, our heads bowed. And coming out of church, the light makes me blink. I want to throw up. I restrain myself. They would take me to see doctors. However I don't want anyone to know anything about the stabbing awareness within me.

I still haven't escaped. What about you, my friend? you all? Who can dare lay claim to the contrary? This claim, this lie, sells well. It entertains and enriches the analysts and the analyzed.

That's what I tell myself, today, as I lay myself bare. That's what I told myself, a year ago, that Wednesday, one day before meeting him. The text records, an inventory. It beckons also, an escape. As one escapes, in the darkness of sheets or in the daylight of pages. They still have a hold on me, with their gravel, their layers of red, their cut lilacs, their silent exchanges and all sorts of dictated fears. Above all, we were never supposed to complain, and with a good reason, we had everything. And we had nothing, nothing but pretty pictures, the kind good pupils receive. We weren't hungry. Everything was raked, clean, neat, trimmed. For the collection? We already gave. I was born in a savings bank. Safe.

Now I take off my makeup, to make my entrance on stage, with Duck. I do everything backwards. I seek out the inside-out and the upside-down of everything. I scrub my face clean so that everything can begin, begin once again. I formally declare my identities. It's all in the face.

I was born as a property owner, in a family of property owners, and I share their frame of mind: I will always be their property. I am made of "this thread and this fiber," as Mariette would say. As for Marie, she says that I was "born like a ready-made layout." These are only passing comments. I have never let myself be treated as a subject by the two of them or anybody else. I slip away without excusing myself. By too persistently refraining from treating other people as objects, I got caught in the snare of passion. There is this one thing reasonable about feelings, it's that you are in the driver's seat. And you sit up straight, as at the table or at mass. Passion, on the other hand, at the wheel of a runaway truck, drives you wildly in every direction.

I was born from the punches I received, in school yards, because I was always the youngest in the class. And I'd punch back, blindly. I hit haphazardly. Once, the school nurse took me back home. I can hear her tell my mother, "Your son shows signs of epilepsy." My mother answers, "It's impossible, there have never been any cases in our family." Farce. Family pantomime. Then I chose, for years, to stay inside during recess. At the end of the school day, I was the first one out. I scurried away. "Hey, Forgue, little Forgy, little faggot, little sissy, you're going to go crying in your mommy's skirts?"

No chance. I was born from the bedroom of my childhood, from its shadows and its mysteries. I was born from the nights of wide-open eyes, wide-awake dreams, and the first wet dreams. I have this bedroom in my head. It takes up my whole skull and I can hear myself walking within, sleeping within, dreaming within. I still haven't come out of that bedroom. They're holding me there. They got me. They have me. I'm still at the stage when I imagine everything about beings, and facts. That room is locked, with me inside, in my head. I did my homework carefully, I know my lessons by heart, and I'm not born. Not yet. So I believed. So I believe. But I'm still there, on the second floor of a bungalow, in Saint-Mandé. I listen intently to the sound of the rain, on the roof.

I was born from lowered shorts, in high school, before gym class, when we had to put on our uniform. I cast sidelong glances at my classmates. I was looking for differences. I wanted to know: their commas, and mine. First in racing, rope climbing and on the parallel bars, I was the first one in the first wave, when we lined up in the gymnasium. And that made those who wanted to beat me up even more furious, more jealous. I respected the body, its bounce and vitality. I wanted to be first. I was. I was first in history, and French too. But these feats made my father peevish. And his peevishness came out in sulkiness and indifference. He wanted me to become an engineer? I'd never be one! I was as determined, in my silences, as he, in his muddle-headed griping. Violent at times, he would toss out hackneyed remarks, at dinner, during an occasional visit from an uncle or cousin: "Artists have become nothing but social parasites," "Teachers have turned into valets." All that was directed against me, as a child. I would be a French teacher. I was also first in poetry reciting. *Jacques le Fataliste and his Master:* "They made their way toward an enormous castle, on the frontispiece of which could be read: 'I belong to no one and I belong to everyone. You were here before you came in and you will still be there when you leave.' "

In the summer, they would send me to England to learn English, or to Spain, to learn Spanish. They picked "equivalent families." Every day I had to write them a letter in the original language. Vacation homework, which would be corrected by my teachers, the next winter, little private lessons. I was born from these little lessons and their privileges. Little math lessons, too, little physics-chemistry lessons. They had me work extra hours. I was born from high-school latrines and meetings on the sly. "Do you spurt?" "No, not yet."

I was born when I "spurted" for the first time. On my bed, in my room, a Sunday afternoon in April. The next day, I could have beat on the whole high school. I was twelve. I could take off, share, offer and receive. I had a normal constitution. Here was the proof! Little larva, all my body responded. I never shuddered so much as during those first times. My teeth chattered when I came. I no longer had any come-backs for my sisters when they made fun of me. I assumed an air of superiority. I watched for the first hairs at the bottom of my belly, in the middle of my chest and on my legs. I was growing up. As days went by, I was getting to be as tall as they were, at the table. Never did I sit up so straight. I had bags under my eyes. I was waiting.

I met Panos Kaftanzoglou at the Lutetia swimming pool. He was a grown-up; he was ten years older than I. He was an athlete. Greek. He painted buildings. He bent me into two in his arms. He stood me up on the bench in the locker stall and bit me all over. He was there, every Thursday afternoon, faithful at his post. And I led him astray. I was the one who led him astray. The last Thursday of that year, he didn't show up. The worker who opened the locker stalls threw me a peculiar glance that day. And the lifeguard too. And our physical-ed teacher made an appointment with my mother. I found out from my sisters. It was over. I was born from that *over*. Everything was beginning. Never at any time did this visit come up. My mother, I'm sure, never mentioned it to my father. I became compliant, frightfully compliant, and went underground. I'd find my opportunities hanging around after school, and meeting people on the street.

I was born from the idea they formed about me, against all proof to the contrary. I was born from the use I made of my body and the virulence of my readings, the virus of texts. I was born from their silences, their never-articulated reproaches, their glances skimming past me at meals when all they talked about were my sisters' high-school graduations, my sisters' first dances, my sisters' engagements, my sisters' weddings.

I could always escape on the train, to Paris. On the metro, once in Paris. And the French Youth concerts. Intermissions at the Pleyel and the Comédie Française. I was born from their trust which was nothing but self-trust. I was born smothered. I am smothering. In your arms, Duck, I thought I could breathe at last. But it was too late. I am the last branch of a dead tree. The only thing I can make is pages. Sing a little. I am not complaining. I observe. I listen. It's all I have left. It's all I had left from the beginning. The rich men's share. All I have is my life to share. Anything else would be nothing but a sham. Those in the highest balconies could certainly tell the difference.

Afterwards, I passed from hand to hand. I was left to pursue my studies in the most scornful silence. I was left to withdraw to the fringes. I thought myself liberated. The ties were only relaxed and now they are pulled tight again. I believed in my freedom as long as I was the youngest of the two, younger than the other. Until you, Duck. Forty years old.

I was born from this little difference. And from this emptiness. From this conformity. I was born from this caste, cut off from everything, in one of those families where you cannot tell apart fear from strength and violence from affection.

November '54, I had just begun my second year. There was no more talk of Indochina. Pleven had said that Dien Bien-Phu would be our Verdun. Mendés-France was in power. The police and the judicial department were wary of one another, a memory of a bad war. Communists were hunted practically everywhere. It was as serious as tuberculosis. In Bordeaux, they fought over a few milligrams of arsenic, "brought in by the kilo." The whole of France was digging up bodies, presumed victims of a lady of Loudun. In Digne, Giono was attending the Dominici trial. Gaston and his sons Gustave and Clovis. Clovis never admitted his guilt. In Algeria, Pasteur's village had just been attacked. I hear Mitterrand's voice on this matter, a beautiful tirade which culminates on an invitation to "safety, prosperity and happiness for all men." There was an earthquake in Orléanville. We listened to the news on the radio. We didn't get TV till much later. My father spoke of the RPF, a right-wing party, and about General de Gaulle. Nostalgia? In our house there were parquet floors everywhere and a few beautiful carpets on which you could slide and which always had to be put back into place. Once a week, my duty was to set up the bridge tables and extra chairs. My parents and their guests played in the politest of silences. Their political conscience was that of the small or grand slam. That's the way it is. I have just turned forty. But that year, that month, I understood that the only political conscience which existed in France was blunted, muted, withdrawn, trampled down. That those in power were either born leaders or opportunists, of the same stamp and the same mold. We were only made to endure and to take refuge in the idea of what we no longer were. Of what we might have been perhaps: the greatest.

My name is Pierre Forgue. Is that my name? I am capable of remaining for whole minutes at a time, in front of a mirror, staring at myself: it's not me. It's somebody else, cluttered with luggage, with principles, with heavy suitcases and catch-alls to break your arms off. The year I received my degree, I left for Diourbel, in Senegal. French teacher. One of the first draftees to do alternate service. Back in Paris, I rented this apartment, rue Boursault, not very far from the school. Time went by. Whom have I known, embraced, caused to linger? As in the street sometimes, you meet someone's eyes, you stop, you turn around, but the other keeps going. I must bear within me and upon me the powerful scent of those whom life has spared. Let this chapter hang me. I blew it at the Nikko Hotel. It was too much. I'm blowing it here. Not enough. But the gallows are set up. And the words will make the knot.

I learned how to play piano, tennis, how to dance rock 'n' roll and the jerk to take out my sisters, golf to make my parents happy. I also learned about the wind, on my motorcycle, fleeing Blue Skies to go and lose myself in the arms of Saint-Nazaire. I learned about the smell of steam in bath houses, and the sound of beer cans being popped in gay bars, weeknights. Inconsequential meetings. I've traveled thousands of miles in the street and in life to meet someone. Rue Boursault, courtyard stairway, fourth floor on the left, I must have, within seventeen years, climbed up the Himalaya ten times.

For my parents I am "a Ph.D. in literature" and I was "the youngest of my generation." Their pride stops right there. For my sisters, I am nothing but "a mistake you don't mention." Nevertheless, I have been a godfather twice, once in Jeanne's family, once in Françoise's. I vote Socialist. I don't know why anymore. I'll never vote otherwise because I know only too well why. It's the slam, for all those who want power for power's sake. In the beginning, and after '68, I went to the teachers' union meetings. Twice I took the floor. The second time, someone passed judgment: "It's good you're brave. But everything you say is too elegant." We all deceive ourselves.

And when I come home, when I rub my feet on the dormat, I tell myself that this is what politics is all about, or what's left of it. And revolutions are not much more than this, dirtying up your doormat, or cleaning it.

That Wednesday, behind the door, I sat on the floor. I took inventory. Before Peyroc, I used to travel. Since Peyroc, everyone else travels, I

don't travel anymore. When I borrowed the money to buy these few
stones, my father told me, "I hope you're not choosing this house for the
friends you have in the village, but rather for the countryside." My
father! Yet once again what he said made sense, his sense. Even when
he speaks, he's silent. Outside of himself, nothing exists and I don't
exist. In Peyroc, I float about the countryside. The Rhône, Mount
Ventoux, the lacework of Montmirail, and in the South, the foothills of
the Alps. You're always your own neighbor. A neighbor to whom you
don't speak.

My name is Pierre Forgue. They came within a hair's breadth of
training me to keep quiet, along with them, my whole life. They brought
me into this world but I haven't been born. Still not. And you had all of
this in your arms, Duck. Your turn. Chapter seven. You arrive, all made
up. And I'm not even going to take notice of it.

7

Thursday morning. I only teach from nine to eleven. It's nice outside, very nice. I go back home to throw the windows wide open. The telephone rings. "Pierre Forgue?" "It's me." "I met you two years ago, on Boulevard Saint-Germain, at the terrace of the Balto café. You gave me two phone numbers, one in Paris and one in the South. I'm in Paris for a training course. So I'm calling you. Am I interrupting anything?" "No, on the contrary." "Shall we get together?" "For lunch?" "OK, but I won't have much time. My class is in Montparnasse. So we'll see each other at the Balto in an hour?" "I'll be there." He laughs. "I'll recognize you!" He hangs up. A draft in the apartment. My bedroom door loudly slams shut. I only have a few minutes to get ready. The porcelain doorknob snapped off. It went rolling on the floor. I pick it up. I try to open the door. It's stuck. I'll need pliers to work the lock. I try, with my fingers, squeezing very hard. Useless. Very quickly, I lose my temper and ram against the door with my shoulders, and then give it a kick: a mark, the paint is chipping off. I stop. The young man's voice and the slamming door, the surprise and the draft, spring morning breeze, gentle outside, cutting inside, cold, mischievous, intolerable, you can't stay still, scent of wisteria, of metal and of small gardens, breeze of early May in Paris. Cast not a cloud ere May is out and do whatever you like.

I don't remember meeting him at the Balto two years ago. Or vaguely, a young man enjoying himself. But I forgot his face. He was with someone. A foreigner. Yes, that's right, someone from another country. But we said very little to each other. His friend left, irritated, because seated at neighboring tables we were staring intently at each other. I had to teach that afternoon. I just gave him my two phone numbers. "If you want to reach me, it's up to you." But his face? What was it like? A smile. And anyway all that was a game. Today I am shaving closely, twice. To be neat and clean, and I wash my hair in a hurry. It'll dry in the metro. Brown velvet pants. A blue shirt. I roll up the sleeves. With my wet hair, parted perfectly, I look like a boy making his first communion. No cologne. A pullover draped over my shoulders, my hands in my pockets, I look at myself in the mirror, behind the bathroom door. As I step back I bump into the sink. Since last night, after Mariette closed her door after me, with a tender look in her eyes, I was not waiting for anything anymore. And Marie, standing in front of me, on the stairway, her hands folded over her belly, her head bowed, counting the steps, humming a tune. Not a thing, I was not expecting anything anymore. I had spent the night making an inventory of my life, my childhood bedroom in my head, with me inside, a Panos for a Tadzio, a Bernard for a Bertrand, Sam, Jacques & the others, mine or anybody's and everybody's. Chance encounters, temporary halts, suburban trains, I wasn't expecting anything anymore. And this voice, over the telephone, animated, open, determined. I can't keep myself from singing. As I rush to get ready, surprised, curious about what will happen, I feel nervous, jittery, the draft, the open windows, the porcelain knob and locked bedroom. A sign? So much the better?

And today, facing these pages, I feel a little like the gynecologist who told Marie, "The child is coming along fine," when in fact the child wasn't.

Out of all the outdoor cafés of Boulevard Saint-Germain, I prefer the Balto because it's ordinary looking, often deserted. Now and then, around meal time, I drop in for a quick bite and watch the passersby. I don't feel like I'm sitting in a display window. You see all kinds of people. No pretense. Time to go! In the metro, I run my hand through my hair to help it dry. I watch the people around me, their eyes. Those who are waiting expectantly and those who aren't waiting for anything anymore. Those who are going to miss their stop and those who compulsively watch for theirs, leaning over the map the whole time. Those watching other people in their reflections on the window and those who stare into the tunnel's blackness. Doors opening and closing. I change trains at Réamur-Sébastopol, and take the Porte d'Orléans line. Another train, other people, same eyes. I am in a hurry. I remain standing. I don't have a watch. But I am always on time. I don't have a car in Paris. I have an old Renault 4 at Peyroc to drive around in the area. Even the subway corridors smell like spring. And spring smells of unhappiness, because you believe in it, every time, and it grabs you there in the hips and it rips your heart out. I get off at Odéon, I start to run the way I used to in high school to be at the head of the rush. Taking long strides.

I arrive at the Balto, a little out of breath. He comes up to meet me. "Hi, it's me!" I shake hands with him, he takes me by the arm. "Let's not stay here. Not enough time for lunch. D'you know where to go?" He looks at me, smiles. "Do you know where to go?" The end of the formal you, the beginning of the informal. An exchange of glances. I wonder what he thinks about me, if . . . I . . . I motion to him to follow me. I lower my eyes, I bite my lips, he . . . He is . . . He says to me, "You didn't remember me?" I answer, "Frankly, no." I correct myself: "Or rather just a little. I didn't believe it." "You didn't believe what?" "That we would meet again." Clumsy, everything I have just said is clumsy. I believe that unconsciously I am smacking my fist alternately in the palm of my hand. He thinks it's a game. We walk along. Heading for the rue du Dragon. "I know a nice restaurant, a menu for 22.80 francs, everything included." Why mention the price?

Sitting at the table, across from each other. I am seated on the bench against the wall. He looks at himself in the mirror, behind me. He has light curly hair shaped like a bowl on his head which he is constantly tussling up. When he smiles, his lips curl up a little, up on the right, a flaw which makes him look gruff and cocky, a little on the macho side. He is playing. He is twenty-one. Twenty-two? He has smooth cheeks, a

square face and broad shoulders. He rubs his hands together, and
caresses his forearms, rolls up the shirt sleeves, a cotton shirt, faded,
grey-and-blue checkered. The top three buttons are open. His pullover
drops to the floor, he picks it up, shakes it, sawdust. We order the
appetizer, a tomato salad. The restaurant door is open. In the street, the
breeze, passersby, and sunlight. He props his elbows on the table,
crosses his hands under his chin and I hear the same voice I heard on the
phone. "You aren't happy to see me again?" I answer, laughing,
"Maybe a little too much." I shouldn't have said that. Like that.
Flippantly. He asks me why. And I tell everything. I warn him.
"Because perhaps I've waited too long, for you or someone else.
Someone . . ." "Because I see us all too clearly as we are and there isn't
a moment when I don't see myself as I am." "Because keeping up a
front doesn't interest me anymore." "Because I was eighteen when you
were born." "Because . . ." All jumbled together.

Say everything. Right away. To get down to the most urgent and serious
matters. To put into words. To toss out. To ridicule your own life, your
habits. To run the risk of having the other person believe you are
playing the role of a victim when all you want to do is warn him—to
warn him off?—warn yourself, to size him up, size oneself up. He
watches me. He is enjoying this. Because in this instance I know how to
say serious things light-heartedly. It's funny and we laugh together. I
say exactly everything I should to make him never to want to see me
again: sedentary vacation, in Peyroc, my salary and the exhaustive
account of my expenses. "I've never been overdrawn, at the bank." The
wasted evenings at the West Side, the affairs lasting a few days or a few
weeks, Jean-Pierre, Antoine, Loïc, fiascos, and exercise, every
morning, the fear of getting fat, like my father, Saint-Mandé, and here I
go talking to him about my family, and my sisters, "those mother hens,"
bridge games, an overview of everything, and then above all "the
butches, the queens, the hustlers, the classic types you see in every bar,
chic restaurants for chic faggots" and "all these clothes I buy and don't
wear." Silence. "What about you?" I ate without knowing it. Before he
starts his own story I add, to make things clear, "I like everything
except scheming."

He comes from Dijon. He is finishing his second year in a school of business administration. He is taking a course in analytical accounting, in a banking firm, in the Tour Montparnasse. "The tuition for the course is deposited directly at the school. For my living expenses, I am doing a market survey in beauty salons in the Côte d'Or, for a new hair spray. And, on top of that, I find ways." His curled-up smile. With the tip of his tongue, he wets his lips. He has three brothers. "I am the eldest." His father is a policeman, "not a real one, he is a guard. A real lecher." As for his mother, "She stayed young. She is a lifeguard during the day. She gives yoga classes in the evening." Silence. "We were poor." Smile. "We still are." A direct open look. "By the way, my name is Duck. It's my first name. It means a lot to me. They say that I had a funny way of walking when I was little." "Coffee?" He glances at his watch. He shakes his head no. I pay the check. We leave. He insisted on splitting the price of the meal with me but I told him, "No, no, you're my guest."

"My" guest. You "are" "my" guest. Where does boldness end and fear begin? Fear, after boldness. The truly shy are those who become more and more so. Over mere trivialities. Duck walks ahead of me on the boulevard. He holds his metro ticket in his hand. "Only three stops, I had better be on time. I have an appointment with the boss. He is interested in the analysis I am doing for the course." Bouncing along, tight-fitting pants, a wallet in his back right pocket. "Be careful, you're going to get robbed." Form-fitting shirt, his pullover in his hand, big round-toed shoes, he turns around to say good-bye. "I don't know what you meant when you talked about scheming." We stop. He holds my forearm. He squeezes it a little. Like a plea. I forget about my fear, the real fear, the fear which makes you stutter and blurt out all kinds of truths. How many times must I have told him my age, in the course of an hour? "We'll get together this evening, if you want." "At your place?" "Why not?" "Good. I'll call you at the end of the day to get your address. All right. I'm going!" He dashes off. He doesn't turn around. Grey-and-blue checkered shirt.

8

You cannot explain what happens when you meet someone; you can only tell about it. And it is not accurate to say that your meeting has happened. It is happening. Everything punctuates it and, in fact, the sentence never comes to an end. Final period, or momentary pause, there is no meeting except in the beginning. Everything is beginning, at every moment. On the last page, the very last line, everything will begin again. We are not meant—individuals, humans, things, beings, bundles of flesh and blood—to meet each other. Life replaces us, perpetually, at the very beginning of everything.

This is the critical condition which calls forth a new stability. Going back to my place to wait for Duck's call, I am beside myself, anxious, as I am one year later, in the very act of writing these lines. This has nothing to do with time lost or recaptured, that esteemed and accurate measure of consciousness and present phenomenon, but rather with something beyond measure, with the time left to us, our share of time, shared with ourselves and in spite of ourselves, by ourselves, with everyone and against everyone. Have I only received what I desired? It's time to be on my guard. The margins are narrow. I must stay within my limits.

Only an attention to detail will spark a certain interest both for one and for the other. I have no other aim but to depict this kind of truth: the color of a shirt, a glance in a mirror, a metro ticket clutched in a hand, and the leaves at the crest of a horse-chestnut tree shaken by a breeze which itself is also inventing a beginning. Within the disorder which Duck brought into my life, within the banality of the facts which will be presented, I will constantly need to hold up—by means of my sentences —what will, to all appearances, be lying down. My only ambition is to make the heart beat faster. One last little jolt to the heart in a world glutted with proliferating images, in which everything is at the mercy of ideas and a reign of terror, of the reproductions of catastrophes and revolutions. But all despair is not lost. I will keep repeating this. It's my way of making my mark. The matter at hand is flimsy, but sharp. The great subjects have all been dealt with. Very greatly. They made me as I am. Yet I want a different time. I want to live my share of time. That Thursday in my apartment I put back into place everything that is already in its place. Not because I hope to make Duck happy, but because I am afraid of making him uneasy with a detail, a personal quirk, a peculiar taste. By putting things in order, I drive away anything that might make itself at home. Am I already driving Duck away?

I clean the windowpanes. The panes of three windows, plus the kitchen skylight. As for my bedroom, the door is still locked shut. I put the porcelain doorknob on the newspaper Bernard left in the study. I file my record albums. I prepare the next day's classes. I dial my own number on the telephone: busy signal. I put the phone on my desk, take out some money, a basket. I am going to pick up a few things for dinner. My mouth is watering. I rush down the stairs.

Drop in on Mariette. Her eyeglasses at the tip of her nose, frail, bent double on a chair, wearing an apron and slippers, she's sewing multi-colored costume jewels onto a crown "which split apart for the third time. It's for the final performance at the Concert Mayol. They're coming to pick it up at five." Mariette glances at me. "We drank a bit too much the other night, didn't we?" She smiles. "But it was nice. And I mean everything I told you. Can you bring me back some bread? And a can for Boubou?" She looks at her cat. "He's always sleeping. He hasn't opened his eyes since this morning. Is it nice out?"

I buy strawberries. And cherries. Some wine. At the butcher's, club steaks. "For one person?" "No, two." "Two slices—thin, medium, thick?" "Two nice slices." A loving detail. As if it was a certainty. An audacity. You feel a little bit better, more handsome than usual. It's all beginning again. And once again, I believe in it. And each time is different: Duck held my forearm. It's that gesture which caught me, stopped me. His eyes also, surprised. Even though I didn't say anything, one is supposed to. I was speaking to him as if everything was over. In the street, I breathe in the air, I smile, I inhale. I make my purchases with an unaccustomed joy. I think about my bill at the Nikko Hotel, the most money I've spent since the beginning of the year. And so what? I only buy the best things. An image: with the tip of his tongue Duck moistens his lips. Mariette's bread. A can of Gourmet for Boubou. And a cake for Marie which I'll leave outside her door with a note: "I'm taking the night off. Thanks. Pierrot."

One day Marie called me Pierrot in front of my sisters, who had dropped by on a Saturday afternoon "to keep in touch." Marie was there so that she could see my "older sisters," at last. "Pierrot?" Françoise glances toward Jeanne. Jeanne gazes back blankly. Marie insists, "It's nice." Françoise smiles, "It's cute." "Cute is the word," Jeanne adds. I'm not telling about this here to get even. What it involves is a deviation and a tenderness. Pierrot is not of their world, and their world only exists in the darkness of voting boxes, crumpled papers, raked gravel, hair smoothed into place.

Duck also kept himself tenderly aloof. When he left me, he did not turn around. I thought of Bernard then, telling me about his friend André's complaints. I would come to know Duck through my wariness, and afterwards. I suddenly remembered Michael, a boy I met on the train coming back from Peyroc. He got off at Valence. He had been drafted and was stationed near Grenoble. We wrote to each other for four months. Then one day, over the phone, he tells me: "Can I come on Saturday, on my leave? I'll get in at eleven." This was seven or eight years ago. Your share of time is not regulated in advance. Unforeseeable, it becomes immeasurable. It is indestructible, like beings possessed by desire. That Saturday morning I waited for Michael.

Everything was ready, in order. Eleven o'clock, a quarter after eleven, a quarter of twelve, noon. I had forgotten to ask Michael if it was eleven in the morning or in the evening. Grenoble-Lyon, Lyon-Paris, I made a few calculations. It was obvious, eleven in the evening! You don't leave a barracks at five in the morning. And I spent the whole day waiting for him. It was the beginning of January. It was raining. I read. I clearly remember the title of the book, *Docteur Martins et autres histoires* by Faulkner. I crept from one story to the next. Time went by. From time to time I got up to nibble on a piece of cheese and bread in the kitchen. It's the only room with a clock, on top of the refrigerator, an alarm clock that I carry into my bedroom and which I put back there, the first step of my breakfast, and leave there for the rest of the day. Then eleven P.M., a quarter after eleven, a quarter to midnight, midnight. I cleared the table, put back the book, finished, in the study. I wasn't hungry for anything anymore. Looking back, I had enjoyed the day I had just spent. Now and then, emptiness is a distraction. You protect yourself as you can. And I went to bed. Very quickly, sleep brought me back to that train, between Avignon and Valence, we are standing in the corridor outside the compartments, glancing sideways at each other, leaning on our elbows, our noses pressed up against the windows, our breath misting the glass. Michael writes his first name with his fingertip and I write mine. And that's how we got to talking to one another. Trivialities about his life. He communicated a fierce reticence like a strong odor, as when you lift someone up, the odor of a whole body. He told me it was the first time he "spoke" to someone like me. His letters remained bashful, like our first exchange of glances and his hesitation about taking my address, scribbled hastily, the train was in the Valence station. "Watch your step! The doors close automatically." Then his leave. Eleven in the morning, or in the evening? He never showed up. He stopped writing me. And so, while arranging the cherries on a plate, I told myself that maybe, maybe Duck, too.

In the late afternoon the phone rang. Loïc: "It's been ages since we last got together. I'm leaving on tour tomorrow. I have a part in a Marivaux play, we're performing under a tent. It's crazy. Jammed-packed every night. I'll call you when I get back, for sure." I couldn't get a word in edgewise. Then my mother: "It's your father's birthday Sunday, don't forget." Then Jean-Pierre, who wants to invite me to dinner at his new friend's place: "It's true love! We're going to Greece together next summer. What about you? Still holed up in Peyroc?" The telephone rings again. First a wrong number, then Bernard: "I left too quickly last Tuesday. We'll get together anyway, won't we?" Why "anyway"? Everybody's calling me up. It's starting to get cold. I close the windows. I start a fire in the fireplace. Ringing. I pick up the receiver. Duck: "So what's your address?" I explain everything to him, the subway, where to change trains. He interrupts me: "Do you mind my taking a bath as soon as I get there? The friend whose place I'm staying at didn't leave me the keys, and . . ."

A half an hour later, he's here. He puts his canvas bag and his pullover on the floor in the hallway. Crouching, he pulls out notepads, a metal ruler, an eraser, a colored assortment of felt-tip pens. "The day's harvest. From under their noses. No such thing as a small profit. Always something accomplished for next year, or for my brothers." He stands up. "That's your bedroom?" "No, it's the other room." "You have all this for yourself?" "Yes, why?" He walks into the main room, pulling his shirt out of his pants. He heads straight for the records, under the bookshelves. "You listen to all of them?" "I've listened to all of them." He looks at me: "My first year, besides my market surveys, I worked in a record store. From time to time I slipped an album into my sheepskin jacket. And then I got caught. That really cost me. Records really cost a lot." I light the fire in the fireplace. "Can I play a record?" "If you want to." "Which one?" "The one you want." He picks out Jimmy Cliff, Bernard's favorite record, no surprise. If you want to, Duck. Our turn to play now. Words can trap us, depending on which ones we choose and say over and over. And don't accuse me of paying too much attention to these things since you didn't pay the least bit of attention. Apparently. "And your bedroom?" "The doorknob's broken. Look!" I hold out the porcelain ball. He smooths it in his hands, tosses it up in the air, catches it. "I'll fix that, but first I want to take my bath, OK?"

Who chooses whom, when, why, how? A little refrain in my head. His round-toed shoes on one side, his pants and undershorts on the other,

Duck puts his blue-and-white checkered shirt on my desk, the beginning of disorder. Everything is beginning. The record goes around on the turntable, the volume is a little too high. I forbid myself to touch anything whatsoever, to change anything whatsoever. "Be careful in the bathroom, you can bruise yourself easily." "I already have!" I bring him a brand-new bar of soap. And a towel, a fresh one. He grabs me by the wrist and pulls me toward him, his kiss grazes me, barely felt. An exchange of smiles. I step back. My wrist is wet. Gained ground. He is gaining ground.

I don't know where to post myself anymore, at my desk, on the sofa, in the kitchen to prepare dinner. "But everything is ready." "What did you say?" "No, I was talking to myself." I'm in my T-shirt, pants, bare feet. I pull the curtains shut. He comes out of the bathroom drying himself. "You know, I called you up in the South of France." "When?" "Two years ago." And he smiles, his lips parted. He is showing me his teeth, gap-toothed, a sign of luck. "That was you?" "Yes."

Peyroc, two in the morning, the eve of July fourteenth. The telephone rings. Jumped out of bed. I grope my way down the stairs. I pick up the receiver. "Hello, is this Pierre Forgue?" "Yes, it's me." "It's really Pierre Forgue?" "Yes, why?" "That's all I wanted to know." And the other person hangs up. The other, Duck.

Duck tosses the towel into the bathroom. He puts his undershorts and his shirt back on. "Can I stay like this?" "Of course." Slight pout. He looks at everything, all around him. I laugh. "And why didn't you tell me it was you?" "Too soon!" "Too soon what?" "Us! Who knows? I was hitch-hiking. I told myself I could stop over at your place. And then . . ." "And then?" "Give me a piece of wire, I'm going to open your bedroom door."

I can still see him, kneeling, his back to me, his heels raised, his legs spread apart, and his hands as high as his face. He takes the handle apart. He twists the wire. The record is over and is making the sound of a heart, dully beating. A click, the door opens. Duck enters my bedroom shouting, "Bravo!" The window is open. He leans out: "Is that a cemetery?" He turns around toward me: "You ought to prop the door open with a dictionary." He closes the window and joins me in the main room. I ask him if he's hungry. "Not really, but . . ." He puts on the other side of the album, sits down at the table, shakes his head, like a puppy. I pour the wine. He smiles at me: "Everything all right?" I answer: "Everything's all right."

Then I remember a sentence, but who said it and in what book? ". . . I was young, I was drawn to twilight skies and shady neighborhoods and desolation; nowadays I like mornings in the heart of the city and peacefulness." Duck whispers: "What are you thinking about?" "Nothing." "Really?" "No, not really." "What then?" Answering coyly, "I'm thinking that . . . I'm no longer very young and not yet very old. I'm thinking that . . ." "Stop!" He laughs. "You're the same age as my mother. The prime of life!" He leaves the table, picks up his pants, takes out his wallet, opens it and hands over a snapshot. "Look. That's her." He sits back down across from me. "Calling you up was a good idea. Don't you think?"

Ground gained by one, lost by the other, or gained by both together, or totally lost by both of them. How can you tell? During dessert, as a joke, Duck hangs cherries over his ears. I can see myself again at Saint-Mandé. My sisters do the same thing, with me. And, laughing, they point at me. Duck takes the cherries off, bites into one, and offers me the other. "Take it, make a wish like me. These are the first of the year." The wine bottle is empty. Duck picks out another record. Silence. I hear Marie's footsteps as she enters her apartment. She must have found the cake and the note. Duck tells me: "We'll clean up later." He points toward the fireplace: "Can I put on another log?" Sitting with his legs crossed in front of the fire he waits for me. "Can I stay the night?"

9

As I touched Duck, pressed my hands against his, sitting opposite him, with my legs crossed, in front of the fireplace, an image came to me, feminine, friendly, or like a brother, soothing, of late twilight, the outskirts of cities, and lovers' misfortunes, the powerful image of an early morning, something like peacefulness. He is here. He says, "I'm happy!" or else, "What are you afraid of?" We intertwine our fingers, stretch our arms out and, forehead to forehead, we gaze at each other. He whispers, "I'm making you cross your eyes?" I kiss him.

Disorder finds a home in the shadows. The whole city has an expectant air. This is only one embrace among thousands and thousands. But due to a body's taste, a fold of flesh, a palpitation, a word forming deep in the throat, the contraction or rather the skin itself, just to touch it—meeting someone is a unique experience, you can't really say why. This is your territory. You nestle down in it. You don't want the other person to realize it. Then, very quickly, you forget your orders. You no longer keep order. You put on your uniform as for a gym class. Everything is given, everything is for the taking. And you, Duck, will seize for me what is not in my power to take. The words ingrain themselves. At least, they believe. Duck smiles, "Relax!"

With a tug he pulls off my T-shirt. I barely have enough time to raise my arms over my head. Then he grabs hold of me, pulls me to my feet, unbuttons my pants and lets them slide down. "You have a blanket? Let's stay in front of the fire." The synthetic rug is dangerous. When you roll around on top of it, naked, you scratch your skin. It cuts into you like glass. You don't feel or see a thing at the time. The next day, or the day after, your skin swells up at your elbows and knees and the soles of your feet. Your skin reddens, inflamed. Like a friend, a lover, like someone who alights in your life. Like Duck. I don't want to tear him apart. What we lived through together tore us apart. I say it again, in the same way, with the same words. There will be those who are only able to read by correcting what they themselves have not known how to live or write, applying the wrong rules to the text in order to point out and highlight the repetitions. When Marie designs a page of advertising, she often explains that "the brand name must be mentioned at least three times: in the title caption, in the text, and at the bottom" so that "the message is communicated."

For this text, I have to sit up straight, as at a table, a holiday dinner, during which everyone has his turn to speak. Words fall into the same pattern as your daily routine: your will must win out. The ritual you follow must be precise. Nothing in a person's life is at the mercy of chance. And the first act of chance. I possess the certainty of being born in a vacuum, I am born within it, it is my cradle. Those who are coddled are the true orphans. Not very kind. I'm not a very kind person. I state here what has always been a matter of good taste to keep quiet in order to make one's confession more touching. But I have no taste for good taste. And to that extent, the story will be a novel, the marketplace for those who cry out when good form dictates that one hush up. It's *The Gold Rush*.

The movie. Charlie Chaplin is waiting for the woman he loves. It's their big date. He creates a palace out of his cabin. He gets everything ready. It's beautiful. She doesn't show up at the time they agreed upon. He waits. Expectantly. Sitting down. At a table. Alone. He does a pantomime of a dance, with his fingers, on the tablecloth. A dance with her. He falls asleep. Happy.

And I am alone, at this table. Typing my novel with two fingers, the pages my tablecloth, one year later. My desk is opposite the fireplace. I see myself again. I come back with the blanket, I spread it out. Duck takes off his shirt and his undershorts. Images stream through my head, as in a dream, what you've lived through the night before. One certain Thursday, Panos Kaftanzoglou did not come back. A certain Michel, one January night, did not show up. When I met Jean-Pierre, an accountant, three years younger than myself, he said that our love was also "true love," and was planning our vacation. Loïc? I was in the theater audience when he was on stage for the first time. He didn't have butterflies in his stomach. He had everything left to learn. The auditorium was almost empty. And Bernard calls me up because we "spoke," of all things. My father's birthday? Next Sunday! Marie is working at home. At her desk. I never did find out which of the three sofa beds Mariette sleeps in, if she ever sleeps. Take a good look at the costume-jewel studded crown, the last performance at the Concert Mayol . . . Duck grasps my hand and licks my fingers. To state things, to state beings and facts. Only hypocrites who are afraid to read about themselves will perceive any sort of provocation. Those kinds of people live outside of themselves, pretending not to know themselves very well. I want to live inside of myself, to be what I am, whatever the cost, to speak, to communicate. At the risk of repeating myself. A whole lifetime, with your arms wrapped around it. True misery is not always the kind people describe. Duck licks the palm of my left hand, then my forearm, my elbow, my shoulder. He is going to bury himself under my arm, in my underarm hairs. It tickles me a little bit. We are standing up, embers in the fireplace.

You never appear alone, before someone. You strip yourself naked, the sum total of everything that has gone on in your life, of everyone who has gone on, relationships which have been passing, fallen through, battered you in all sorts of ways, bruising you, brushing up against you, images from your dreams. Each caress is the continuation, which itself will be followed by all the other tender moments we have already shared, more or less willingly, along the surface or deep within, violently, silently, held close or at a distance. Now, Duck holds me and I relax in his embrace. He moistens me from my head to my toes. From time to time he pulls himself away from me, draws back and observes me. He is watching me, enjoying himself, and his eyes are full of approval. Then he nestles on this or that part of my body. He retraces his steps, pressing his mouth down or letting his lips skim my skin. Motionless, surprised, now and then I stroke his head, his curls, but he shakes my hand loose. He is moving all around me. He is only touching me with his lips, his tongue, and now and then the tip of his nose. It's only a game. An idea for a game. Or maybe much more.

Much more as far as I'm concerned since, little by little, I have the sensation of being completely seen, accepted, almost known, circumscribed, his prisoner, liberated from everything else, absolutely everything, my past attempts, my failures, my expectations, my imperfectly expressed words so perfectly misunderstood. Duck's smile, especially, strikes me when he draws back only to come down upon me more surely, a furtive smile, twisted, turned up, with that crease on the right cheek, a dimple. He does not get hard. Small naked animal, he draws me into him as if he wanted to swallow me whole. The enemy is not the other.

The enemy is not the other, it is the third person ashamed, non-existent, he is the one outside, judgment, he judges. He ridicules. Duck does what he wants to do with me and I relax in his embrace. Then he gets up, tangles his feet in my pants, almost trips. He starts the Jimmy Cliff record over again, very softly, takes a dictionary from my bookshelf and props my bedroom door open. He walks through the hallway rubbing his hands together. In the kitchen, I hear him drink from the faucet. He comes back. His mouth is dripping. I am leaning, my two hands grasping the edge of the mantelpiece above the fireplace, unsteady but still on my feet, trying to find the questions, all the questions that I was always asking myself, trying to locate the fear within me, the fear of the other, growing fear, the interrogations, the suspicions. Perfectly at ease, Duck puts the blanket back down, smoothing it out. Then, a few logs in the fireplace. His hair brushes my leg when he leans down to blow on the fire. A burst of flames. He stretches out. He tells me, "Come here!" I turn toward him. He holds out his arms toward me, straight up. I feel both wet and dry at the same time. Over my entire body. His tongue fluttering. He smiles, his tongue goes back behind his teeth and repeats, "Come here!"

The dictionary stayed there for a long time, propping open the door. From time to time I would consult it, on my knees, whenever the need arose. The porcelain doorknob, also, stayed for a long time on top of the newspaper in my study. Duck has arrived! From the morning telephone call to the moment I stretch out alongside of him, in the evening, a whole story, already. His curling hair. I kiss him, the faucet water, then his saliva, and gradually, a taste, his taste. We still have not used our arms. When I lie down upon him, he tells me: "Be careful!" Then, "Gently . . ." I get hard. He doesn't. It's a beautiful thing to say. It's not dirty. It is. It is the way it is. No, he doesn't get hard. He doesn't get stiff. Above him, my back arched, I close my eyes. With his two hands he opens them: "Look at me!" He says the right things, at the right times, at the precise moment. He has a knowing touch. I was going to abandon everything, get up, stop, good-bye, good-night, and then, farewell. As Marie would say, "He was the Sam, Jacques & Bertrand type, so . . ." Duck gets up, lays me back down: "Just relax. . . !" He strokes my forehead: "It's nothing serious, it's giving me pleasure . . ." He places a finger across my lips, I bite it. He whispers, "It's really nice like this." He jumps back, spreads my legs apart and positions himself on his knees, facing me, leaning down. "Don't think about anything . . ."

I only see the top of his head. Back and forth. A mouth, that mouth. The entrance. That entrance. A movement. I let him spread me apart. Hands placed flat against the blanket, I watch the ceiling. Who lives on the fourth floor, the fifth floor? Who lives above and below? Who lives all around me? And myself, here! And Duck at his task. I am going to come alone, yet once again. You always come alone. How is it possible to "not think about anything. . ."? I come, without even realizing it or having the time to announce it with a moan, or only a faint sound in my throat. The back and forth movement slows up. Duck stops. He pushes his head between my legs very hard, his ears pressed against my thighs, his nose in the blanket. And he lunges at me savagely, as if he wanted to come into me. Then he throws himself on top of me, his arms stretched out on both sides of my shoulders. He laughs: "It was good . . ." He wants to kiss me. I turn my head away. Semen. My semen. No. It is. It is the way it is.

He didn't want to sleep in the guest room. "I don't like beds." When I left the bathroom, he had shut out all the lights, he was already asleep, wrapped up in the blanket, facing the fireplace, his fists clenched against his lips.

The next morning, we shake hands at the top of the stairs leading to the Europe metro stop. We didn't say a word to each other. As he leaves me, he simply blurts out, "As for *schemes*, you've never explained what you meant." And he disappears.

There is no unit of measure for measuring what is new, nor a standard nor a frame of reference. Duck and I said nothing to each other and we didn't arrange our next date. I arrive at school right on the dot. The students are waiting in the classroom. Voltaire. A student reads a passage from *Zadig* out loud: "But chance does not exist, everything is either trial or punishment or reward or omen . . ." In the margin of my notes, in pencil, I write: "Friday May 5th. A touching meeting with Duck. And then, failure. Why? How? He doesn't know the answers himself. Maybe the blue sky, the threat of spring, his age and mine. *Misfit.*" Silence in the classroom. The students are watching me, expectantly. Voltaire? *Zadig?* I leave the podium and take a seat in the last row, leaning on my desk, my chin resting on my crossed arms. I tell the students: "Let me hear what you have to say." They smile, buzz of conversation, then they fall silent. They have all turned around to face me. A name, on each face? An age, too? They are sixteen years old, seventeen. Almost Duck. I won't see Duck again. A certainty. "Sir? Can we open the window?" Sir. Mr. Forgue. I smile, my lips twisting up, on the right side, like a tic, already. Caught red-handed.

10

Friday morning. Upon the school walls, graffiti, written in tar: ANARCHY = LIFE, THROW DESCARTES EUCLID INTO THE GARBAGE CAN, *A*s ARE FOR ASSES. In the faculty lounge, all they can talk about is this "defacement of a public building!" "And you, Mr. Forgue, what do you think about it?" A twenty-year-old student was questioned in his home yesterday. Another, in his sophomore year, was interrogated this very morning by a detective, in the principal's office. The students are threatening not to go to classes tomorrow, Saturday, in spite of the academic inspector's intervention. The deputy of the public prosecutor handling the investigation has announced that all further interrogations will take place only in the students' homes. Everything happened during the day, while I was teaching. I hadn't the slightest suspicion. As far as the girls and boys in my class are concerned, my students, I am neither young enough to be in their confidence nor old enough to be detested. And if I sometimes allude to current events, in the heat of an analysis of a text from the past, if I take sides, I am on guard against becoming vehement and I do not get carried away. As the years go by, I grow farther and farther from them, my voice restrained, no precautions, the very beginning of devotion. I have only grown closer to myself, to what I have not been, what I did not know how to be in my share of time. My share of time is still to come. I forgot how to relax. From now on I attempt to instill knowledge. "You're not saying anything, Mr. Forgue?" "What do you want me to say? It's serious, because tar can't be easily wiped off." "We don't see you often at our meetings . . ."

You have no choice but to go into the faculty lounge. Peyrat, Barbaroux and Arondelle are always there, of course. It's their club, their castle. They have fifteen or twenty years seniority over me. And they always address me as if I had just arrived. Or with polite chatter. "You're going away for the weekend?" "No, I'm staying in Paris." "Still happy with your house, in the Midi?" "Still happy." "My wife and I will drop by next summer, if you like the idea." Each year in May, it's the same promise. Courtesy. Empty gestures. I want to go home. Barbaroux approaches me, drawing me aside. "You were very close to our friend Roussel, am I not right?" Irony. I smile calmly, to avoid giving a direct answer. Jean-Claude Roussel, celibate, holding his position at the same high school for forty-two years, also a literature professor, retired for a year now, retreated to the village where he was born, in Alés. Sometimes he would accompany me to the Balto. He would speak to me about life before the war, when everything was still possible for him. And in one of his letters I read again, "I don't know if I'll be able to hold up here. This retirement is offensive. Paris hid me. Here, people, my people, my cousins have lost all contact with each other. Loneliness works away at them, and as soon as a great titmouse lands in a cherry tree, it's a dramatic event. Everywhere, they write DO NOT ENTER. Yet I have come back to this land, clump of nothing, on which like a small seed I have been sown. The silence of the vineyards is deafening. How lovely the sidewalks of Paris were, even if no one looked at me anymore. Have you found my notes useful? Are you minding my advice? I speak to you as to a friend. Now that I am far away, I can caress you . . ."

"So, your friend Roussel is seriously ill. A complete breakdown. He's taking a sleep cure. Here's his address. He's in a clinic at Uzès. His brother is a doctor there. His sister-in-law is the one who informed me. Maybe you will be able to do something for him?" I don't like Barbaroux's baldness or his razor-thin lips. I thank him and say, "See you tomorrow." "Only if the students condescend to attend our classes,

Mr. Forgue!" As I was leaving, I bumped into the principal and the academic supervisor. "This is a serious matter, Mr. Forgue." "I know. Would you please excuse me." Duck. Misfit.

Would you please excuse me, not excuse me. A memory of Saint-Mandé. I am a well-respected man. Celibate, I don't trouble the administration. I keep my hands off my students. Curious respect. I go home. I want to take a drink of water from the faucet. Duck: misfit.

Very quickly, I put everything back into its proper place, and it's exactly as if Duck had never been here. A note from Marie: "5:00 P.M. I'm going back to Chantilly. Even if I get bored there. Don't forget the flowers. They're thirsty." Signed, "Marie and her two-ninths." I slip the Jimmy Cliff record back into the album jacket. In the kitchen I eat a strawberry, a few cherries. I fold up the napkin Duck used to wipe his lips. I get undressed. Seven o'clock in the evening. Friday evening. I'll go to the movies, or maybe take a walk. In the shower, standing up in the bathtub, I splash water around, too bad. The nozzle in my mouth, I take a few gulps, I choke, I cough, I laugh, all alone. It's over. I remember Loulou, "my real name is Louis," twenty-two years old, a three-day relationship, how long ago? Loulou was covered with tattoos, "a souvenir of prison, fifteen years old to eighteen, Nancy, Laval, Fresnes. I really screwed up. I walked the line. The tattoos were just to be like everybody else." He swaggered when he walked, a real body builder. "I'm superman. But it's only to give the impression I can defend myself." He shows me a black dot, on top of his left hand, at the base of his little finger. "It's the lonely man's mark." And on his cheek, a little below the eye: "This is the pimp's mark." On his forearm, a cross: "This is the punk's cross," and two dots in a backwards S: "It's going back to prison." Olga, "my mother's name," a sun above a highway, "it's the path of freedom," a compass, "so I won't get lost." And on his thighs: "March or die." Loulou is proud of his tattoos. "But at the same time, I'd like to get rid of them. But electrolysis leaves scars. Anyway, when I did it, I believed in it. It's insane how I want to tell the story of my life . . ."

In the shower I scrub myself, I lather up with the wash rag, in front, behind, and everything starts over again. Someone walks into your life, and the whole world with him. You feel like you're at a crossroads, horribly exposed. I have to do something for Roussel. Pay him a visit. From Peyroc, by car, not more than an hour away. And Loulou, you didn't do anything for him because he didn't ask for anything. He used to say, "And when you ask for nothing, you get nothing." On his chest, another tattoo, an "I love you?" "The question mark is important. That means, *no such luck*." And around Loulou's belly button, lines, radiating, "It's the punk's sun." Roussel had introduced me to him. "He's nice. He lets himself be fondled. Something should be done for him. Something else." From time to time, Roussel would invite a gigolo home. He would say, "I've asked over a young man who . . ." Asked over! And he would admit, "Imagining it is worse, or remembering . . ."

Tattoos. In the shower, I rub, wash, scrub, instinctively, willingly, too. I feel myself tattooed from the night before. As I am drying myself, patting my body with the folded towel, the doorbell rings. I go answer it. Duck. "Am I disturbing you?"

Duck walks in. I close the door. He puts down his canvas bag. He's wearing another shirt, a white one. A white shirt? He rummages through his bag, takes out an enormous eraser, brand new. "Look, it's for you. I swiped it at the office. I'm sure it'll come in handy." I don't move. He walks over and puts it on my desk. "I think my course evaluation will be very positive." He undoes a shirt button. "Can we spend the night together?" He smiles. "Do you have any plans?" He takes off his shirt. In three movements, he is naked, he runs into the bathroom. "Ouch!" He shouts, "Can I?" And there he is in the shower. I feel good. But I don't say a word. It came as no surprise.

At times like these, you assess your life, you sum everything up, you would like to push everyone else away, but everything happens too quickly, and everybody rushes in. Massacres, wars, famines, summit meetings, daily lottery, tar-written graffiti, demonstrations, strikes, official statements, murders, royal weddings, hike in the price of gold, own your own house by the seaside, gulags, receptions, the latest trends, car accidents, accidents: the only true drama in a person's lifetime is the courage and the fear to meet people. Duck is here. He came back. "Where is the towel?" He leans over my desk while drying himself, moves the eraser, finds my course notes. He reads, smiles, looks at me, "Misfit, what's that mean?" He throws the towel on the floor, clenches his fist and pretends to box me. My first punch, answering his, lands on his shoulder; after his second, I punch him twice, like a madman, blindly, my lips tight together, as a joke. Hysteria? Epilepsy? Most of all, don't go out during recess. Duck grabs my wrists and squeezes them tightly. "But what's gotten into you?"

Out on the street. We are going to a restaurant. "I felt like seeing you again, because . . ." He laughs. Knocks into me. I knock into him. Like two children. Silence. We walk on. "I felt like seeing you, because . . ." He thinks, pouting slightly, "because . . ." A gesture of helplessness. He pinches my arm. "You should know why better than me." Then, "If you like, we could spend the weekend together."

A deserted street, parallel to the Grands Boulevards. A gay restaurant. Inexpensive. Smell of french fries. The waiters shout: "Ple-e-ease be careful, it's hot!" The bar is crowded, a waiting line. At the tables, we are piled on top of each other, there is just enough room for the plates, the glasses and the ashtray. The menu is written on the wall, on a black-board. Posters everywhere: International S & M Meeting in Amsterdam June 8th, The Only Sado-Maso Boutique in Paris, James Dean, Marlon Brando. We are sitting opposite each other. This time Duck is against the wall. There is no mirror. He plays with his curls, aimlessly. My eyes stop him. He smiles awkwardly. It's touching. I am touched. At the table to the left, two guys in leather jackets, in costumes. They are talking about the "bungalow" they are going to build "at the far end of the garden" in the "Touraine style." On the right, three guys, in leather jackets too, a scent of perfume betrays them. They're talking about a "baroness" who is "fun but bitchy." Silence. Then, "especially during a cruise, if she hangs around the whole time." On the left and on the right they are looking at Duck. In shirt-sleeves. We forgot to dress up in leather. I don't have the proper attire. Duck neither. And since the others are talking loudly, since we cannot not listen to them, I glance at Duck questioningly, I assume a deep voice, the proper intonation, an act, my arms crossed on the table. "Listen, listen to me good, you leave, just like that, for three years, without a word. Poof! the gentleman vanishes . . . and you come back, tonight, you ring the doorbell, three years later . . . and I have to be there, I have to be free, as if it was nothing . . . as if nothing had happened?" Duck, gaping, a look of false discomfort, glances to the right, to the left: they are listening. Duck has joined the game. I go on, calmly, very audibly, "So then, I guess you still leave the toothpaste cap on the edge of the washbasin. . . . You know, it takes as much time to fold up a towel as to throw it on the floor. . . . You still throw all your towels on the floor? Maybe you're going to tell me, three years later, that I'm still as old as your mother?" Duck lowers his eyes. Raises them. We look at each other questioningly. I fall silent. Silence at the neighboring tables. It's no longer a matter of "bungalows" or "baronesses" or "cruises." Duck can't take it anymore. He laughs. We laugh hysterically. Duck unfolds his napkin. We order dinner. The smell of eau-de-toilette and french fries. Duck whispers, "It would have been better to stay home."

Home? He let it slip. Or maybe that was his way of starting the game over again. His sincere way.

Out on the street, afterwards, he raises his arms, takes a deep breath of air. "I don't like those kinds of places." I slip into my pullover and check to see if my keys are still in my pocket, my money, my ID card. I pull down my shirt sleeves. Duck is waving his arms around. His eyes closed, he shakes his head. I watch him. "You want to go to a club?" "If you want to." "It's a little late for the movies." "So let's go back home." We take a few steps, and in the street, suddenly, he grabs me by the neck, gives me a quick kiss, a bite. Refrain: Who chooses whom, when, how, why?

We go back home, very quickly. And it all begins over again like the night before. I do, he doesn't. "It's nothing," he whispers afterwards, "nothing. . . . The important thing is that we felt good together. You work tomorrow morning?" I place a finger across his lips. He bites it. "Can I sleep in the other bedroom?"

11

Confessions. "What's nice with you, Pierre, is that I don't have to lie. Usually, I lie all the time, it gets the best of me. It's my wild side. But with you, I can't. Every time I'm about to lie, you already know it."

Words. "It's the first time I feel good, at somebody else's place. I feel protected. I accept it, though it's against my nature. I won't stay a long time, it's perfect like this. Anyway, you'll kick me out the door before I leave. All because of a toothpaste cap on the edge of the washbasin." Silence. "Can I brush my teeth with your brush?"

"When you're in a couple, it's true, you become a target. And so what then? All you need to do is to trust yourself. Each person is free. Yesterday, at the restaurant, I admit it, there are two or three of them who would have done anything to get my attention. The scent of fresh blood. Like in a hunt, the game. Why not?"

"While you were at school, a guy called, Bernard. He sounded surprised to hear someone else on the phone. He told me he'd call back in the late afternoon. He insists on seeing you, talking to you. You've known him a long time?"

"You remind me of Larry, the friend who was with me at the Balto café.

He's American. He is a member of the New York City Ballet. He invited me twice to his place. It was nice, but every day was planned ahead of time with him. He didn't do what he wanted to anymore. As for me, I didn't do everything I would have liked. I met him in Geneva. His troup was on tour. He's thirty-seven years old, and for a dancer, that's not very young anymore. He wanted me all for himself. Well, I didn't understand. And why, anyway? When I was there the second time, he took me to dinner at some friends' place. I left with one of his friends. Only because the guy made me laugh, and with Larry, I didn't laugh anymore. Hee-hee, I have a stupid laugh, but it's my laugh. It's like the way I walked when I was little. My real first name is Daniel. You didn't ask me, so I'm telling you."

"And my last name is Carbon. It's a Northern name. Originally, it was Charbon. So there, my name is Daniel Carbon. And you, Forgue, where does that come from?"

"How handsome Larry is! He still writes to me. And he's so very nice. You've never been able to sleep with someone, in the same bed? Well, I slept with one of my brothers until I was thirteen. We only had one bedroom for four people and two beds. One day I decided I'd rather sleep on the floor. It had started to bother me."

"For Christmas vacation, I went to Egypt. A friend from Lyon was a tour guide there. I tagged along. As an extra member of the group. No one noticed. Zero francs, everything included, round-trip Dijon-Dijon. There were only doctors, lawyers, Rotary-Club style. That's where I met the guy who has me doing these surveys in beauty salons. I fudge the answers a little, but when all is said and done, his hair spray will sell. The important thing is that I be able to pay my tuition."

"As for Larry, in fact, it's not true. I understood very well what he wanted. And the same goes for my friend in Egypt. The least one can say is that if the trip was beautiful, things didn't work out very well with him. I had become everybody's friend in the group. Especially the women. They all had a son or a daughter my age. But I was the one on the trip."

"I almost even went to Tokyo. It was last year. For Easter. Another friend who worked for Japan Airlines, in Amsterdam. He sends me a ticket, prepaid. Off to Holland. Four days, I hitchhike to Orly. I take the plane. I only had my bag, that one. The plane was full. They put me into first class. Stewardesses in kimonos. In Amsterdam, I fell asleep. In fact, no, I woke up, but I didn't move. Stopover. I played dead and the plane took off. It was only after an hour in the air that they noticed I was there. Because of the dinner trays. They had already served me champagne. The whole crew got involved. They spoke to me in English, I pretended I didn't understand. They spoke to me in French, I sat there gaping. They made me get off at Anchorage. I waited seventeen hours for the next plane, in the opposite direction. They paid, of course. When I arrived in Amsterdam, it was two days later. They kept the ticket. My friend wasn't home. I had just enough time to hitchhike back to Dijon. And get back to school. First year, you couldn't fool around. You had to maintain a B average. But anyway, I made it to Anchorage. And I sent a postcard to my mother and another to my brothers from there, so that they wouldn't understand."

"My parents don't say a word. I ran away for the first time at sixteen. But I had just graduated from high school. I went to Munich. To earn some money, I washed dishes in a restaurant. Like yesterday's restaurant. Eight days later, I was in Berlin, with one of the waiters, at his place. It's the first lover I ever really had. He still writes to me, too. I keep all the letters. Ashtrays, theater tickets, stationery with headings, road maps. I carry on at customs, to get a really good stamp on my passport. In my room, in Dijon, there's a map of the New York city subway. And one of the world. I draw lines where I've traveled, afterwards. What graffiti."

"Who is this girl who has asked you to go water her flowers? More than a friend? I have a woman friend, too, in Dijon. She's in prison. Accused of conspiracy. She had a German lover who lived with her. They arrested everybody when Baader died. She's awaiting trial. I took over her two-room apartment. Seventy francs a month. In the old area of Dijon. Before I left, the hot-water tank exploded. The apartment's on the second floor, facing the courtyard. The toilets are on the stairway landing. I should really fix the place up a little. Or give it a good painting. And most of all, make a real room for myself. For now there's only a mattress on the floor and cushions everywhere. But it's really nice. It's my home."

"Last weekend, my mother was with me, in Paris—supposedly. Well, that's the official story. In reality, she wanted to go to Strasbourg, to see some friends, women friends, who were married, too. But my father is jealous. It's the only cop-side of his personality. So I had to write my mother "General Delivery" to give her all the details of her trip. I even enclosed a restaurant bill and some used metro tickets to put in her handbag in case my father goes through it. At the place where I'm doing my training program, I photocopied the syllabus. When I go back to Dijon, at our first family meal, my father will ask questions. Mustn't make any mistakes. When I think that my mother didn't even go through all of this for a lover."

"The friend I'm staying with, in Paris? I never really knew what he did. A student association? He dropped out of college. But, ever since I arrived, he's been asking me too many questions. He wants to know where I've gone if I don't come back at night. The day before yesterday, he took back his keys. I have my things in his apartment. I'll go get them in a while, if you don't mind. The training course is over in two weeks. Is that all right with you? In the beginning of June, I'll go back to Dijon. I'll have two weeks to write up my evaluation. Then, I'll go to the seashore, at one of my uncle's homes, near Béziers. Just like that. To recharge my batteries. So the saying goes. A week there. My aunt's a very good cook. I spend my days in a rowboat, on the pond, surrounded by oyster parks. After that, I'll go back up to Dijon. I have to put in my long weekend. For the army. I'm going to get a discharge. I'll come up with something. I have a psychiatrist friend who'll help me. And after that, away I go, trucks, freighters. I want to travel around the whole Mediterranean. And you? You have any plans?"

"I really like it, when you look at me like that. You looked at me the same way, at the Balto, the first time, and the day before yesterday when I forced open your bedroom door, or when I showed you my notepads and everything I retrieved at the office. You have no idea all the things these companies throw away. And anyway, you have to manage as best you can. That worries you?"

"You're wrong. You see, I'm not lying to you. I'm telling you everything. The important thing is that we gain something from the time we are going to spend together. Gained time. And right now, I'm not being very sincere. I'm kind of saying what's going through your mind. It's not all that easy, to stop lying."

"And so we'll see. Before or after Béziers, maybe. I'll come to your house, in the Midi, if you're there. Peyroc? I spent all my vacations, until I was fifteen, with my parents and my brothers, in a policemen's campground, on the outskirts of St-Raphael. So now I want to move around."

"At home, five men, and my mother. Every time somebody hollers, we break up laughing. My father is jealous, but he's jolly. In reality, he doesn't give a shit about anything."

"Can I call up that guy? If he's home, I'll go get my things right away. If not, there's a chance he'll go away for a few days, and I won't have anything to put on. Tonight, we'll eat here, won't we? And tomorrow, I'll take you around Paris. Only Parisians never know where to go."

"Can I put the Jimmy Cliff back on?"

"And most of all, don't think about anything. Don't ask yourself too many questions. I've just made 'the' decision. Two weeks, or two years. Here, I feel good, very good. I feel like, I don't know. . . . You don't mind, my holding your head, like this, the tip of your nose against the tip of mine? This is how the Chinese used to say hello. You're crossing your eyes. You're funny. Are you listening to me? You're not saying a word?"

12

Lovers. There is always one who talks and the other who doesn't. And when both of them talk together, they often go their separate ways too soon. "It's plain as night," Marie would say. They talk together and everything becomes obvious: too much of a feather will not flock together. Or else, arguments, everything is continually deferred, they don't want to admit to anything so the game itself serves as a distraction, carries them away. You analyze love too much when you live it. You try to bring it to reason. It is not reasonable. Even the word *love* has become suspect. But only in the mysterious depths of each being.

That Saturday morning when I leave the apartment, Duck is sleeping in the other room, naked, sheets and blanket thrown off, on his stomach, his face turned toward the door, his left arm hanging over the bed. In his hand, on the carpet, a spoon. Near the spoon, an empty yogurt container. So he got up during the night, to eat a yogurt. Small white specks on his lips. So beautiful asleep, hesitating between hunger and repose. I cherish that image, my world tour, my graffiti.

At school, no one, student strike. Barbaroux is fuming. Arondelle and the others pace up and down the corridors waving their arms about. All they talk about is "tar," "defacements," "ineradicable marks," "unwarranted atmosphere" in "this institution, which has never, thank

God, been contaminated by leprosy." In my classroom, I stay behind
my desk. I write. You don't decide to write: everything gets written
suddenly. You execute. You are executed. And the fear of love, of the
word *love*, the fear of what is suspect has prompted me, for this first
text, to speak of the embrace. Everything leads back to the original
gesture. Little to do with eroticism or pornography. Little to do with an
affront or a scandal. I will place this text in chapter thirteen. I am
waiting for it expectantly. It will be the cornerstone. The true decisive
moment. And already I don't care much for this chapter twelve. A fact
is going to fit in here, a drawer within a drawer, a bad memory in an
obsessive memory. Why pause at Duck?

To reestablish a logical order: I came home around twelve, that
Saturday. Duck had just woken up. Chapter eleven. The chapter you've
just read. He talked. I listened to him. I didn't say a word. Distrust is
perhaps the first proof of affection. Duck is the one who made the
decision to move in with me, by talking. Or perhaps I myself invited him
to do it, by keeping silent. How can you tell? The text shouldn't dictate
the order of things. The way one orders an execution.

Around five, Duck calls up his friend: "You're there? Then I'll drop by
immediately to pick up my stuff." Duck asks me for a metro ticket and
leaves. "Happy?" A hurried kiss on the cheek. He dashes down the
stairs. At Marie's, I water the flowers. Through the windows, the
perfect calm weather surprises me. The good weather lasts suddenly.
On Marie's desk, between the layout of an industrial magazine *Flash
Engineering* and drafts of a direction manual for a water pump, lies the
prenatal catalog. On the door, as I leave the apartment, a note which
Marie put up with transparent tape: "the flowers thank you."

I ask Mariette if she needs me to do some shopping for her. She has
opened up all her hatboxes. She's looking for her glasses. "I must have
put them down but I can't remember if it was in the pearls or the
ribbons." She looks at me smiling. "I lose everything, I forget everything. That's how it is when you're old." Frail voice, almost shrill. I
think about Duck's "hee-hee." Same youthfulness, same carefree
attitude? As for Duck, he keeps everything and forgets nothing. I am

going to buy some bread, fruit, and ordinary steaks. Jean-Louis, my hairdresser, sees me passing in the street. He waves to me from behind his window. He has got customers waiting. The neighborhood customers, the Saturday afternoon children, with the parents' orders, "Cut it short, please." I follow the rue des Dames to get back home. My neighborhood is a village. You hear bursts of conversation, and you can see real faces. Duck is moving in with me?

I put everything away, in the kitchen. I hang the basket behind the door as usual. The phone rings. Bernard. "I am at The Lizard across the street, can I come up?" A minute later, he is here. "You're expecting someone?" "Yes." "Can I stay anyway?" "Why not." "I've seen André again. Things went badly. At home I'm alone and I can't get used to it. However much I tell myself how terrific it is. But no. Can I drink a glass of water?"

Chapter twelve, the lovers' trial. Chapter thirteen will be about the real embrace. Real? Words are only beautiful when they fall short. The perfect word is comfortable. It doesn't live life. Roussel often used to tell me, "We're cankers on cultivated culture. I would have so dearly liked to lay my life bare as I have lived it and to lay life itself bare such as it is." Bernard and his glass of water. "You look worried."

Roussel would also say, "It's easier to silence historical truth than to prevent its commercial exploitation. After all, we only teach the business of letters. And literature is the echo of history. There are no innocent bystanders." Sometimes, at the Balto Café, Roussel's hand would brush against mine. "To understand that everything happened to me in a world which thinks it is civilized, to understand it can happen again." Roussel would rarely finish his sentences. He punctuated his fits of silence with some "I am alone" and "I don't want it to happen to you," about which I still wonder if he articulated them consciously. Bernard puts down the glass of water on my desk. "What are you thinking about?" "An old friend. He was a teacher with me, in the same high school. He retired a year ago. Nervous breakdown. He's taking a sleep cure." "Because of someone?" "Perhaps." "Of you?" "No. But I guess that . . ." "That what?" The door bell rings. It's Duck. With a big suitcase. He's out of breath. "I'd like you to meet Bernard. Bernard, this is Duck."

Three. One, two, three. Duck puts down the suitcase in his room. I did write, *his room*. Bernard wants to leave. I stop him. I stopped him. To live as a couple, with a peacefulness, an attentiveness one for the other, an affection which speaks the language of real love? A fantasy, a trial, or perhaps an invitation, I no longer know. Or else a rejection. No doubt, by asking Duck to stay, I was rejecting him who had just arrived, put down his luggage. Or perhaps I wanted to see them together, same age, and understand? Never cease to understand.

Life, nothing but life, lived through, experienced, with its funny touching moments, sometimes traumatic, always sincere. In a letter from Roussel I read over again: "How to express it? How can I prepare my soul to accept what chance sends my way? Let something happen, let someone appear!" The three of us, sitting on the floor. Duck looks at Bernard. "What do you do for a living?" Bernard talks about his work at the hospital. "And you?" Duck stretches out, his head propped on a cushion. "I am studying for a degree in management so I can wave it around later." His training? "Analytical accounting, a new accounting technique for reconciling balance sheets. A matter of money-supply forecasting. I have an idea about that. But that's not what counts." I look at Bernard, then Duck. "And what counts for you?" Duck answers, "To bum around." He laughs.

Duck's "hee-hee" amuses Bernard. It makes me smile too. I remember it like an exclamation point, always out of place, unexpected.

Duck took out all the records. Bernard helps me to prepare dinner. "You're sure I can stay?" "Absolutely." "But I get the feeling that . . ." "It's only a feeling." Duck sat at my desk. He is looking through the index cards, the notes for my classes. He flourishes the sheets. "What's that, 'the mystery of the sources?' " "It's a text I wrote, this morning, about you, or rather because of you." Bernard smiles. "You've known each other long?" "No, three days."

Duck gives the sheets back to me. I slip them in my notes. He wants to
take them out. "First tell me why it's called, 'the mystery of the
sources.'" A fight or a game. Duck grabs me. Bernard separates us.
We sit down for dinner. Our feet on top of the records. Bernard says,
"Good thing I have you both tonight."

Later. Inevitably. On the blanket. It's grown dark. Footsteps in the
courtyard, a plane passing above Paris and the trains coming and going,
open windows, turned out lights. Bernard has a bandage on his chest,
right side. He doesn't want to take it off. "It's still sore. What shit."
Everything is said in hushed tones. One, two, three. Duck rips off the
bandage. A little gold ring pierces his nipple. Bernard protects himself
with his hand. "Careful, it's not healed yet. I don't know why I did it,
but . . ." He smiles. "But I felt like it!" And he lets himself be fondled
by our fingertips, Duck's and mine. Duck takes off the medal from
Bernard's neck and reads in the darkness out loud: "Neither compel me
nor prevent me." We kiss. And gradually they forget about me. It's
neither a torment nor a vision. Voyeur. It's the way it is, simply. It is.
And I stretch out alongside of them. From time to time they pull my
hand for me to join them. Duck takes Bernard. He takes him.
Completely erect. And Bernard arches his back under Duck. And it's
the way it is. It is. Duck wakes me up in the middle of the night. Bernard
has left. He forgot his medal. A piece of paper on the desk. He wrote:
"Thanks." Duck shuts the windows. "Do you want me to sleep in your
bed?" He takes the wine bottle and holds it out to me: "Drink, you're
cold. And me too. Why did you tell Bernard to stay?" I answer, "So
you'd leave, so you'd stay, I don't know. I wanted to know." "What?"
Duck enters my bedroom first, throws himself on my bed. "I want to
stay."

Daybreak. Duck whispers, "You'll read me what you wrote?" Chapter
thirteen. The mystery of the sources.

13

Sunday noon. We've just had breakfast, in my bedroom, on the bed. Duck went to get the pages on my desk and handed them to me. Like a command: "Don't skip a single paragraph, a single word." I read.

"The mystery of sources, who can fathom it? And as for the man who expresses himself, is there anyone to listen to him? We blame ourselves for all the time we have not spent together and lived with the other. The person we expected. When a man alone remembers an embrace, he relives it and continues to conjure it up, and to wait for it expectantly. Strange youthfulness which teaches us, as the years go by, to become wiser and wiser and, at great risk, younger and younger. The memory of bodies is never obliterated. It's the first and clearest of all our readings. The most incomplete also. Therein lies the source, and its mystery. The text once read, we fall or we fly. There is the kind of artist who produces and another who produces himself. The latter mimics himself; the first uncovers and discovers himself, growing more uncertain. His doubt increases inevitably along with the mastery of his art, and makes him grow . . ."

Duck: "That's beautiful. But perhaps only because you're reading out loud."

"The text, here, wordplays, a last scar, a sly smile, frozen, of those who have used too many words, will never be a pretext. In our efforts to bring all things within our grasp, within our expectations, have we not reached this stage of analysis where everything becomes incomprehensible, and where the unexpected makes its demands? The artist, faithful to his original impulse, defined by the intensity of his daily suffering, is always one step ahead of the avant-garde, one step ahead of his risk. This classroom in which I have been teaching for years, this morning, empty, is listening to me, dangerously. I want to talk about meeting people, meeting someone. About an embrace . . ."

Duck: "I don't understand. I don't want to understand." He smiles. "Go on."

"The empty classroom is watching. The possible young man of the summer to come is inaugurating my guest room. This empty classroom is listening. The young man of the summer to come decided to stay, for the night. He got up to eat a yogurt. The spoon is still in his hand. His left arm is falling off the bed. He doesn't move. The image is already planted in my memory. Meeting people, someone, maybe him. The empty classroom is watching, listening, with the eyes and ears of a person who is awaiting his share in the work, a person who is sharing, and who wants to express, to express himself. Art transforms man. Man, completely transformed, gambols about, purified, informed. Or perhaps, moved, possessed, he cannot leave the contemplation of the work of art unscathed, when it exists, when it offers, when it shuns calculations and affectations, codes and modes, when it leaps up, surges forward. And as the other breaks into your life, the one expected so fervently, confronting the art work of his presence, and confronting these words, here, laid down as we ourselves lie down, one against the other, the individual, either he or I, now, has no choice but to ask himself once again the important questions of life, torture or joy, transformation. At the source of the art work, he seeks its mystery, just as he seeks his own mystery. We always feel different, prepared to make other choices. Austerity, renunciation, negation are not always completely foreign to us, even if we defend ourselves against them. We have all ceded to the temptation, as you almost always do, when you're twenty."

Duck: "Don't stop. I'm in the classroom. I am looking at you. I am listening." He moistens his lips as if he, too, was preparing to speak.

"Now voices, the sublime voices rise up. Those that I attempt to make heard, here, rows of seats, desktops, blackboard, podium. I've succeeded Roussel, who himself had succeeded. . . ? And so the misunderstanding goes on. The sublime voices which guide, beckon, inspire. An essay topic: I'm satisfied with the human; I find everything in it, including the divine. There is only one point about which I feel superior to the mass of men: I am altogether more free, and more dutiful than they dare to be. Superiority is not a matter of caste but a matter of generosity. It's not the product of ambition, but of the raw gift of yourself. The gift of life is enough. Would be enough. Excess can only be expressed sparingly. And what is human, in the narrowest, most restricted, most direct sense of the word, serves the daring intentions of whoever wants to exist through self-expression. Here, I am expressing myself. They may well wave their arms about in the hallway and take offense over some graffiti. I have a memory completely covered with names, in tar. And they can't be erased, Mrs. Superintendent. And they'll come to question me in the privacy of my home. They are already questioning me. Between the words, they station themselves and point their fingers at me. And even the possible young man of the summer to come squeezes in. Sooner or later, they will accuse him along with me. Scheming. Conspiring. Thickets. Lies. At the very moment the meeting occurs, everything has already happened. I am afraid of it. I don't want to believe it. It's a fact. I mean, the embrace . . ."

Duck is silent, naked, his back against the wall, curled up, his arms wrapped around his legs, his fingers intertwined. He rests his chin on his knees. "Go ahead. I shouldn't have . . ." And so, my voice clear, very distinctly, I continue. I transcribe these sheets, today, word for word, without changing anything. On the bottom of each page, silence. I go on to the next page. And I heard Duck speak, because suddenly silence rips off his mask and embarrasses him. I hear him repeat everything he told me between the reading of each page. His voice, today, and the exact words: "Go ahead. I shouldn't have . . ."

"Here is the embrace. The risk is taken. Taboo rituals attract misdirected stares, a horde of ideas bristling with scandal, this method skillfully undermined, subtly recognized, for ensnaring the freaks, the raving fanatics, those for whom liberty and subjection go hand in hand. I am free to tell of the embrace and subjected to the desire of expressing it. First contact, this very first reading of beings, when they meet, or if they meet, palpitate, listen to each other, touch and penetrate each other. Absurd hope of coming back to the place from which you have never really wholly emerged. Voyeurs may break their glasses and scandal mongers grow more strident: another kind of embrace does not exist. So relentlessly has morality conceived itself as open or closed, it has forgotten to be what men are. How beautiful it is this morning! How full this empty classroom is! I've never had so many students willing to listen to me, so many professors willing to keep quiet. Everything can be written down. I am. Duck is expecting me . . ."

Duck: "It's true. I was expecting you. I even wonder if . . . But no, read what comes next."

"Free then, here, I neither expose nor expose myself. I impose a vision, on paper, a support, print it, implicate myself, apply myself, and propose. The Nikko Hotel hallway leads to this meeting, that day, day before yesterday, yesterday. Him. The unexpected one. And it's necessary to give advance warnings since we are all frightfully warned in advance. The voyeur, within ourselves, is a constant companion, a part of ourselves uselessly shielded, waiting only to be aroused by a tragedy which has no subject, a commotion whose only scenery is principles, precepts, vague dried-up ideas. Necessary to cast off your armor, to forget the social game, the interplay of points of view, preconceived ideas which are often the most solidly anchored, and lay ourselves bare. To be naked, confronting the embrace as we lived it, knew it, forgot it the very moment we were experiencing it in order to bear it within ourselves, later, a whole lifetime through, our lifetime, the strange memory to come. Why shouldn't we tell what we are and the way we are, when we draw near the other's body to touch it, to stroke it, to caress it, to embed ourselves within it? At this very moment, as we stroll through our lives, everything that does not exist authentically, ceases to be and disappears on the spot. Essay topic: When I am with you I am not alone anymore, but I am not yet two. Within the embrace, the voice of the individual rises up. A gesture. He's about to speak. The gesture suggested, affirmed, insisted upon, brings us back to ourselves. So little and so much at the same time. Stubborn as we are. A couple?"

Duck looks at me. "The Nikko Hotel?" "I'll explain." "It was last weekend, wasn't it? I saw the bill on your desk . . ."

"Laugh then, sideshow villains, servants of hypocrisy, tacky voyeurs, enforcers of worn-out morals. Re-cap your pens, glutted theoreticians, crowned with intelligentsia, that flower which, little by little, crumbles into grey dust. Blend all the colors of nature and you will obtain grey. Brown, the optimists say, like earth. No, grey. Laugh and re-cap your pens: art is not in the province of the worldly, and particularly of the worldly man who insists that he is not. In the tribunals of the absurd comedy which is being played out all around, the creator, each man, in order to clear his name or assert himself, pretends he is superior to the other, to his neighbor, his rival. And this comedy has been playing for centuries, may my classes bear witness to this fact, fiercely determined as we are to remain at the outpost which we haven't occupied for quite a while. The organization of taboos functions flawlessly. Surely it's by this feature that we recognize civilizations which are breathing their last . . ."

Duck: "If Bernard doesn't come back and take his medal, I'll keep it for myself. His motto suits me. I'm listening, you know."

"You construct ramparts so as to better keep on the lookout, to vilify all the while looking on, to vilify, to vilify, and especially never vivify anything. I write, everything can be written. I want to speak of the embrace and, even now, the silence of this classroom is vilifying. Beware of the unruly. They lie. The artist's gesture, pushed off to the side, can no longer help but to bring together, haphazardly, those whose freedom is bound to their subjection, the lunatics, tramps, the hard-headed, those whose hopelessness is the only possible hope. From behind the ramparts, you foresee everything. You quantify. You

despise the success which escapes the sentinel's eyes. You plot failures.
You block roads. You write of death, the dead. You gain mastery over
the creative enemy by analyzing him too much. You're unaware of one
thing, of one single fact: lyricism will prevail. The very kind which
carries me away, today. They wave their arms about in the hallway. I,
for one, subject myself to the call of these pages. It is my turn to write.
We all write, always, one day. If it only be a letter which believes itself a
love letter. And if censorship no longer means robbing the power of
speech but rather giving it to those to whom it is given, if fascism no
longer means gagging people's mouths but forcing words to their lips,
the fact still remains that the artist, guerrilla in service to his art, says
what he has to say, rejects the idea of forbidden subjects, the maze of
social fortifications, the constrictions set by worldviews rated highly in
the Stock Exchange, and seizes the whole world in the palm of his hand.
At the source. The original water. He drinks, quenches his thirst, and
transcribes the emotion."

Duck: "Anyway, about this medal, I'm sure Bernard left it on purpose
and that he won't come back. Everybody to his own message, right?"
Silence. "I've just finished, Pierre, what I had to say. Go on!"

"These lines, for me, come in their own good time. Like a song. A
whisper. These lines are listening. Listening is necessary. The
embrace: the startled body is waiting. Double surprise, double
constancy, couple, the surprise is unpredictable. It's not a matter of
what's written, reproduction of the real, not very realistic, all things
considered, and which shows too much, but of writing, a reality in itself.
To draw with words. The sketch approaches the completed work, the
rough draft structures the precise outline, this choice of the body's
geography that we make, while embracing, blinded, surrendered to the
other, as if it was possible to enter the other wholly, and erase oneself
until you are only flesh of the other's flesh. To come back. Point of
departure. The body's surprise lies in that reaching out. You touch each
other, you size each other up, you bury yourself in each other, deep.
You know that the dream is not going to come true. You look for your
double, your twin, brother, sister, father, mother, an ordinary couple,
two identities, or two identical beings, what's the difference? I'll tell the

possible young man of the summer to come not to stay. May he leave
before it's too late. Before I have my chance to caress him and he comes
the way he made me come. Alone. As soon as he gets back, I'll tell him
to leave."

Duck smiles. "Except for one thing, I gave you an eraser!" He bites his
lips. "Read to the end, please, even if I don't understand, even if I don't
want to understand."

"Here, sentences, my sentences, what I write, what is being written, the
body is listening. Ordinary eroticism manipulates bodies in strained
postures, frames, partial concealments. And pornography focuses on
outskirts, folds, borders, the mound or the phallus, a contrary frustra-
tion. Here, sentences, my sentences, I don't want either of these modes
of representation, but I am aiming for something beyond that, for the
sense of touch, I want to tell of this bodily presence, sensual, so that
there is nothing which contracts or relaxes at cross-purposes, it is
indeed a matter of listening. Hands are so many sexual organs.
Attitudes, so many invitations. Regions, all the regions of the boundless
geography of sight and touch. Therein lie the truth and the emotion. The
swooning embrace when, a split second of life, we attempt to fuse
ourselves, lost as we are then, surrendering to the oars of our arms, to
the sources of our saliva, to the soft wetness within, to the illusion of
accessories, to the task of exploring, of seizing, of ripping apart, to the
violence without which, at this intensity of collision, tenderness cannot
express itself in any other way . . ."

Duck merely gazes ahead, his lips resting on his knees.

"It's our bodies' feast. A dizzy spell, the plunge. And I plunge into other
men. And what is different about my twin couples, and the way our
identities clash, have nothing abnormal about them except the
extraordinary normality of our outburst, and nothing moving except the
determination which we display by choosing one another with no
purpose in mind. The idea of procreation still prowls around. But the
self-contained purpose of the other, embraced, and his self-contained
rapture, are as beautiful and human as the being who is engendered,

created. Two beings can generate each other, transform each other. During the supreme silence of embraces, do we not learn of dissatisfaction and failure, what an individual may accomplish most successfully? Chest, neck, hands, the feel of skin, the titillation of tongues and lips, mouths, all the mouths, the body knows no filthiness. Its topography does not encompass any badlands. The other's body always remains to be discovered. A whole lifetime is not enough for the task. Where are my crayons? Whispers, moans or sighs, poorly disguise the fact that a life, strictly speaking, would not be enough for the task. Sublime feast. To find the proper words. And let them frolic, far from eroticism and far from pornography. The other and I, here, bound to these sentences, we are. They are. They are here. Look at us. Look at them. They are going to melt into each other, one into the other. Is it possible? Orgasm, sarcasm, will arise to interrupt everything like a retribution. But the feast goes on. We devour, we bite, we bend, break, mold, caress, moisten, moisten each other, we lick, we cleave, we scratch. With our whole being we do everything to open our eyes wide, to seek out the sister-image, the brother-portrait, we want to produce and present ourselves with the other. Very different from reproducing ourselves and representing ourselves. Within the other and for the other. To no purpose. Renunciation. It's a matter, here, of a mystery and a source, the same mystery and the same source as for all of us. And you, the possible young man who is expecting me, and for whom I waited expectantly, for so long, go away, quickly, go away! There's still time. Before I grab you the way you grabbed me. Before we hold onto each other, together, and we find our pleasure one in the other."

Duck looks at me: "I love you, Pierre." "Excuse me?" "No. I didn't say anything, but you heard me perfectly well."

"A light is dawning, transparent, delicate, a light like gazing eyes inviting us not to stop at appearances, at details which, in the intimacy of an embrace, have never been banished, filthy, guilty or reprehensible. The mind's militia knows this. The only militia that has as many soldiers as there are human beings. Each person, within himself, knows the truth . . ."

Duck stretches out on his back, his hands behind his neck, right up against me, he stares at the ceiling. He smiles.

"We will never be happy. But happy doesn't mean anything. So, we'll never be satisfied. Those who claim that they are are lying to themselves. We will never totally get back to where we've come from. The brother doesn't exist. The brother, the sister, the father or mother. No, we'll never meet our twin. We know this. But we look for him. We stumble along. We crash into each other. We tear each other apart as much by waiting as by embracing. We fall from on high, orgasm, then once more the upward path, we brush up against each other. And art, when it exists, when it doesn't compose, when it doesn't impose, speaks of dissatisfaction. Thereby, it leads us on, inspires. It breaks into your life, like a being, and everything can be written. I wish so intensely that, in the embrace of these lines, curves, tensions, touches, ink, script, raw desire for writing, there may be a rising and a falling, the round-trip ticket of any love, a desire wherein nothing is gained, a desire at its origin, above all not original, in a world, a society, the skirts of a very old Europe, which speaks of desire only in the hope of selfish gain . . ."

Duck jumps up, goes toward the window and opens it wide. His laugh. High-pitched. He turns around: "Hey, across the way they saw me stark naked. Anyway, that's what I say to myself. Go on!"

"To speak of the embrace adequately, hitting the right note of distress, depicting the most authentic joy. Orgasm will catch us unprepared. It's about to catch you unprepared. Words never cease weaving their intrigues. Nothing ever really reaches a denouement. Going away and coming back at the same time. And everything begins again, stubbornly. There remains the idea that they formulate about a difference: I am their faggot, the faggot. Barbaroux has just stepped into the classroom and asked me if I was working. I answer that I was preparing for a class. To measure out the right amount of restraint and audacity, of submission and rebellion, of fierce demands and perspicacious compromises. Come back home, and tell the young man to go away, quickly. Quickly . . ."

Duck slips Bernard's chain and medal around his neck. He had the whole thing clenched in his fist, like loot. He rubs his forearms. "I'm cold, it's barely spring." Under the window, slanting sun rays strike downwards, silhouette, curls, he shakes his head and whispers, "It's lovely . . ." Last page.

"Bodies stumbling into each other, tracking each other down, questioning, staring, grabbing hold, everybody and all of world history in two beings and in one single instant. At this time, nothing is too risky or matters anymore. They are here. We are here. In our image. One against the other. Embracing. Wild hope haunting us and before which we no longer behave as we are wont to. The body, territory of the mind, beckons. Mysteries, we will never really take possession of it. Neither our own nor the other's. Down with taboos, prejudices. Take action, here, an event. The pen is both tender and violent. The marks on the page are watching, the embrace is listening. Tell the young man to leave while there's still time." I look at Duck: "That's where I stopped."

Silence. Duck puts the medal in his mouth. He speaks to me. I don't understand what he's saying to me. I ask him to repeat. He takes the medal out: "Why do you say everything, right away?" I answer without pausing to think: "Because I'm not expecting anybody anymore." He gets up, gathers the papers together, puts them in order and returns them to the desk. I hear him whisper, "In that case, I'm staying."

14

Sixteen days of happiness. Album. Or sixteen days of wariness. A ritual established itself, an embryo of a shared daily life. For breakfast, Duck does not get up until everything is ready. Nothing surprises him, neither the brioches nor the wild-strawberry jam. Small treats. But, crooked smile, knowing glance, Duck isn't really unappreciative. At times, I even tell myself that he's testing me this way, a revenge for the reading of my text, which *he* demanded. "Anyone else, in my place, would have run away on the spot. But I like to break down doors, be there when I should be gone. I was born gone. It's one of my mother's expressions when she scolds me for not looking after my brother enough. When I was born, my mother wasn't eighteen. I have pictures of her, I'll show them to you. Are you working? Have your students come back to class, like little sheep?"

Whenever Duck enters my room, he pretends to get his foot caught in the dictionary, to trip, and flying forward, flings himself on my bed, motions to bite me on the chin. "I sleep next door, it's better for you. If you have a very, very bad dream, call me or rather get up and come and shake me. With a little luck, you'll wake me up. Good night!"

Duck goes to bed and falls asleep instantly. At times I get up. His bedroom door is open. On the floor, his suitcase, unpacked, stacks of books. "I read everything. Right now I'm finishing *Gilles* by De Drieu and I'm going to attack *Aurélien* by Aragon. They wrote their books at the same time, you see, I know, see which one would finish first, a race for prizes. I didn't like *Dreamy Bourgeoisie*. Everything in the preterite, like a bad translation from English. I read, but I don't retain anything. I just want to know why they all want to have power. That's what novels are all about: power or death. Rastignac or strychnine, at the end of *Man's Fate*. It was strychnine, wasn't it? You see, I'm giving you a lecture. Actually, when someone is about to die, everything becomes very interesting. You have to be crazy to write a novel without any character dying. And clever to sneak in a petty upstart. Proust makes me laugh, how about you?" Around the suitcase, bundles of envelopes, ballpoint pens, sheaves of paper, multicolored cardboard folders, carbon paper and a stapler: "My war treasure. In the firms where I am doing my training course, it's insane how much they waste. So I pilfer. The secretaries love me. I'll have to come up with an idea of a present for them, the day I leave. A teapot maybe, because they have tea every day at five. It's air-conditioned, you know. Thirty-first floor. Every day there is somebody who blacks out or gets a nosebleed. They don't let out a peep. It's either this or no job. You, in teaching, you don't risk anything. We'll see about me. But I'll do everything except analytical accounting. I'll try to bum around as long as possible. Am I bothering you? Still a lot of papers to correct? Tonight we eat out. It's my treat! That means I feel like going to a restaurant and I'll be your guest. Anyway I'm flat broke. OK, I'll shut up. But you still haven't told me, why, the Nikko Hotel."

Scattered around the suitcase, the grey-and-blue checkered shirt, the white shirt, undershorts, two pairs of jeans, pullovers in a heap, a jacket, and hanging from the window handle, "my beautiful suit, to take exams in, especially orals, it's the tie which makes the difference." A wool suit, burgundy colored. "Look at it, it looks like a hanged man." Sometimes, at night, I stand in the doorway to Duck's room, beautiful disorder of the sheet and blanket. "I don't need them." He sleeps naked, on his stomach, his head buried in a pillow, the way he buries it sometimes between my legs while ramming into me. Battering ram. Standing on the threshold of his room, I dare not enter. Tomorrow morning, I'll need to shake him several times. "Get up, Duck, you're going to be late, and me too!" He jumps out of bed. "Oh boy!" He stretches. "In Dijon, I have three alarm clocks. I always wait for the third to ring. And its sound. I'll show it to you. They're everywhere, in windows. But I'm never late. For next year I found work as a night clerk in a hotel. The pay is good. A friend from school is handing over his job. You better believe mornings are going to be rough." I can't remember when I gave Duck a set of the keys. He gets into everything. He found them. He took them. I must have said, "It will be simpler."

The phone's ringing? Duck answers before me. "I'll see if he's here!" Then Duck holds the receiver out to me: "It's your mother, she seems surprised," or, "A guy, but it's not Bernard. I would have recognized his voice." The doorbell's ringing? Duck gets to the door before me. I barely have time to get there. "Marie, I'd like you to meet . . ." "We've already introduced ourselves." Duck insists that Marie stay with us. "And then, afterwards, we'll go see if your flowers have been properly watered. Pierre has already forgotten to phone his father Sunday. It was the Saint-Mandé's daddy's birthday, his glorious bridge-playing daddy!" Duck amuses Marie. Marie tells me, "He's a natural, your little pet."

One evening, I meet Marie at the top of rue de Rome. We walk home together. Marie tells me, "This time, keep him. Do you feel good with him?" "Yes." "Yes-yes or yes-no?" "Yes-yes." "I don't believe you, but keep him all the same. As long as possible." "He'll be off in ten days." "He'll come back. Or else you'll go meet him. And Roussel, any news?" "I wrote his brother. I'm expecting an answer." Third floor, on the landing, Marie takes a teasing tone. "I'll leave you alone, this evening, the two of you." "If you wish. But Duck'll come and get you." And that's what happened. Later, the three of us come out of a movie theater. Duck takes Marie in his arms. "I'll be the godfather, won't I?" "Why not?" Marie glances at me. "Are you jealous?" Marie wants to pay me back for her ticket. Duck prevents her. "No, no, we're his guests." Marie puts the money in my jacket pocket. "You don't live in Saint-Mandé anymore." Duck says nothing. He is a few steps ahead of us. He imitates a duck's waddle. Marie bursts out laughing. He turns to her. "It's not funny, it's the tragedy of my life. From now on I forbid you to call me Duck. My real name is Daniel." "But of course, my little Duck." They laugh, both of them. We burst out laughing, the three of us. "Shall we take the metro, or walk home?" "Walk!" On a street corner, Duck stations himself and motions us to stop. "Be careful, watch out, we're going to be attacked." Marie whispers to me under her breath, "There are times when I wonder if he's not worse than Sam, Jacques & Bertrand. In any case, he has Tadzio's hands. When's he leaving again?" "In a week." "Have you spoken to him about Peyroc?" "Not really."

At Mariette's, Duck plays with Boubou. "This cat is not so old. Look, he scratched me." Duck holds Boubou in his arms. "So, Boubou, you're still scratching?" Duck kisses one paw, then the other, alternately, ten times, twenty times. Boubou, aggravated, scratches him on the forehead. "You see? It's bleeding. Are you happy, Boubou?" In front of Duck, Mariette looks even smaller, frailer. She takes me aside, in a room, and tells me, while holding my hand, "I understand you, Pierre, but he's too young for you. You . . ." She falls silent. She smiles. Duck bursts in, on all fours. He pushes Boubou around on the floor, on his back, petting his stomach. Mariette watches. "Not so rough, he's old, you know." "I know, I know, Mrs. Mariette, Pierre also is always telling me that about him. But . . ." Boubou bites his hand. "You see, he's happy!"

Two weeks. Album. Images. Adoptions. A clock broke at Mariette's. Duck repaired it. "I don't know anything about it, but the wheels know me." The four of us have dinner together, at Marie's. Duck insisted on carrying Mariette in his arms, on the stairs. "But." "But, yes, Mrs. Mariette, you are our little bride." At the table, Mariette glances at me. "Is he nuts?" Duck comes back from the kitchen with Marie. Mariette winks at me. "Or not nuts at all. How can you tell? I could never tell the difference." Duck sits down at the table. "The difference between what and what, Mrs. Mariette?" "The difference between you and you, Mr. Duck!" "In that case, there isn't any, Mrs. Mariette." Duck glances at me. "Or else there is: when I lie. But *that* is the mystery of the sources. You always dream about what you don't have."

We go back to my place. As soon as the door is shut, Duck takes my hand and presses it against his belly. "You see, here it goes. Don't turn on the light. No, don't say anything."

Blue sky. Unbroken sunshine for two weeks. If Duck comes home before me, he opens my mail. "There isn't much money left on your account." Or, "Is that all you earn, every month?" Or else, "Your sister wants to know if you'll go to your goddaughter's first communion. Does she live in Le Havre? Sainte-Adresse? That's a lot of saint-somethings in your family. The other one lives in Saint-Cloud, doesn't she?" Duck sprinkles detergent on his dirty laundry in the kitchen sink. It'll be my job to do what's left. As I do for myself. "It would be nice if I could leave with everything, everything clean, because in Dijon I won't have time."

A letter comes. Daniel Carbon, c/o Pierre Forgue, 113 rue Boursault, 75017 Paris. "It's my mother, since for once I have a set address . . ."

The three of us. We drink a beer on the terrace of the Balto. Duck is telling Marie about everything. "I even went to Marrakesh with a Swiss man, from Geneva. Thirty years old. An architect. But it turned into the sourest vinegar, all because of love and money. He had paid for the trip. And as for love . . . he was of the Sam, Jacques & Gilles type." Marie interrupts him. "No, it's Sam, Jacques & Bertrand." "Have you read *Gilles*? and *Aurélien*?" Later, we go home, in the metro. "I even went to England, at an old beautiful woman's house, haughty and domineering, Johnny Walker's lover. From her house, you could see the ocean." The next day, Marie meets me after school at noon. "I want to talk to you. Does he lie?" "Not with me." "When is he leaving?" "In three days." "Does it hurt?" "No. Let him leave! I haven't really grown attached to him." "Is that a promise?" Marie grabs my arm, her head on my shoulder. We walk along like two lovers. In a coffee shop, Place Clichy, she opens her pocketbook. "Look, my pregnancy calendar. I've just had my third month checkup. The gynecologist said everything was going very well. I won't come to Peyroc this summer. I'll stay in Paris. A little free-lancing. Some extra money. And then I'll fix up the bedroom." "I'll help you." "No, I want to do it all by myself." She rests her hands on her stomach. "For him? Everything, all by myself!"

Duck arrives late. "I was at Mariette's." He's lying. He glances at me. "But it's true!" He goes into his room, throws his bag on the floor. "You shouldn't have bothered to make my bed . . ." He undresses, flourishes a book. "I bought *Aurélien*. I started reading it in the metro. So I missed my stop." He goes into the bathroom. "And then I gave Mariette some flowers. But I don't think she likes me. No mail for me? I called my psychiatrist friend from my office. There is nothing official I can do to get a discharge. But he has a few tips. I have an appointment to see him, Wednesday evening. What will you be doing on Wednesday evening, here?" He takes a shower, gets out, dries himself. "You know, everybody telephones, all the time, from the office. You've got to take advantage of it. I even called Larry. It was five o'clock in the morning over there. His contract with the New York City Ballet was not renewed. He's going to open a dance studio." Duck tosses the towel to the floor. The telephone rings. He picks up the receiver. "Yes, yes, I'll put him on!" He hands over the receiver to me, his hand covering it tightly. "Hi-hi, it's your sister. You also forgot to answer her letter."

Duck puts the records in order. "Can I take this one?" Duck rummages through the clothes closet. "This short-sleeved shirt, do you still wear it? Dark blue is perfect. When you travel, you don't wash and you don't get washed." Duck turns off all the lights. "Are you coming?" He enters my room, brushes up against the dictionary, a game, he trips, throws himself on my bed. "I'm waiting for you."

Correcting papers. "Give everybody a passing grade, they all deserve to pass. But then again, no, we don't deserve anything. That's what you're thinking. So flunk us, F-." We? He jumbles up the papers on my desk. "I don't know which one of us bothers the other more." He stretches out on the sofa, propped up by the cushions. "Masochism! Masochist! My psychiatrist friend is always coming out with those words. I'm bothering you, right? But I don't know which one of us bothers the other more. And which one of us loves it more. And which one of us . . . Excuse me, I'll be quiet. At any rate, there's always one person in a couple who talks, and the other who doesn't. Two mysteries and two sources. Never the same bed. Hee-hee!" Silence. He turns toward me, a finger over his lip. "Shhh . . ."

In the shower. "Scrub me." He laughs. "Harder than that." Then it's my turn. Standing up in the tub, he sprays me, soaps me up. "Tonight . . ." He works up a lather, my back, my legs, my feet. "Tonight . . ." He wets my hair, shampoo. "Tonight . . ." My eyes are stinging, he laughs, water everywhere, I splash, he rinses me off, he straddles the edge of the bathtub. "Tonight, I want you and me to . . ." I kiss him. Later, outside, we leave a Chinese restaurant. He tells me, "You didn't let me finish my sentence: tonight I want you and me to . . ." I kiss him again. He starts running. "So, hurry up!"

Like a struggle, a fight. Is it possible we are so clumsy, or else is it our rough approach which leads one along, attracts the other? We slam up against each other. His bed, mine, in his room or in mine. And always the same record, Jimmy Cliff. I take him and he whispers, "Gently, I . . ." He glances at me, smiles. A smile like a laugh, tossed off. Given. A smile flung into my face. He asks me, "Do you feel comfortable?" Or, "Is it good?" Then, orgasm, my orgasm, and once again I hear the rumble of the city, of the trains, the heartbeat of the record which stopped long ago. Duck strokes my forehead. "I'll have to come back to give my presentation, in September . . ." Silence. "I'll visit you in Peyroc." Then, "All you'll need to do is come and pick me up, it's near Béziers. You'll see my aunt and uncle, at last, they aren't really married. They're the rich members of my family. And you'll see for yourself! OK?" Shadows in the bedroom. "Everything went by very quickly, didn't it? I'm sure you've counted the days. Me too. Sixteen! A real record."

Tuesday evening. End of May. Duck has gotten home before me. His smile is forced. "You shouldn't have bought the teapot. I won't say thank you because I make a point about never saying thank you. If the secretaries kissed me once, they kissed me ten times!" His room is empty. "I came home in the middle of the afternoon. I gave my suitcase and my boxes to friends who were leaving and passing through Lyons. They had room for me, too, but I wanted to see you again. I'll hitchhike home." He props the dictionary against my bedroom door, a kick, and places the duplicates of the keys on my desk. "I've said good-bye to Mariette. She had a funny way of wishing me good luck." He lowers his eyes, rubs his nose. "I think it's better if I leave right away." He steps back, opens the door. "No, I'll find my way. I have your telephone numbers. I've left you my address." His canvas bag over his shoulder, he shakes his head. "If there are any letters, you'll forward them?" He seems embarrassed, or happy, I can't tell. I don't move. I put my briefcase on the desk. He looks at the stairway through the open door. "I'll send a postcard to Marie and to her three-ninths." He laughs. "Anyway, I'll call you collect if you don't mind . . ." Blows me a kiss on his fingertips. He shows me Bernard's medal hanging around his neck, then his fist clenched, raised, "Ciao," he pulls the door shut. I hear the footsteps on the stairs. Four by four. He is in a hurry. He has friends. A lot of friends. He just lied: his hair too nicely arranged, his curls knowingly tousled, the look in his eyes brighter, somewhere else, already.

Through the window, by the desk, I intently watch the courtyard. He passes through quickly. He doesn't turn around. Over. It's over. I tidy up his room, I put away the Jimmy Cliff record, I throw away an empty bottle, his shampoo, for his curls. On the desk he put the eraser in a prominent place. And on a piece of paper he wrote, "Daniel Carbon, 5 rue Jean Jaurés, Bât. c., 21100 Dijon. See you soon. Duck." He drew a little figure spreading his feet apart. Over the face, a balloon. "Hee-hee!" It's over.

And I find you again here, Duck. And I hold on to you. And I question myself. And it's so very much you, it's as though it's someone else that I had loved. Conjured up. Not you. The Tuesday evening you left, I went out right away. Just to go out. To breathe. But I caught myself unawares looking around to see if I still might not spot you at the other end of the street. It was getting cloudy. It was going to rain. And it rained that night. Anxious, I told myself, "I sure hope he gets a ride right away." And I repeated, as if to convince myself. "But it's over, over. And it's just fine this way."

15

You tell yourself that it's over. You erase the other, but he is there. He is holding fast, he is hiding out, especially in what is not visible. You pass in front of a restaurant, an outdoor café, a movie theater, and you remember, the other is there, you see him again, he smiles, he laughs, flippant mood, or else he says nothing and looks at you in a strange way. Mariette tells me while petting Boubou, "But what goes on in a cat's head?" She thinks it over, stares straight into the eyes of her companion, smiles sweetly. "And in the meantime he is wondering what could be going on in a human being's head." Mariette strokes her face. "Look, Pierre. Since your young man passed through, Boubou has been scratching me over nothing. He started up again." She holds out her hands for me to kiss, a lady's gesture, sudden, so very moving. And Mariette whispers, "Have you at least heard from him?"

End of a school year. I eat more often at Marie's than at my place. She's working on her layouts. "I've got to completely redo the *Flash Engineering* project." And I stand in her kitchen, another living-space, other pans, other plates. I dare not confess to Marie that everything that pertains to my living-space, one floor above, has been possessed, touched by another. It would also be honest of me to write here that the thought occurred to me, too, that Duck, by living with me a while, by touching everything, had dirtied everything. The idea of dirt. Meaning sin in Saint-Mandé.

I was thinking about this while preparing those meals which I ate, sitting across from Marie, and during which I felt her powerless to speak to me, to find the appropriate word, so that everything could be restored to the way it was before, before the passing through, the breaking in. A hardness in Marie's eyes. "You should have known better!" One evening only, under the pretense of speaking to me about herself, her life, about Sam, Jacques & Bertrand, Tadzio and the others, she speaks to me about myself, and tells me, "The important thing is to make yourself master of your solitude again. To still be able to do it. And to do everything so that it won't turn into solitary confinement. I dreamed about you, Pierrot, last night. I was seeing you all alone, in a hallway, isolated. And I don't like it."

Marie raises her glass and drinks to my health. "I know you too well to know that you're already looking for Duck everywhere, all the time. That you're even wondering if he really left for Dijon, if he's not staying with friends, his friends, in Paris. I know myself too well because I've gone through that, a few times, and to know that in such cases, one person can't do anything for another. The lonely person's path does not run into any other path. An endless corridor. And even when you stop, even when you think you've stopped, in fact, you're still moving. You are sinking deeper. You know the joke, you have to tell it with a Swiss accent, a slight drawl. I'll sum up the situation in three words: BE-CARE-FUL. And when I say Swiss, you're already thinking of the architect in Geneva, in Marrakesh, and the sourest of all vinegars. So, I can't do anything for you, except thank you for fixing dinner. 'Thanks.' "

In the faculty lounge, Barbaroux comes up to me. "Any news from Roussel?" The question bolstered by a smile, a tone shrugging off all responsibility, his way of saying, "Let them all drop dead, by the roadside." There's always someone closer than yourself who should have held out his hand. Stopped. The novel which is not a story, also throws, too easily, dangerously, responsibility onto other people's shoulders. The other person. Elegant aloofness. Indifference.

In the kitchen cabinet, at home, I find two dried-up brioches, forgotten. From a Wednesday morning, had there been one. I throw them away along with the jar of wild-strawberry jam. The porcelain doorknob is still on Bernard's newspaper, the dictionary to prop open the door and Duck's last kick, along with it. There is the eraser on the piece of paper, with the address, rue Jean-Jaurès, Bât. C. And a record put away with the other records. You can only see the cover edge, but it's there. The guest-room sheets need to be changed, the towels thrown into the laundry, a list drawn up for the laundromat, the iron put away, the one we used so that his things would be "all clean, because in Dijon, I won't have time." You hear the voice of the one who passed through. Defend yourself as you may, act as tough as you can, but the voice is there, and so is the laugh. You always feel better than the stories you live. You shouldn't always feel better than the stories you read.

You tell yourself it's over, yet it still goes on, insinuating itself. Memory begins to crumble, everything falls apart everywhere. I don't intend here to describe the phenomenon of depression. I leave that to the spineless novel, with its preterite, which Duck spoke about, with its aloofness, its pretension of not getting its hands dirty, the way it has of not dealing with beings and facts, its so very undaring tone.

I wish ever so much, here, to express how, like bowling pins, a being can knock over the other without falling himself. And sometimes the other doesn't get up again. He rolls into a corner. I want the present of the indicative.

As a matter of fact, I caught myself during those days, shortly after Duck left, sitting in a corner of the main room, on the floor, crawling to dig up a book from my bookcases, or notes from my desk. I didn't want to sit in an armchair anymore, on the sofa or at the table. At times, I didn't even have the strength or the desire to stand up. Once you've closed the door, in such moments, you quickly bump into walls. And furthermore, I had just stripped these walls bare. Their whiteness dazzled me, in the evenings. I turned off all the lights. And in the shadows Duck was even more present than in the light. Then I'd go out. I'd stay in the West Side until closing. I drifted about Paris. I thought I spotted Duck in a group of men, but no, or else dashing into a metro station, to avoid me, the metro at that time was closed. Absurd. Visions. I saw daybreak over Paris. This town, in the early morning, is quite endearing. Deserted, it seems to be playing hide-and-seek, it seems to be hiding someone.

I'm afraid of the mail. I forbid myself to expect a letter, yet I'm expecting it. The phone rings. I forbid myself to think of Duck, but I'd like to hear the operator's voice: "Do you accept a collect call from Dijon, Daniel Carbon?" Several times, I started a letter "Dear Duck, a short simple note . . ." Then I tear it up. "Dear Duck, I'll be going down to Peyroc on the 17th of June. You . . ." I tear it up again.

Eleven days after Duck left, one Sunday, late afternoon, it's raining. I neither feel like listening to music nor reading nor going out. In the fireplace I light a fire. I tell myself this will be the last before the summer. I pile on too much kindling without even realizing it. And everything blazed up like a match. High flames which fascinate me. I put on a log. And I tell myself that everything that's happening to me doesn't matter, that Duck won't write, won't phone, that his is a pleasant moment, and then *basta*. I even say, "punto e basta!" very loudly. And I rub my arms, I smile, I hold out my palms to warm them. Very quickly my cheeks are burning hot. And here I am on my knees, throwing even more wood on; the fire impels me. I repeat in a whisper, "It's over, really over . . ." Suddenly embers fall from the chimney, I hear strange crackling in the wall and a scream in the courtyard, "Fire!"

Five minutes later, emergency squad, the firemen, the building super-intendent, and on the courtyard side, people at their windows. The fire is quickly put out. I am questioned, identity, insurance policy number, "Owner or tenant?" "Name of the landlord?" And in the apartment, hustle and bustle, boots, helmets, uniforms. In my files, I hasten to dig out the chimney-sweeping bill. Once a year, it's mandatory. I had it done, I have the proof. And all these people, at the windows, neighbors whose faces I didn't know, are staring at me, from afar. Focal point and commotion. There's a lot of people in my place. At last the firemen are about to leave, everything's in order, extinguished, police reports, I'm even amused at my good mood, offhand way of saying, "punto e basta!," when the captain hoists himself up into the chimney, taps the wall, a little to the left, on an angle, "It's scorching hot. It's still burning. There's a bend in the flue." He looks at me. "Everything that was cleaned dropped there!" His finger leaves a smear on the white wall.

They go up to the fifth floor. "We'll have to make about a two-inch hole. I'll douse the fire by twisting the hose." The firemen talk to each other, from one chimney to the other. "Go ahead! More! It's running! Stop!" For the first time in seventeen years my upstairs neighbor and I speak to each other. He listens to me, furious, with a smile. My apologies aren't to his liking. They've made a hole in his wall, and I am, I am, what am I to him? I know his smile all too well. Mariette is there, on the landing. "I came up." A real feat. "Nothing serious?"

Mariette stays with me and we have dinner together. In the fireplace a mush of ashes. We have to wait till tomorrow to clean it up. Clean up. Once in a while, I feel the wall, above the fireplace. It's warm. It's cooling off. I open a bottle of wine. Mariette doesn't want to drink. She wants to eat fruit, nothing but fruit. And drink a herb tea. "One lump of sugar, two?" "Two is too many but it's good." I kiss Mariette on the forehead. She says in a hushed tone, "Why so troubled? No one's worth the trouble." Twice the word *trouble*. She holds out a hand which is all scratched up. "See me back home, would you? I can't make out the steps very well anymore, especially on the way out."

That night, restless, I accuse Duck. In absentia. While at the same time, I forbid myself to accuse him. Accuse him or wait for him, it's the same thing. Two more weeks of classes, and Peyroc. But I have just brought attention to myself, in the building, for the first time. And the people at windows were watching. I still wonder what they could possibly have been saying to each other, or worse, what they could have been thinking. Marie, Mariette, and myself, as luck would have it, are the only three single people of 113 rue Boursault. A woman alone is a woman who's suffering or who's brave. But a man alone is always strange. *Punto e basta, via, via!*

Dead fireplace. A few logs for appearances' sake, only for show. Marie tells me, "You should have come with me to Chantilly. It's boring. But then there's always the strolls."

A letter from Roussel's brother. "Uzès, May 27th. Dear Sir. The news which reached you in Paris was serious. The reality is even more so. My brother began a sleep cure the day before yesterday. He's being well taken care of in a clinic, run by one of my colleagues. My wife Eliane and myself have striven to pull him through, in our home, these past two months. But he's unruly. And we know so little about the origin of his problem. We have barely a few suspicions. I wrote down your address in Peyroc. I will not fail to get in touch with you and to request you to visit Jean-Claude when he feels better, when the time is right. Yours sincerely. Léon Roussel." Jean-Claude, Léon, Eliane, first names are ageless. Nicknames and diminutives on the other hand . . .

Suspicions and stares, the family's suspicions and the neighbors' stares. Is the phone ringing? I pick it up: they hang up! Perhaps it was Bernard. And so on and so forth. Everyone struggles. Only dizziness is dangerous, when it seizes you, spinning, and staring eyes when they probe and peer into everything. Why stop at one individual? Then you only think of him in terms of ransacking. When Jean-Pierre left me, we were stopping at Patmos, a crisis, how did I react? Dizziness! Jean-Pierre should say about life, "It's a jungle. All you want is dreams and you try very hard not to see reality!" And Loïc who played his breaking-up scene to the hilt, as on a stage, better than on a stage, he was good, a good actor, suddenly. He would say about life, "It's a marketplace and you'll find anything. Exotic spices and rotten fruit. But in our special world, there are only fruits!" Jean-Pierre, Loïc & Duck. Dizziness.

June 17th, I take the train to Avignon. Early, in the morning, early. The weather's nice. It's stopped raining. The air smells good. Mariette laughed as she kissed me, for fear of crying, as she does every year. Marie helped me pack. She'll water the plants while I'm gone, and she'll forward my mail. "I'll keep you posted about my sixth-month visit." "Listen, Marie, I want to know why you kept telling me to hold on to Duck." Marie shrugs her shoulders. "Because I thought he felt good with you, and you with him. But . . . ." "But?" Marie places a finger over my lips. "Punto e basta. You told me yourself." Jean-Louis, the hairdresser, cut my hair short, very short, for the summer. Marie laughs at me. "You look ten years younger."

The train stops two minutes, in Dijon. "Please be careful! The doors close automatically." I can't help looking to see if there's someone on the platform. And to take my mind off things, I tell myself that, all things considered, Nikko and Duck is the same story. You simply wake up a few days later, you feel more or less good. "Tuckered out" as my neighbor in Peyroc would say. Full steam ahead, for a brand-new summer.

16

A rock mountain, the rock, and a village at the foot of the mountain, Peyroc. Only one street, the main street, and at the narrowest point, my house. It's not really my house either: I am its owner, its guest, its grateful servant. I belong to it. And it's an affectation to acknowledge it. Whenever I arrive, it does its routine for me. With its eyes closed, it sees me come back: I feel a little like a lover, barely loved, frightfully expected, who's been scolded for being away too long. I like the shade of this house when I close up the shutters, the air when it whips up the chill of absence, the sunlight when it brings warmth. Everything bursts into song. I am here. I'm back. Flaubert: "I'll go back into my den . . ."

Facing the street, a door, a window on the right, a window on the left, and two windows on the second floor. The street is in the shade, the whole day, until sunset. I've planted ivy on the front wall. It overhangs the windows, they are my curtains, and through the course of the summer, it clings and grows on the opened shutters. White shutters, everything is white, here too. In the beginning the ivy was a subject of concern for my neighbors. "It's going to attract bugs" (with their accent); now they say, "It's our village's pride and joy" (with their accent). Emilienne, my neighbor across the way, spots me with my luggage. "Oh, Mr. Forgue, you're here? Now the summer can begin! I'm on my way down to kiss you." Always at her window, she keeps watch over who's going, who's coming, or else simply watches. We are in the middle of the village, she on the mountain side, I on the valley side, in the middle of the main street, and at that spot, narrow, a truck wouldn't go through, a van ripped off one of my shutters once, the faintest whisper, as people go by, echoes can be very clearly heard. I lean over to kiss Emilienne. My house blocks her view on the valley and the Rhône. "Are you going to put flowers at the windows this year as usual?" I leave Mariette, I find Emilienne. "If you need anything at all, call me . . ."

On the ground floor, the living quarters. The darkest. The windows look out only onto the street. The kichen area on the right, the fireplace on the left, a round table, four chairs, a small love seat and two trunks. Under the staircase, the toilet. Opposite the door, four steps, a little landing. On the left, half-way up the stairs, an extension, last floor of a neighboring house, a room, with the only window facing the Rhône and Mount Ventoux. In this room, my desk and an extra bed between two bookcases. I put down my bags. On the right, the staircase is a little steep, here I am above the living quarters, a small bathroom, with a real bathtub, not like the one in Paris, you can stretch out your legs, not get cold knees, and my bedroom, a single bed, barely enough room to move around it. I put down my suitcase. The bedroom ceiling is the house's roof. I had the attic cleaned out, like a loft above my bed. A ladder leads up to it. A door opens onto a small terrace, above my study. Barely enough room for two deck chairs and some potted geranium plants. There is the view. It took me four years to get the ivy to go up that far. It attracts wasps and bees. From July on, you can't stay there anymore in the broad sunshine. Silly? From the terrace, you can make out the highway. Down below, behind the rows of plane trees and Italian poplars, there are vineyards and farms and more rows, the Rhône, and on the other side of the Rhône, the plains of Comtat Venaissin, a steeple, Carpentras, and Mount Ventoux about which it always tickled my fancy to think of as an extinct volcano, with its peak of everlasting snow and this little cloud whose disappearance heralds the Mistral. Under the door, a telegram. "To scare you. Stop. You left alone. Stop. Learn how to live alone. Reconquest. Stop. Marie and her three. Stop. Ninths. Stop." For starters, unpack, hang the clothes, put away the socks, the underwear, the T-shirts, white, 100% cotton, tics, fetishes, the fear of synthetic material, skin diseases, perspiration, inherited ideas, faithfulness to the past of Saint-Mandé. And everything begins again, all the time. The memory of my mother: she knits me underwear. She has never come to Peyroc. My father neither. But a tribute from Daddy, a lamp, for my desk: "It will come in handy, I hope, for preparing your winter classes during the summer." It was written on his business card, attached to the gift. The members of my family compose. Everything that we say is carefully modulated. A trifle declamatory. We dare not remember our Gascon heritage, but sometimes we betray ourselves. And, a gift from my mother, a blanket, multicolored patchwork, crocheted "with all the leftover wool from your childhood sweaters. It'll keep you warm."

Next step, empty the bags of books and place everything in the bookcases. Files, folders, a single color, blue. At my place everything is white and blue, little rectangles of sky scattered everywhere. Music, played softly, not to bother the neighbors. Stacks of envelopes, the writing paper, the sheaves of linen-finished paper, the one I like, I pile up everything on the desk. Third step, go out with the bags and the empty suitcase, a slight hump on the house, a low door with the letter box, you must bend down, go in, it's the cellar where the septic tank is enthroned, and in the corners, a pile of wood, bottles of wine, the trash bin. I put my luggage away. Fourth step, leave the cellar door wide open and greet Mrs. Beylac, Mrs. Santienne, Mrs. Vérini, Mrs. Luc or Mr. Carolon. There's always someone passing by when I emerge. In the village, there are only widows and one widower. "The Mistral is going to blow," or else, "Did you know that Mrs. Raillou died?" You must never say about someone or yourself, he's sick, I have been sick. Mr. Carolon explained it to me. "Someone who's sick is someone who's going to die. And you don't look like you're going to die, Mr. Forgue. You're just a little tuckered out."

Go in. Put things away. Sweep up, wax the floor tiles, in the living quarters and on the stairs, clean the windows, make the bed, put towels in the bathroom, put on another record, a little louder, I am here, after all, it's beautiful music, Mrs. Beylac, it's classical music. Go up and down the stairs, new sponges, so more Ajax, make a list for the grocery store, another for the supermarket, climb up to the terrace, the river and the view, the village mayor's farm. "We're fond of you, Mr. Forgue, but you will always be a foreigner."

The accent of the passersby. "Has Mr. Forgue arrived? Emilienne? Have you seen him?" Knock, knock on the door. Mrs. Olaya, with a basket of cherries. "I put them aside for you. I knew you were about to arrive." Olaya, the Spanish woman, the emigrant. Mrs. Beyron says about her, "She doesn't have the real accent. She'll never have it. But she never misses Mass." A smile. Thank you. Far from the Batignolles, already. I bite into a cherry. Duck's coming back? Via, via!

In Peyroc, people still talk about everything with a tinge of super-stition. "Satan's brew" is one of Mrs. Santienne's expressions when she speaks about the doctor and drugs. Nikko Hotel. Corridors. Dijon, nobody on the platform. And Marie's telegram. I roll it up into a ball, I'm going to throw it away. No, I uncrumple it. I keep it and put it on the desk. Overpowering smell of polish, of pinewood furniture, and late afternoon sunlight. Shake out, fluff up the cushions by the study window. Seek out order, order. Knock, knock, it's Olaya coming back. "If you have any laundry, as usual, I'll be happy to do it for you."

Step by step, the commotion of settling in, and the house playing the awakening beauty. A tiny, tiny house. Mr. Carolon doesn't understand why I travel "so many miles for this stump." The terrace of his house overlooks the valley. When I visit him tomorrow he'll say to me as usual, raising his arms toward the countryside, "All this belongs to me. It belongs to the person who knows how to take it. There is nothing bigger anywhere else." He'll look at Mount Ventoux: "It's my barometer, it tells me everything."

In the village grocery store. "Shall I put aside a *Provençal* and a small loaf, every morning?" Life, this life, takes its course, once again, a course, a lesson. And the neighboring river, "Bathing Prohibited." "Danger," or else "Private Property." Roussel is sleeping, not far from here, behind the hill, to the west. They're making him sleep. The shopwoman goes on, "Within two days you'll feel yourself again and within three, we'll already have forgotten that you're here. But I'm sure you're forgetting something!" "Yes, Ajax and new sponges." Bread, cheese, butter, two slices of ham, enough for one person, this evening, first evening.

Peyroc is joined to the highway by a side road which traces a half-circle, winds a little through the vineyards at first, then rises, narrow, buckling, cracked in places, a forgotten road bordered by blackberry bushes. You follow the cemetery, the road becomes steep, on the left, first houses carved in the mountainside, and on the right, a terrace, plane trees, parking lot, "Please Park Vertically" handwritten on a sign, with the mayor's seal. I leave my Renault there. 1899 QA 30. Le Gard. Then a very small square, the church, the town hall, the post office, the washhouse and the street which heads back down, bottleneck, my house and Emilienne's, a few beautiful residences, the grocery store, the boule players' ground, and the café, three tables on the sidewalk, Pampryl umbrellas, an old Casanis sign. Further down, a few prefabs, the school, warehouses, and once again the vineyards, blackberry bushes, a few young olive trees, you're back on the highway, and at the crossroads, the Esso pump, but there is still on the sidewall the brand name of Desmarais Fréres. Peyroc hangs to the highway by a jump rope which seems to have caught in the rocking hill. On one side, "Peyroc, .5 km" and on the other, "Peyroc .5 km." What accuracy. Justin, Mrs. Beylac's brother, runs the gas pump. About the cars and people zipping by on the highway, he says, "So much the better, they no longer have time to take time. They only stop if they need to fill up." He's been there for forty-seven years. "And when I started out, Mr. Forgue, I could hear the grass growing between the cobblestones!" Justin has an odd way of constantly twitching his mouth as though he had just lost a tooth. "Nowadays, the road is pink as asphalt. My dog doesn't dare lie down on it, it's so scorching hot." Sometimes, if I talk to him about the village, anecdotes, meetings, flippant remarks, Justin repeats his inevitable, "Oh, you, Mr. Forgue, you're a stranger, and you're lucky: you can talk to everybody." Every summer I bring him my car the day I get there. "I'm going to give the baby an overhaul. She'll still give you her 50,000 kms." And he spends the night with her.

I walk back up to the village. It's growing dark. If you listen closely, you can hear the river flow, or is it the wind, always present, ready to pounce, running up against the rock? Night magnifies Peyroc's rock. Houses seem even more sheltered. As soon as the news comes on, the streets are empty. It then becomes a village of dogs and cats, fights, mewings, night is given over to ambushes and the hunt.

I have fled Paris. Tenth summer in Peyroc. I didn't dare light a fire in the fireplace. I ate alone. After doing the dishes, I set the table for the next day's breakfast, bowl, spoon and knife. Ritual. And I put my napkin away in one of the two pouches, the one marked with my initials, P.F. The other one is slapped with an X. A gift from Emilienne, embroidered, sewn by her, offered with a smile. "I put an X because the other person is never the same one." No irony intended. In Peyroc, irony doesn't exist. Mr. Carcolon says, "We're civilized, just enough to make us attractive."

I tidy up the desk late into the night. I file away Marie's telegram in the folder labeled "current." You uproot yourself from everything and you never really put down roots anywhere. Love as it's lived has nothing chivalrous about it. Chivalry is only love which resembles love. Often, in Peyroc, on a linen-finished paper, rough to the touch, this beautiful paper which slightly impedes the fountain-pen point, resists writing, reminds the smallest word about the importance of the word, I am writing a poem. But every time, I throw the poem away. It's too declamatory. It's always full of drunkenness, tenderness, setting suns or whispering dawn, so early in the morning, the river, you can hear it, it glides by like a solid mass, it's become unnavigable. A poem, always the same poem. A prisoner in the bedroom of my childhood, all I'll ever be able to do is imagine what the world once was, what it will be, and what it is. Coddled, too coddled, a low hidden branch, which the wind snaps off. I took my childhood bedroom to rue Boursault, I take it to Peyroc, I drag it along everywhere I go, and me within it. And I confess it: I haven't escaped, I'll never escape. World news, or local news, what's happening everywhere, all the time doesn't matter much to me if I can't once at least get out of myself and touch the other, another, and by listening, paying attention, or by his presence, to go into him. Get out of myself and go into him. Or is it the other way around? Who, then, will bring me back to myself? Waiting for the other keeps me beside myself.

I could very well write, "That evening, Pierre Forgue felt himself free of all responsibility toward other people. He had received too many knocks to get bruised anymore. He had just given up. He'll never touch any other consciousness but his own, in the prison of his being, prisoner of what others had made out of him, a family which had produced an offspring, ugly duckling, an assembly-line defect. That evening, Pierre Forgue remained on the terrace a long time. He observed the rock, the river, and the shadow of Mount Ventoux, the summer breeze was rising, a breeze already smelling of the harvest and the approaching end. He told himself, "The seasons are cruel," and, startled to hear himself talk aloud, he took a deep breath, like a sigh of joy or relief. He was going off to reconquer his solitude. Around the lamp posts of the bowling ground, at the bottom of the main street, he watched the circular flights, whirlwind of bats fascinated by the electric light. At times, due to a stretch of silence, widening, when everything in the night seems to grow peaceful, they would stop, wild flights broken off, and cling in bunches to the edges of the lamps as well as to each other. A fit of barking, and everything starts over again. Their flights like graffiti in the night. And Pierre Forgue, due to this image, thought about Daniel Carbon, alias Duck. He saw him again on his knees, naked, in front of him, an obscene position when it's described. However, there comes a point when everything can be reduced to this desire, when the other agrees to let himself be taken, or when he too desires it. How can you tell? It was the night before he left. Pierre Forgue shook his head to get rid of the image. Just as Duck shook his own to let his curls fall into place. He decided to go in, and in the darkness of his bedroom he stretched out on the bed and fell asleep, all dressed in the body of another, within. But this was only a dream . . ." I don't write this way. Duck smiles about the preterite of the dreamy bourgeoisie. Everything is always in the present in a story. And story means two.

I write. I say "I" and I insist on this in order to run a greater risk, and to achieve a greater distance, the distance of soaring flight. I go to bed, my first evening, everything is polished, put away, spruced up, ready to live for a new summer. On the blank page of the book I was reading on the train while passing through Dijon, which is on my night table, I wrote, I reread, "Spontaneity exists, doesn't it? And the kind of an outburst which is not masked by calculation? I refuse the suffering which comes from the kind of game which you are forcing on me, Duck. I am growing cool. I wanted you sincere. But I merely find you to be a perfect guest."

I go to bed, happy, telling myself that I'm not expecting anything anymore. Tomorrow, when I get up, I'll go get the *Provençal* and my little loaf. Peyroc, a cradle in the rock.

17

"Dijon, the 17th of June.
"My Dear Pierre.

"I expected a note from you, but it didn't come. It just occurred to me that today you were going down to your South. So, I take up my pen, and it's not easy. I simply tell myself that you'll receive this letter tomorrow morning. Neither too early, nor too late: tomorrow morning.

"For a long while, I used petty lies like so many bricks with which I constructed a rampart around myself. A rampart for my protection, for my safety, for securing hiding places, not allowing anyone to grab me, to come close to me, no matter how briefly. I took this streak of wildness for independence and self-sufficiency and I could never depend on anything but my own strength. I defended myself, to preserve my integrity, and I learned how to conceal myself before knowing how to give.

"This was probably necessary but this attitude acted as a brake, preventing any real meeting, and warping, spoiling the relationships with others. So I gave it up, at least with the people I love and who are my friends.

"I understand perfectly why you feel suspicious, and afraid, and distrustful, and vulnerable and cynical. And it doesn't bother me, because it does not destroy what's left, namely, no matter what you say, your warmth and everything you are willing to share. With you, I am uninhibited, at least, I try to be, and I know that you're there. I don't know what I can offer you and you have me understand that you never really touch another's consciousness. I hesitated before writing to you, for what matters is this presence, sometimes.

"I need that 'wholesomeness,' so I won't be left behind or impressed by the sideshow of the unliving. I felt good in your home. Sheltered for a brief moment. And I was very happy to get to know Mariette, a real lady, Marie, whom I love dearly and who possesses all of life's principles within herself, and Bernard, honest, mixed up. I hope I'll see them again even though at times I have the feeling and the apprehension of existing for them only through you. In fact, all these misgivings are ridiculous, and experiencing these moments is already a lot.

"This 'wholesomeness' gradually deteriorated during those last days in Paris, because my body didn't follow. I lied to you. I stayed for another few days at a friend's house. You must have suspected it. I'm sure that you were looking at me through the window when I left and I didn't turn around on purpose. During those days I saw you everywhere. I don't thank you. And I'm not proud of myself either. Now, I feel the weariness. I think it's this whole year, overburdened with jobs to do, sleepless nights, which suddenly snowed me under. And then you. Going to Béziers is important, and I'm counting on the wild birds to tend to my wounds.

"Life in Dijon is a little dull and makes me see Paris as an oasis. All my day-to-day problems are here. I'll get by as usual, and I'll do it alone because it's better that way. I won't do any work this vacation, but I'll need to readjust to this mad pace once school starts.

"I'll hitchhike down to Béziers tomorrow evening, and I'll get there some time during the night, if I'm lucky. I'll stay there a few days and I'll call you from there to decide on a time when you can come pick me up. I'm very happy to see you again in Peyroc. I think that the way things go with us, everything is structured in this way: presences following presences.

"I received my draft notice to report for the preliminary days of testing: it's for July 2nd. Before that, I have to devote five or six days to my marketing surveys in the Saint-Etienne region. Concerning the kinds of hair sprays and beauty salons. A poll. I committed myself, and it's necessary in order to cope with some trivial matters. After that, around July 6th, I'll go off to bum around. I'll come back in August, around the 16th. Perhaps we'll be able to see each other at that time for a longer while. We'll discuss it.

"And to think that at this very moment you are on the train, you're passing through Dijon. My apartment is in quite a state, the water heater hasn't been fixed yet for lack of funds. And I'm putting up a friend who had to evacuate his dormitory, closed for the summer, and who's taking advantage of it to clean out the refrigerator. The records are scattered around, lent out all over the place. And I'm pushing myself to go spend a few days at my uncle and aunt's. If you'd like to write to me: Daniel Carbon, c/o Mr. and Mrs. Pertuis, Villa Toula 34990, Le Petit Pont. Tel: 55.67.13. I'll be spending all my days there, except for the boat. Anyway, see you soon. Love. Affectionately. Duck.

"P.S. I'm sending this letter special delivery so you'll have it tomorrow for sure. You can, in fact, call me at my aunt's at meal times. Bernard's medal is a hit."

The *Provençal* and the small loaf, the water is boiling for the tea, the bowl, the spoon and the knife, the napkin and its pouch P.F. and the other pouch marked with an X, there, on the table, I should have put it away, breakfast, the first morning. I've just read Duck's message. I was awoken by the sound of the letter falling into the mailbox, Emilienne's voice at her window, telling the mailman "he's arrived," and the mailman answering, "I already knew, saw the shutters." First I went to the grocery store, in the paper a full-page headline "IT'S WAR!" but where, in which part of the world, and this exclamation point? A folded newspaper, holding my bread, I went back up to my place. "Hello, Mrs. Vérini," then, "Hello, Emilienne." "There is a letter for you, Mr. Forgue." In Peyroc, everything is dreadfully announced beforehand. The door closed behind me, swallows' cries, in the sky, above the house, coolness of the living quarters, I fix the tea, I spread butter and jelly on the slashed bread, I almost cut myself with the knife, nerves. Sentences of the letter echo in my head: "neither too early nor too late: tomorrow morning," "streak of wildness, independence, self-sufficiency," "bumming around," "alone, because it's better that way," "I don't thank you. And I'm not proud of myself either," "presences following presences," and this present of the indicative: "I'm very happy to see you again . . ." Scalding hot tea, a few sips, I'm not hungry. I go out, a walk. The letter sits on the table.

Behind the washhouse and the town hall, a path, strewn with pebbles at first, a former exercising ground for horses, and then packed-down earth, flint and fig trees along the border, whose branches you must push out of the way to pass through. Sloping path twisting around the rocky hill, twines, very quickly you tread carefully, you count your steps, then you forget to count them, suddenly gusts of wind lash out, you emerge onto the chalky plateau, barren soil, stumpy vegetation, cane apple trees. You don't see the rocky hill anymore, nor the village, but down below, the valley, vast, the river, wide, silent, and in the distance, to the south, the Charter house of Villeneuve, the Palais des Papes, the foothills of the Alps, and the high waterfall of the Luberon above Cavaillon and the Durance River. Mr. Carolon always remarks, "Ah, that's our lookout point up there," and with a laugh, in a slightly nostalgic tone, "when I could still go up to see that panorama, with my cane and my panama." For an instant, bewildered, I look at the countryside questioningly. It's over, really over. I see myself again as a child, coming home from school, bleeding above my eyebrows. My mother dabs my forehead with Mercurochrome, mechanically, with no real worry, "You didn't manage to do this all by yourself? Tell me the boy's name . . ." I keep quiet. A tear runs down my cheek. It's stinging. A tear only because it's stinging a little bit. My mother would like to make light of it, but she remains distant, preoccupied, all the while applying herself. "This evening, we'll tell your father that you got hurt playing soccer, during gym class. Our two versions should match. Repeat." And I repeat, "Playing soccer, during gym class, Mommy . . ." She pinches my cheek. For a second, I think she's really going to look at me or take me in her arms. She wipes away the tear with her thumb. "It's really not worth crying. Over anyone. Ever." A cottonball, a bandage, she whispers, "There you go, you little troublemaker!" And her evasive eyes, not even daring to meet her own eyes and see herself in the bathroom mirror, unconsciously she says, "I'm not very happy either . . ." Then, "You are right, you should never give names." But my ears were not deceived. I remember it. To Jeanne and to Françoise who'll bombard her with questions right before dinner, she will toss out a "leave your brother alone. He got hurt. Playing soccer. In gym class." What can a mother do when her son is not really the son she wished for, a son who would reflect her in ways other than silences or attitudes? She senses it. It pains her but her life is painful. She doesn't give names. She has nothing to concede, there is nothing she can do but keep quiet. She fully recognizes that everything escapes her, just as her life escaped her. I am the son of this torment and this silence. I am the son of her obstinacy, she who knew how to keep quiet and never make accusations. Life bore her, bears me and rejects me. Above Peyroc, the soil is barren, both the wind and the river swirl toward the sea, swirling from everywhere, overflowing, flooding, scraping, eroding, polishing the walls and the garden terraces, clinging to the trunks of the green oaks, dwarves, their whole weight also bent toward the Mediterranean. "I am counting on the wild birds to tend to my wounds . . ."

I know this path well. It leads toward the west, the tiny village of Fontaubes. There is the country-style house of the Waterfields, John and Ruth Waterfield, the Roberts' house, Robert and Gérard, and Betsy's reconverted windmill. They often have me over in the summer. Around Ruth and John's swimming pool, the days go by quickly. We talk about concerts in Aix-en-Provence, Avignon's art festival, dance performances in Orange. They play gin rummy. I don't. They swim. They dry off in the sun. At one time Robert was John's lover, Betsy was in high school with Ruth, once Ruth ran off with Gérard. They live in London (the Waterfields), in Lille (the Roberts), and in Zurich (Betsy).

She says about herself, "I am the one-and-only Betsy, in a class by myself, like each one of us here. Fontaubes belongs to them. When I drive, I have to make a four-mile detour. When I walk, there's a direct path, twenty minutes at the most. I was neither the lover of one nor the lover of the other. They have me over because I lend them books. If I don't say anything funny, they worry about my health. And if, with a witticism, I make them laugh, they lead me to understand that I'm going too far. When Marie comes, we aren't asked over anymore. Ruth feels that Marie 'always passes judgment with her eyes.' "

Fontaubes is in sight. I pause. There's John's car. They are here. Already. I shrug, kick a pebble. I hear Jeanne telling me, on her wedding day, "Do what you want with your life, but you'll always be unhappy," and Françoise, on the same day, next to me, in the first row, in church during the ceremony, whispering, "I'm ashamed of you, of everything people say about you. So I too tell stories, make up things. It's the only way of giving the impression that I know everything about you and that you don't exist." As for my father, he repeats to me, resentment over Blue Skies, "I hope you didn't pick this house for the friends you have in the village, but for the scenery." They're there, the family, surrounding me, all the time. They read Duck's letter with me and they don't want to concede that it is touching, sincere, they don't want any evocation of embraces, they condemn everything that escapes them as a sign of sexual obsession; they, on the other hand, reproduce, during the night. As for me, in broad daylight, I try to produce, but I can't bear myself. I hold out my fist, I speak alone out loud, the wind intoxicates me. I head back. The cloud above Mount Ventoux has vanished. The Mistral is going to blow. Noon, already. I have to go pick up my car at Justin's, I have to plant some geraniums in the terrace flower pots and place flowers at the windows for Emilienne, I have to stop at Mr. Carolon's "to say hello and out of common courtesy," I have to give my laundry to Olaya so she won't worry, I have to, I have to, I have to say no to Duck. And everything screams out for me to say yes. I am not making my way back towards the village but towards his letter. It is waiting for me. I have to read it over, alone, with no one around, from the vantage point of the past, to peer over my shoulder and pass judgment the way Marie passes judgment when she watches the

Fontaubes's crowd.

On my way down, the scent of the fig tree is powerful. I almost
trip.

18

A letter, you fold it up, like a napkin after a meal, you slip it back into the envelope, as into a pouch, you put it away, you tell yourself, "All this doesn't matter," or else, "Tomorrow it won't get me this worked up." But you keep it. You hold onto it. You're always prospecting for the gold within the other. The words glitter or weigh heavily in the crux of your hand. You hold the letter, you read it over again. The magic words take effect: ". . . to see Paris as an oasis." Stendhal: "The suburbs of Granada form something like an enchanted oasis in the midst of the scorched plains of Andalusia." Everything always brings me back to my classes, to the writers, to fragments of my readings. I have no memory whatsoever for famous quotations, and only remember trivial details, at times crucial, those pertaining to emotion, to chiaroscuro effects or to confession. The function of objects and the description of places fascinate me, because at their level, the crossroads of real actions, nothing dictates anymore, nor aims to represent. Everything presents itself. Everything takes place. A little like the way the story of the young man of last summer is happening here, any similarity with people who exist or who have existed is due strictly to chance, any similarity with myself appearing to me to be more and more unlikely: passion eats away at you, disfigures you, it's him, it's me, it's two people who have lived nothing but an ordinary story, a story other than the one they had believed in or wanted to live, and nothing more, and one person seeking to love the other, and vice versa, each in his own way. A failure which ricochets. Between the two of them, nothing durable can be concocted. They are not living, nor have they lived, the same span of time. Seventeen years separates them. The mark of history isn't the same, neither for one nor the other. On top of Peyroc's rocky hill, overlooking the village, the only place from which my terrace can be seen, midnight, there I sit with my feet dangling, hands gripping the edge. I brought the letter with me this time. It's in my pants' pocket. The Mistral blows in roaring gusts. I put on three pullovers, one on top of the other, and I cross my arms, my hands buried in the sleeves as in a muff. I don't want to get dizzy. The Mistral whips at my face. Beyond the Rhône, a dark shadow which seems to swirl even faster with the wind, a train is going by, heading south, and the highway, tiny shooting lights, following one another, relentlessly: I am waiting for Duck to pass by. I am imagining. In a truck, in a car, who knows? I could have gone to pick him up and we would have made the trip together. But he didn't ask me to. I never suggested it to him. And suppose we left together, in my car, to travel around the Mediterranean? The two of us together, visiting Italy? The wind blows in gusts, the tip of my nose is frozen.

Perhaps I could call Marie, at the studio offices, tomorrow morning, read the letter to her, and ask her what she would do in my place? Marie who has within her "every life principle . . ." No. Marie would say no. The fear of creating havoc. I uncross my hands, push myself back and stretch out on the hillside, rising moon. The wind strikes the top of my head, slips down along my nose, my cheeks, insinuates itself along my neck and under the sweaters' wool, I'm cold all over, my knees like two rocks, I kick my feet one against the other. Once there used to be a large cross at the summit of the rocky hill. The only thing left now is the base. Mr. Carolon says that on one day of gusting wind, "someone didn't take off with it, it just took off." Carolon juggles with words. "It restores nature to itself and me, a human being, to what I am, a sideshow performer, an acrobat of the countryside . . ." Within the darkness, I smile. I hold on to the letter, in my pocket, in my hand, so that it won't take off. Justin says he knows the ironsmith who stole the cross. "It was the year the 'Vateurfields' bought Fontaubes. And it was no accident.

There are bars on all their windows. Those kinds of people are scared of being robbed."

The time? Duck passed by, he is passing by, he is going to pass by, how can I tell? Stretched out, I watch the headlights in the distance on Highway 7, the procession of fireflies on the road, yet another train. I stand up, shiver, flap my arms hard around my shoulders, jump up and down, a feeling of dizziness, the village far below. I'll go as far as Fontaubes. If the lights are still on, I'll go in.

A walkway bordered by cypresses. The Roberts' house on the left, Betsy's windmill on the right, John's car in front of the back door. The copper plaque "PRIVATE PROPERTY" has been recently cleaned, streaks left by the rag, reflections in the darkness. The sound of the latch, the squeaking of the hinges, I close the gate behind me cautiously or suspiciously. "Come over when you want to," the Waterfields always tell me. I've never figured out if that was a way of telling me never to come. "You're not disturbing us, on the contrary!" I'm disturbing them.

Lights in the dining room. I walk along the swimming pool. The filter motor is working, the water touching the skimmers seems to be trembling, as if churned up. Night labor to insure a greater purity for the following day. I knock on the windowpane of a door. They're playing gin. There are four of them. John, Ruth, Betsy, and a stranger. Ruth gets up. "Pierre, our Pierre!" Betsy: "He ventured out through the Mistral." John: "Did you just get here?" John insists on using the formal *you* with me the first day of each summer. The stranger's name is Oswyn. With three exchanged glances, they sit back down at their card table. "We'll finish up the game, and then we're all yours." I gather that Oswyn belongs to John for the summer. The women are playing against the men. Betsy wants to sip her drink, Ruth pulls the glass out of her hands. "No, you're making me lose too much. Win a little bit and I'll give you your glass back." Standing, I observe them. "Sit down, Pierre, help yourself to a drink." The neutral scent of this living room, the softness of the sofa cushions. Once I heard Betsy say while stroking them, "Buttocks or cheeks, I can't tell, but it's soft." I wait. I'm always

waiting when I'm at their place. I often catch myself thinking that they
too are waiting without knowing for what, nor for whom. Ruth has
money. John is handsome, but he's sixty. Betsy puts on too much
makeup. "When I don't leave anything behind in the bath water, I get
the impression that the bathtub is empty . . ." Betsy has been married
three times. "And when you hear what people hear, when you see what
people see, you tell yourself that you're right to think what you think."
Betsy has a whole collection of this kind of nonsense. She always says
them with a Swiss accent. To make people laugh. To help time go by.
"And it never goes by fast enough." Betsy is expecting her fourth
husband. "The last act, the most beautiful."

The game is over. Two in the morning. Here we are flopped down onto
the sofa. Betsy made Ruth lose fifty-seven francs and Ruth tells her,
"You'll pay for that." John comes up to me. "Come on, Pierre, tell us
about your winter." His formality intimidates me. John smiles.
"Excuse me, I forgot . . ." And he repeats his question using the
informal *you*. I have nothing to say. I smile. "Nothing . . ." I repeat,
"Really, nothing." They laugh. Betsy says, "Us, too!"

I'm never really myself, anywhere. I lived at Saint-Mandé like a
stranger. I am neither their son, nor their brother, but someone else who
still has no identity. I only rent a place on rue Boursault and am passing
through. It's as if my neighbors' staring eyes, provoked by the fire, have
turned me out on the street. I don't truly read Marie's life. And the child
she's expecting frightens me. She wants to get revenge. John's formal
you reminds me of Mariette's. This kind of distance, paradoxically,
doesn't allow you to escape the conspicuous emptiness, even when it is
affectionate. No one is ever really there. There are only imaginary
presences. Mariette told me before I left, "Don't torture yourself
anymore, please. Everything's like this . . ." And Jean-Louis, while
cutting my hair very short, "I get the feeling that you're still about to
screw up." Barbaroux, the last day, let drop a "if you see Roussel, give
him my regards." That's all. The school's director, summarizing the
year, as she flitted past, in the hallway, "We don't see each other often
enough." And my mother, over the phone, "You ought to come back to
Blue Skies." The knot is tied, the knot is continually being tied. No one

ever takes a risk, really, with the present, unless it be superficially, by manipulating ideas, nothing but ideas. I'm never really myself anywhere, with anyone whomsoever. Everybody drifts away, everybody passes by, no one ever really gives of themselves. We are coddled, doted on, catered to, each and every one of us, from every class, from every background, of all ages, every civilized person, we are capable of being no more than the idea we send back to ourselves about ourselves, and the survival of one diminishes the other, the exploits of the self make saying "I" impossible. I say I. It's a rather trivial tale, but I want to pull it up by the roots. It will revive, it will grow back, but I will have ripped it up once. I only feel really myself at Peyroc, in my house, when it puts up with me putting up for the summer, when I air it out, clean it up, and set everything in place. Ruth takes me by the arm and tells Oswyn, "You'll have to go see Pierre's house. It's tiny, but quite tasteful." Tiny, but tasteful, that has been making us laugh for years. Betsy pinches my hip. "You've gotten fatter." John wants to pour me a drink. "No, thank you."

"What are your plans for the summer?" "The same as always . . ." "The same? Us, too!" John glances at Oswyn. Ruth leads me into another room, supposedly to show me the new dining-room table. "Oswyn is only a friend, for both of us. You mustn't think that . . ." "I don't think anything, Ruth. Why are you talking like this?" "Because . . ." She sets two silver candlestick holders in the middle of the table. "Because I love John, and . . ." She smiles. "It's a lovely table, don't you think? An extravagance. We'd been dreaming about one for such a long time. Yes, I said *we*. Wait till you see the dinners this summer!" We go back into the living room. "I'm handing Pierre back over, I'm going to make some herb tea. With fresh mint?" Betsy shouts, "Oh, yes, it's an aphrodisiac," and Oswyn, thirty years old, impeccably dressed, blank eyes, a tall Englishman with dangling arms, follows her to the fireplace. "How about lighting a fire, I'm cold, what about you?" Oswyn doesn't understand. Instinctively, I offer Duck's letter to John. "Here, can you read this and give me your opinion?"

That's the way it is. You turn toward anybody, the moment is of no importance. At times, you surprise yourself. And if you draw up an inventory of all the people you've known, if you ask yourself who's left in your memory, who is present, you don't discover who mattered, as far as appearances go. Never once have you known how to turn toward those who were expecting that you turn toward them, and you only approached those who could neither understand nor listen, so rarely share themselves. You choose the others in your life poorly. Undoubtedly because you want to choose them. John has donned his glasses to read the letter. He finishes it. He rereads it. He folds it up, gives it back to me. "When is it you're going to pick him up?" He smiles. "I'm already impatient to see him, if you feel good with him." He takes off his glasses, nods toward Oswyn. "If you think that I'm happy with that creature! He's here, because if he wasn't, it'd be even worse. And anyway Ruth likes to be jealous." I put the letter back in my pocket. I blush and smile at the same time. John gives me a friendly pat on the back. "Have you already put flowers at your windows? On the terrace? All over, at your place?"

Late into the night. Betsy goes home. Oswyn has gone to bed. John throws acid pills into the pool. "If I don't, when the first storm comes, the water is going to cloud up, and I want it to be more beautiful than ever." Ruth sees me to the door, sound of the latch, squeaking of the hinges. "How is Marie?" "She's expecting a baby." "Not yours, I hope?" "No, not mine." "So, great for her. Does she have what she wanted?" John, in the background, shouts to me, "Come swimming tomorrow. We'll talk about your letter again. And you'll get a little tan, you need it badly." I kiss Ruth. Slight, dry, hard, suddenly I see her as an old woman. She whispers, "What letter?" "A letter, a friend, and . . ." "Don't say any more. Good luck!" She closes the door. "And come over whenever you want to! The Roberts arrive tomorrow!" Ruth doesn't pronounce Robert, but Roberte. She, too, will always have an accent.

The path back. And the Mistral so strong, you think to yourself that it's going to dislodge stones and rocks. The moon has disappeared. A glow, already, in the east. Whatever place it may be, money, power, each one of us wants to take possession of the other. A game, nothing but games. And the wind doesn't give a damn. I gulped it down that night, on the path back, to the point of losing my breath. Here is my text, my novel, first novel, and it isn't an idea. Here, I lie down, I deliver up, I want to deliver myself; I am wholly inside, burrowed in, my feet in the ground, half-buried. I am Pierre Forgue. And I say my name. I almost got skinned alive, once again. Why?

I'll call Duck, tomorrow at noon.

The table is set for breakfast. The letter is on the night table. A rooster starts crowing. Dogs bark. I forgot the alarm clock, it stopped. In bed, my hand slides on the sheet. I am groping. I am caressing. Duck has soft lips. A flavor. A flesh. A feel. When I left rue Boursault, I closed his bedroom door, and I tell myself, while trying to let sleep overcome me, that it is "closed for repairs," smile, "for internal repairs, indefinitely," laughter. And I laugh alone, in my bed. I squeeze the pillow tightly against my stomach. At Fontaubes, they drank heavy white liqueurs. As for me, no. Heart palpitation, it's the mint tea. I hear and I see everything, very well. Duck must have arrived in Villa Toula. I twist, turn; sleep doesn't come. Dawn is breaking. I hear the wind sliding along the roof. In a while, before or after the telephone call, 55.67.13., as I lean out the first floor windows, I'll need to trim the ivy pushed back by the provencal-style frieze, and which is hanging down, like a fringe. "Like in the army," Mr. Carolon will say. While Emilienne, at her window, will say, "I'm afraid you might fall. But it's all for the best to do it, because if it grows under your tiles, you won't have any roof left." Who are my friends? Damp pillow. Sleep at last.

19

"Hello, Mrs. Pertuis? Could I speak to Daniel, please . . ." "He is out on the water." "Can I leave a message?" "Yes, but I can't tell you when Duck will come back. When he is here, he takes a boat and off he goes." "Then, simply tell him that Pierre called. I'll call back around . . . two o'clock? Two-thirty?" "I'll tell him." "Thank you." A cheerful, sprightly, amused voice, an echo, tiled room, and a setting which I can already picture in my mind: Mrs. Pertuis sees Duck far from shore, but he is too far to hear her if she called him, a villa, the pond, the oyster parks, at the horizon, the sea. I look on a map to find Petit-Pont. I am already on my way.

Olaya stops by to pick up the laundry. "I'm going to make it whiter than the white of Paris, the grey-white of your laundromat." She carries away everything I brought. "You'll have it tomorrow morning." There is no arguing with her. The *Provençal* headline is not about war anymore. It's about the price of gas. I cut off the ivy where it was touching the frieze. I sweep the front steps of the house. Emilienne goes to the grocery store. "Was it your footsteps I heard last night?" "Yes, Emilienne." "That's what I told myself: it can only be him."

At Carolon's, we have our pastis. His elder sister is sitting in a corner. She doesn't say a word. She doesn't move. She looks at us vaguely.

Carolon says of her, "The Mistral keeps her alive. She'll bury me you know." He hands me a drink. "It'll perk you up." And we clink our glasses together. "I was just telling myself that you would surely remember to come and see me. All these widows, they talk, they talk! All they talk about is you, as soon as you arrive. Come." We go up to his attic, he shows me a trunk. "I'm going to clean it, and this time I'm going to sell it. They've made me spectacular offers. I'm going to make it glow. It's all eaten away, look, it would crumble into pieces if I sneezed. But I'll sell it for its weight in gold. All these guys are crazy about anything that's old. Very old. Except us. When they quote a price, I play dumb. But my price is set. A fortune, Mr. Forgue." On the terrace, a moment later, Carolon explains, a confidence, "And this piece of furniture, I showed it to you because I'll sell it the way we sell ourselves: all glowing on the outside, and all eaten away in the inside." He fills up my glass a second time. "You see what I mean, don't you?"

"Mrs. Pertuis? I am the one who called a while ago. Is Daniel back?" "No, still on the water. His boat hasn't moved." "I . . ." "Call back in the late afternoon. Who's calling again?" "Pierre, ma'm, Pierre." The cheerfulness of this voice makes me feel uncomfortable.

Around the swimming pool, Ruth wipes her sunglasses. Oswyn dives and does a belly flop, splash! Betsy, naked, massages her chest with a suntan oil. John puts his newspaper down and slips his sun hat over his eyes. The newspaper flies away. I pick it up. They haven't heard me arrive. Quickly changing into my swimming trunks, I dive in. "Pierre!" I swim under water, I swim up to the pond. Then, my head out of the water, my forearms on the edge of the pool, John glances at me. "Well?" "Nothing." "You mean, not yet?" "I am supposed to call back in the late afternoon."

Robert and Gérard arrive with two friends from Paris. Ruth asks me to go get some plates and some extra silverware, a lunch on the edge of the swimming pool, mid-afternoon, taking it easy. Ruth whispers in my ear, "Still quite a lot of men here, considering it's summer." Mrs. Vérini is fixing the meal. "And I don't understand why Mrs. Vateurfield wears a two-piece swimming suit. With the bust she has, she doesn't need a holder!" She laughs. "And that Englishman, who doesn't even make his bed and clean his sink. It's quite simple: all of Mr. John's friends, they're good neither boiled nor roasted!" I take the plates and silverware. Mrs. Vérini puts down a salad bowl on the top of everything. "Good thing you're here, Mr. Pierre. I'll bake you a chocolate cake. I'll bring it to you tomorrow morning."

These words matter, for everything reverts very quickly, too quickly, to a comedy of manners. Proust makes Duck laugh? End of Swann's love: "To think that I have wasted years of my life, that I have longed for death, that the greatest love that I have ever known has been for a woman who didn't please me, who was not in my style!" This time, in a need for precision, a parenthetical quotation, I go into the Waterfields' library, Proust in a deluxe edition, and I read the passage over again, find the words, very exactly in their place, a beautiful design. The copy of the book is new. Nobody has ever opened it. But it's here, like bars over the attic windows, so that everything in the house be perfect. And I read the passage aloud, in front of everybody. There is a "it's marvellous all the same" and a "nobody will ever top this. Do you know that it is still more beautiful in the English translation than in French?" Word by word, word for word, how can I express the state of being in love, a state of disappointment and rebellion, a state dreamed, terribly experienced? Robert, Gérard, those from Paris, a little stuffy, Oswyn and John, eat, look at each other, smile at each other. Ruth picks up the dirty napkins. "Otherwise the wind blows them away into the swimming pool and the filter gets clogged up." Betsy does not eat lunch. Two little globes of plastic over her eyes, she tans, like a blind woman. Now and then she sprays water over her whole body and wets her lips. She would like to speak, but she says nothing. Slanting sun rays. Late afternoon. I want to go home. Ruth wonders, "You're not staying with us?" John smiles. "No, he has a very important thing to do."

"Mrs. Pertuis?" "He's not here yet. He must be sleeping. Call back a little later. I know him, as soon as he gets hungry, he'll come back."

On the terrace, I set up the two deck chairs, one for him, one for me. But

I don't sit down. He's not here yet. I water the flowers, I set up some propping sticks, I check to see where the ivy is clinging and guide it so it will finally grow on the railing, all knotted, braided. June 19th. I haven't slept, lying awake all last night. There is sweetness, sometimes, in exhaustion. I stretch out on the bed. I see the high school again, the classroom, classes, students, my notes, reading of texts, I see staring eyes, I hear silences, expectant pauses, more students, classes, homework, the year passing by, the strange noise of beer cans which are popped open behind the bar, at the West Side, the smell of dirty feet in steam baths, a movie ticket at the bottom of a jacket pocket, the garbage can you must take down when you leave, Mariette's eyes when I forget to drop by, the day before, Marie's footsteps on the stairway, she has just closed the door of her apartment, she's on her way up to see me, and I also know, by the sound of the phone, if it's my mother, my father, or else Françoise who calls me from Le Havre, or Jeanne from Saint-Cloud: the state of being in love is universal only in its lies. My life, my whole life won't be enough. And yet, my time is here, yes, Carolon, it doesn't glow, it's all eaten away inside. Stretched out on my bed, I fall asleep. I do my own textual analysis, the text of the day coming to an end. There is also the holder, the neither boiled nor roasted, Mrs. Vérini's chocolate cake. Justin says of my car that I could still "go around the world with it!" I twist, turn, I'm looking for Duck. My bed, like a boat, out at sea, coolness of a body. His. I don't like mine. It counts off the passing years.

When I wake up, the sun has set. Eight o'clock in the evening. I run water over my face. I dry myself with a towel smelling of lavender from Olaya's garden. In the mirror, above the sink, I dare not look at myself. I'm afraid of seeing myself as Duck sees me. The phone rings. Ruth: "So, really, you're not coming? Gérard and Robert say they haven't even had time to speak to you. And it's our first big dinner, on the new table!" I say no. "See you tomorrow then. John has explained everything to me. You must get a tan, be handsome." I hang up, lift up the receiver, and dial 16, dialtone, 99, then 55.67.13, I already know the number by heart.

"Duck has left again. He wants to spend the night on the boat. But he told me to tell you that he'll be expecting you a week from Sunday, at eight o'clock in the morning, here, near the small bridge. There's only one bridge, you can't miss it."

Calculation: A week from Sunday? June 29th? There are only thirty days in June, a gap between the left hand's ring finger and little finger, a child's game, for counting. So Duck will only stay three days with me. John will tell me, "It's still better than nothing. Prepare yourself carefully."

To dream at night, head buried in a grey-and-blue checkered shirt, a memory of a Thursday morning, of a Friday evening, of a Sunday noon, days gone by and still going by, filing past, touching, questioning. The little refrain: who chooses whom, when, how, why? And above all, the impression that everything else is nothing but a backdrop. So there is no truth, nor nature except in the other. Everything is decided outside of oneself. You tell yourself that distrust is nothing but the first expression of trust, and surrender, a venomous form of suspicion. "He told me to tell you . . ." Duck was afraid to speak to me. Or else was it a frankness, more beautiful yet, the real nature of making a date? To fix a time. To create a duration. "He is on the water." He's sleeping in a boat. He is dreaming of going around the Mediterranean. He'll do it, for good. A wanderer. But where are the real journeys? He's sleeping. He's on the water. He said to tell me. Is there really no celebration but in the preparations of a celebration, and affection only in expectancy? I'll go walk along the river, I'll go in the cedar-tree forests of the Luberon, I'll go lose myself in the gorges of the Nesque, I'll go, I'll go, I'll go to Fontaubes too. Money and boredom, power and death, the subject is always the same. On a scrap of paper, I begin a poem: "How sweet, this time we're not going to spend together and which I'm going to live without you . . ." Carolon says there is Mistral for nine days. "Three, six, nine, this time it's nine!"

There is only a small bridge, you can't miss it. Chapter twenty, a beautiful day, in the course of a lifetime.

20

Sunday, June 29th. One hour early, seven o'clock in the morning. Villeneuve-lès-Avignon, Remoulins, Nîmes, Montpellier, freeway exit Béziers-Est, a maze of secondary highways, a sign "Petit-Pont, half-mile," a bridge over a canal, the ruins of a rampart, a few wooden shacks along the pond, and, in the distance, the mountain of Sète. A happy happiness doesn't exist. The companion of the rising day, intoxicated by the morning air, I legislate, I formulate, impression of being born. An impression only. But it's in me, fleeting, a mere trifle would blow it away. The blue of the sky catches you unawares at this moment, shimmering light, the gamboling sun. The Mistral has died away. I feel new, expectant, regenerated, clean, clean hair, clean-shaven, a light tan, hikes of the past few days. I feel clear-headed and ready for all kinds of generous deeds. Those, mostly banal, of a lovers' meeting when time has just sharpened it like a pencil, to make more distinct marks or to correct. Everything about waiting is concerned with making corrections. Precisions. There is no risk for that morning's truth: I feel like a boy making his first communion. A forty-year-old boy.

And, sitting on the railing of the small bridge, I breathe in the air, inhaling it, a white short-sleeved shirt, cream-colored cotton pants, barefoot in tennis shoes, bare-armed. I shiver a little, but the sun warms me up, gradually. Whenever I see the sea again, I tell myself I had forgotten the sea. The repetition, here, is voluntary: to see the sea again, and to forget the sea. I have become such a product of cities, of sidewalks, hallways, stairways, the ant of a never-ending winter. The affectations of city life, around the Fontaubes swimming pool, also prevent me, sometimes, very comfortably, from once again striking up against rock and soil. Here, my legs dangling above the canal, my whole body turned towards the sun, for one instant I feel like I am towering above the world, that I have reached the end of the roads, railways, prescribed directions, of everything that has been built, designated. The morning is designating me. I don't know any stillness more poignant than that of the pond, the prelude to the sea. Like the end of a very long journey, harrying, I feel like I can erase everything. I breathe. Marie, on the phone, told me, "Do what you want. Try, one more time. By the way, you had forgotten your laundry at the laundromat. I picked it up, it's paid for." Paying what's due for clean laundry. And the accompanying moral lesson.

A quarter of eight, wearing shorts, bare-chested, barefoot, rubbing his eyes like a kid tumbling out of bed, Duck appears suddenly, between two houses, one white and the other blue. He doesn't see me. He shakes his head, scratches his shoulders, he's peeling everywhere, over his whole body. He passes in front of the R4 not knowing it's my car. He scares away a dog which was coming near him, then he raises his head, opens his eyes wide and spots me. A slight wave of the hand. I don't move. He draws near, says in a low voice, "Too bad, I would have liked to be here before you." He is standing there. His hand brushes against my shoulder. A hello. He looks at the villas, somewhat as if, behind the shutters, we were being watched, listened to. He pretends to punch me, a little tap on my head. "Are you happy?" "What about you?" "Me? I'm taking you back, right away. I want you to meet my uncle and aunt. You are going to see the rich folks in my family." I get up. Duck smiles. "You're dressed for a wedding? White becomes you." And he dashes off. In front of the R4. "Is it your car?" Then, "You didn't forget your swimsuit?" Finally, "Here, as a child, it was a kingdom. All this appeared to be very big to me. Paradise, my feet in the sand. Now it's a shrunken paradise, with slime everywhere."

Villa Toula, a pergola, you enter through the kitchen. Mrs. Pertuis is making coffee, a flower print blouse, an apron, her hair up, all smiles. "So you're Pierre? You're lucky to find Duck, because for the past ten days, I haven't seen him." Duck shrugs, chews a lump of sugar, and motions me to follow him. A dining room, a TV set in one corner, a dresser, a grandfather clock, tiled floor, and a small balcony, very narrow, overlooking the water. Mr. Pertuis is there, reading the newspaper. Duck teases him. "It's been the same one for eight days. The paper is passed around all the villas. It's last Sunday's. I warn you that my uncle is stone deaf." Introductions. Duck imitates me shaking his uncle's hand. The cheerful voice, bright as the tiles. "Coffee is ready." In the morning, that morning, the grandfather clock struck eight twice.

Who am I, for them, at the end of the world, on the other side of the small bridge, there, their world, villa Toula, odds and ends thrown together, everything is spic and span, touching, the dream of a lifetime? What about mine? Mrs. Pertuis says proudly that all the houses of the neighborhood have been built "squatter-style," "in a few hours," "overnight." Duck looks at me. "It's true, you know. There is a suit that's been going on for twenty years. In every villa, there is a machine-gun, for the bulldozers, in case they show up one day." Mrs. Pertuis hands me a piece of toast. "I never know if Duck is making fun of us or not. But these guns scare me. They're the ones that are going to bring in the bulldozers." She lifts a jerrycan and pours water into the sink. "The important thing is that we haven't been kicked out yet. It's beautiful, here, in the evening, when the sun sets. You won't see it, but you will stay for lunch, won't you?" I look at Duck. He smiles, his nose in his coffee cup. Mrs. Pertuis watches him a moment, then staring at me straight in the eyes, "We would enjoy it. Since for once Duck is introducing a friend to us. Until the time comes that he introduces us to his fiancée . . ." Mr. Pertuis enters the kitchen. He folds the newspaper, puts it on the waxed tablecloth, looks at us, Duck and me. "Are you going out on the water?"

A narrow punt boat. I am sitting in the front, straddling the seat, my feet in the water. Duck in the back, with a pole which he pushes alternately on one side, on the other, propelling the boat forward, awkwardly. "I never knew how, I'll never know. There is not enough water for swimming and too much slime for walking." From the distance, Mrs. Pertuis watches us. Duck laughs. "My uncle is deaf because he spent his whole life at the marketplace, calling auctions, and my aunt, who is not really my aunt, has had so many fiancés that she can't think of anything but my fiancée. I am sure you like them, if for no other reason than that." Shallow water, the punt boat comes to a standstill. Duck thrusts the pole into the slime, knots a rope around it and sits down. I turn toward him. Face to face, both of us sitting, our hands on our knees. I cross my arms. Duck crosses his arms. I bend my knees. Duck bends his knees. Duck closes his eyes. I close mine. Two kids who dare not admit anything to each other. Petit-Pont might be watching. Duck says, "I could stay here a whole lifetime, like this, like them. I admire my uncle and aunt. I've always admired them. Every time they came to Dijon, they would bring something to eat. Do you understand?" From time to time Duck leans down and splashes water on his shoulders, stomach and thighs. The tip of his nose too. He says with a laugh, "I am burned, I get burned like this at the beginning of every summer. But I'll never put anything on my skin. You're not saying a word?" I smile. Duck unties the rope. "Let's go back." He hands me the pole. "It's your turn, we're turning back."

Noon. Lunch. Mrs. Pertuis places a leg of lamb on the table. "Not every day is a special occasion." She looks at Duck. "And I can tell you in front of your uncle, he's jealous, but he can't hear: I love you as much as I love him, like the first day." She sits down, passes me the dish. "I'll show you our photo album. Duck was cute when he was little. I even have a naughty picture, which I am keeping for his fiancée." Laughter. Then silence. Water lapping under the house. Burst of sunlight on the corrugated roof. White wine, red wine, coffee, liqueur, and the photo album. Mrs. Pertuis shows me a snapshot of Duck, five, six years old, someone has just dumped a bucket of water over his head. He is stark naked, facing the camera, he's going pee-pee. Duck wants to grab the picture. Mrs. Pertuis puts her hand over it. "No, it's exclusively for your fiancée."

Duck goes off to throw a few things in his bag. Mr. Pertuis picks up his paper again and dozes off in an armchair, by the TV set. One o'clock strikes twice on the grandfather clock. Mrs. Pertuis browses through the album. "This is my sister-in-law, the year she graduated junior high. A month later, she met Duck's daddy. Love at first sight and a real disaster; they were too young." She flips a page. "This here is Duck and his three baby brothers." She points to a snapshot. "And Duck, from behind. I babied him enough to recognize him. He was always making mud pies for his father. This here is his father. We used to come swimming here, in the old days. It was still sandy there." Duck calls his aunt. Mr. Pertuis is snoring in his sleep. I steal Duck's baby picture, naked, from behind, crouching across from his father and I slip it in my left pants' pocket, like the letter. Duck comes back, closes the album, pinches my arm. "Let's go!"

Duck ahead of us with his duffle bag. And I behind, my hands in my pants' pockets. Mrs. Pertuis sees us to the car. "Here, we live on a tight budget, but we live well. As long as it lasts. Half of 1000 is 500 and we don't have that either." Cheerful voice. High-pitched. In front of the R4, she and I kiss on both cheeks. "And don't let him cause any trouble because he's always getting into trouble." She kisses Duck. "You'll stop back, right?" We get into the car. She leans down by the door. "Your uncle is a lucky man, he's always asleep when people are leaving. I still have a lot to learn from him." On our way. We pass over the small bridge. I glance in the rearview mirror. Mrs. Pertuis, swiftly, undoes her bun and shakes her head: she had fixed up her hair.

Duck says, "Let's play hookey . . ." We drive around the pond. Sète. The seaside cemetery. We look for the poet's grave. Behind a mausoleum, Duck pinches the nape of my neck. Surreptitiously. A few minutes later, in front of the museum; it's closed "for repairs." Duck says to me, "What are you thinking about?" The sun is scorching hot. The asphalt is scalding, rippling light, haloes, not the slightest breeze. In the car we're suffocating. We stop in a gift shop to buy a sunburn remedy and a "total sunscreen." Duck immediately dabs his nose with it. They sell swimsuits there. He looks at them. "A new one? It's a good idea." Forty minutes of trying on. In the dressing room, Duck laughs at himself. "I don't mind the expense, but it'll have to last for years. Any purchase is important. Hee-hee!" He wants to pay. I stop him. He says, "Fine, if you wish." And he picks out two postcards in addition, "One for Marie, and the other one for Mariette." Writing the cards at the terrace of a deserted bar, siesta time. To Marie, Duck writes, "We didn't find the poet's grave. The future godfather sends his love. Duck." And to Mariette, "We're about to go swimming. No buoy for Boubou. With love from the young (too young) man." Duck hands me the cards. "And what about you, what are you going to say?" I sign my name, that's all. Stamps. Mailbox. Duck is proud. "We need to have the postmark of the place. This is a big trip, isn't it?" And we're back on the road. Heading for the beach.

Palavas-les-Flots. I had often told myself this beach didn't exist. It does exist. Campsites, vans, cars, it's a big parking lot, and thousands of children, balls, stretched-out bodies. Duck asks me to rub some lotion all over him. Shouts, faint clamor, sunshine. Duck smiles. "Petit-Pont is paradise! Shall we go?" He adjusts his swimsuit. "Do you like it?" A pattern of interlocking chains.

In Frontignan, Duck can't understand why I insist on stopping to buy "at least one bottle of that aperitif wine." Saint-Mandé, after the war. On Sundays I was allowed to drink a sip of that brewed wine, sweet, sugared. I blushed instantly. In the car Duck says to me, "Now, no more stops till we get to Peyroc." He pinches my knee. He whispers, "Watch out when we get there."

We're getting close to Remoulins. On the other side of the highway, a stream of cars and campers. The setting sun in my eyes: I adjust the rearview mirror. I glance at Duck. "Listen. We're going to spend a few days together and I won't bring it up anymore. But if you'd like, after your three days' military duty, we can go off together, with this car, where you want to. Italy, if you want . . ." Duck doesn't reply. He is staring straight ahead at the highway. He's growing sullen. He's sticking to his own idea of a trip. Toll, ticket, change, no answer. Duck rests his head on my shoulder and falls asleep holding my forearm. I switch gears, very slowly, so as not to wake him up.

In Peyroc, vertical parking, between two plane trees. I put on the emergency brake. I switch off the engine. Duck wakes up, rubs his eyes. Seven o'clock in the evening. The hour of the swallows' cry and of their restless, dizzying flights. Emilienne is at her window. "Mr. Vateurfield dropped by with some friends a few minutes ago." "Emilienne, meet Daniel." "Welcome."

In the house, Duck goes up, goes down, touches everything, opens everything, puts on some music. "Here, on the other hand, it's really *your* place. I feel like I'm meeting you for the first time." In my bedroom closet, under the pile of sheets, I hide the snapshot. A day of peace and war booty. Duck is on the terrace. He points out the other bank of the Rhône. "I passed by there the other day . . ." He doesn't use the ladder to go back down. He jumps with his feet together into the bedroom. "It's even smaller than I pictured it. Shall we take a bath?" He sets the water running. In my study, I turn the volume down. The phone rings. John: "Has he arrived?" I say "yes" with a laugh. "In that case, no point inviting you over this evening, but we're counting on you tomorrow."

The table is set for our dinner. There is one of Mrs. Vérini's chocolate cakes "since for once you have friends over." Once again a plural for a singular. Duck is here. The house breathes and I breathe. Three days with him. From the bathroom he shouts, "Come on! We're going to make it overflow!" Emilienne heard. And so what? Close the bedroom shutters. Emilienne has two television sets: her own and my bed.

End of dinner, around midnight. The chocolate cake is half gone. Duck wipes his lips, folds his napkin. He's going to put it in the other pouch. "What does X mean?" He places his napkin on the table and the pouch beside it. "X isn't me!" He kisses me. "I feel good, what about you?" Happiness is a happy thing. Sometimes, you believe this. Duck is burned all over. "Be careful!" Then, "I'm shedding my skin, like snakes do."

A beautiful day, in a lifetime.

21

One's share of time is imaginary. There is nothing in this story which resembles us anymore, Duck, our story, which I relive and live here. The transcription is bound to accuse, assign roles quickly, thrust us violently into the spotlight when in fact, you and I were lost in the enormous throng of individuals. We did not want that share of time, we were not aware of living it. I nearly interrupted everything at the end of the last chapter. It's not in good form to acknowledge it: the reality of the text is a reality in itself, a world apart which does not tolerate that the painter step back to contemplate his canvas. And yet, the writer I am becoming here (where did I read that one is always in the process of becoming a writer?) asks questions for which he can neither find nor hear any answers. I reread each chapter after finishing it. I correct it, trim it, polish it. I even remember chapter thirteen with anxiety, the most directly transcribed of them all, the mystery of the sources, I remember it as an obstacle to the reading of the whole work, if indeed one day there is a whole work, and with every final period, the silence rushes me on. Where are we going? Which of us is being led and leading the other along? We have in common, with the collective consciousness, a combination of memory and forgetfulness. Sometimes forgetfulness is as important as memory. The author is the only judge. He is also the first reader. As I read us, it's not my intention to judge us, but as for the text, whose structure I am apt to announce from one chapter to the next, by the very way it is organized, designates, transfigures, alienates us from each other, gives right to one and not to the other, or vice versa, following the mood, the resonance of details. But these are only rationalizations, tricks of lighting. The stage is nothing but the smallest part of a theater. And behind the screen of the page, there is many an impulse.

Monday, Tuesday, Wednesday: my calculating is indeed accurate, we're only going to live three days in Peyroc together. Together! However, there were two of us to live this story and I am the only one to write it down. Or rather, did we live that story two by one, each in his own corner, each in his own body, two fields which will never be one, one single one, a single soil, turned up, worked upon, absurd efforts of our nights and our embraces, the sullen stubborn work of our days, guests, silences, visits, gazing eyes or confessions? Two by one to live this story through, and perhaps two to write it down now, one year after meeting each other, because you're still here, because I don't understand why you paused at me, and I at you. Because I neither want nor can admit that a true source, or secret, or meeting, or union cannot exist. We all more or less fashion one another in our imagination, but only to ultimately strike up against each other, wounds, the masts are broken. And start all over, start all over.

Monday. Betsy adores you. She even decides, what an extraordinary thing, to go swimming because *you* go swimming. Ruth adopts you from the very start. Because you jump into the swimming pool like a madman, splashing everybody, and you make her laugh. You're a disruption and you're a pleasure. You want to appeal to the women first because the others are watching you, those from Paris, Robert, Gérard, Oswyn with this look he has of not seeing or understanding anything, and John, who tells me, "Hold onto him," just like Marie. You take, you hold on to, you throw away, you believe you're the owner, you're either rich or poor, you make assurances, you insure yourself, you hunt each other down, you lie in wait for each other. I know that language by heart. It is not the language of the heart: it doesn't share, it robs, striking at your weakest point. You don't want to take that tone, but it takes you. You don't want to transcribe it, but it comes back and imposes itself, a

mental attitude. During our first visit to Fontaubes, no sooner had I
arrived than I wanted to go home, our home. It's clear to you. You
watch me, from a distance, smiling slyly. You are playing. Or else,
sincere, you're testing me. When Betsy leads you off to visit her
windmill, one of the two boys from Paris tells me, as though he were
spitting out a black pearl, that he saw you "hardly a month ago in a
club." And he asks me if we've known each other a long time. When we
left Fontaubes, in the late afternoon, you tell me, "Together, they're
awful. One by one, they're all right. Did you know Stéphane?" "Who?"
"One of Robert's friends, because . . ." You fall silent. I walk ahead of
you. You catch up with me. You throw stones into the brush. You say,
"My undershorts are wet." Then, "I should have kept my mouth shut,"
and finally, "Anyway, I said what I said."

Monday evening, full moon. A stroll along the Rhône. You're cold. I
offer you my pullover. You slip it on, whispering, "But what about
you?" You take me in your arms. Two gay men, together, will always be
two gay men, together. And when we come back into the village, you
say in a hushed voice, "I'm sure you're thinking about that jerk, but
you're wrong, because really, considering what happened . . ." The
light's still on in Carolon's bedroom. Emilienne is watching television,
a Western, gunshots. Olaya dropped by while we were gone. You go up
to the bedroom, come back down with a surprised, amused look on your
face. "She took all my stuff." "She'll bring them back tomorrow."
Music. Naked. Night. You stretch out on the little bed in the study. You
hand me the tube of magic ointment which Betsy gave you. I have to
cover you with moisturizer. Very gently. "Be careful . . ." Your body
seems scalded. Without being aware of it, you say to me, "Thanks."
And you fall asleep. Almost instantly.

Tuesday. "I want to bum around with you. Call up Fontaubes and tell
them no!" La Nesque, Sault, Apt, Lourmarin, we stop and visit the
abbey at Sulvacane; we arrive in Aix, toward evening. You look at me
and smile constantly. You are wearing Bernard's chain and medal. You
keep asking me if everything is all right. I am dazed. Dazzled. Trusting.
Because I have the feeling that you are finally going to confide in me. I
return your gaze, your smile. As we walk down the street, you grab my

hand furtively, and you squeeze it, pulsation, hidden from sight, kindly. But then hidden from whose sight? In front of the cathedral, for the concert. "It will be the day's highlight!" We meet up with the Fontaubes tribe, each and every one of them. John says, "And yet we only made up our minds at the last second." The seats are not numbered. You sit between Betsy and Gérard. And I between Ruth and Stéphane, with John and the others. Sometimes I get the impression that you're going to turn around, but you no longer dare to really look at me in front of them. I am writing this text alone, what's your version?

Only those who accuse others of being selfish are really selfish. Jealousy is other people, when they made up their minds at the last second and when the seats are not numbered. There they are, to the right, to the left, trapping you with their eyes and their irony, their schemes and their envy. Jealousy is them, their handcuffs and their games. At moments like these, passion becomes exacerbated. You would go so far as to break your wrists to escape, not to be there anymore, not to have met the one you love.

Tuesday, middle of the night, driving home. You want to take a cold bath. Olaya has placed all your laundry, clean, on my bed, carefully pressed, it smells good. You sniff it. "It's a luxury . . ." You undress. Out of your pants' pocket, you take a scrap of paper and hand it to me. Robert scribbled his address and phone number, in Lille. And with a laugh, "I'm showing it to you because it doesn't mean anything to me . . ." And I go down to the study, pound the walls with my fists, hit my head on the floor like during recess, in high school, or some evenings in my bedroom, at Saint-Mandé. A nurse came by to warn my mother, but we never had any cases in the family. You're scared. You come up to me. You hold me by the shoulder. Breakdown. I am prostrated. I don't know what to clutch onto anymore. I see white, all white, opaque, blurry. Dizziness. And you whisper, "I don't understand." Here, the two of us are writing, because there was no way you could understand.

Wednesday morning. A few hours later. Naked, stretched out on my back, at the edge of the bed, and you, naked on the stomach, you're taking up all the room, you're asleep clinging to my forearm. I dare not

move. I hear Mrs. Santienne, Mrs. Beylac and Mrs. Vérini, a long
conversation. Something about the butcher "who's going to come by
late again," and an accident that happened on the highway, "two
seriously injured, but they're only Germans." I also hear the mailman
come by, the sound of letters falling into my mailbox and Emilienne's
voice, "They're not up yet." They? The truth is that I like all of this,
because it is. In Fontaubes, people watch and people are watched. In
Peyroc, people stand watch, attentive gestures, a first affection. You
stir slightly, you turn your head, open your eyes and say, in a faraway
voice, as in a dream, "I am going to fix breakfast." I slip out of bed.
Music. Sunlight. Last day. You fall back asleep.

Three o'clock in the afternoon. Fontaubes. We planned to arrive in
time for coffee and they haven't started to eat lunch yet. You wanted to
say good-bye to Betsy, at least, "who is so funny." Betsy takes a picture
of both of us. "Smile. Better than that. A little tenderness!" To show
some tenderness, I kiss you on the forehead. Betsy shouts, "Perfect!"
The men are watching us. John asks you, "Why are you leaving so
quickly?" And you stand at attention, in front of him, like a soldier. A
military salute. A button of your grey-and-blue checkered shirt, the top
button, pops off, because you puff up your chest too much while
repeating, "But they'll never get me!" Then you explain to Ruth that
you want "to take off," "bum around," "backpack and without any
money," that "that's what traveling is all about," and that, and that?
Stéphane, a few steps away, is pretending to be asleep, stretched out on
cushions, a book opened over his face. Ruth goes into the house with
Oswyn. Gérard sets two salad bowls down on the table. John looks
upset. He glances at you, at me, he smiles vaguely, and when Ruth asks
us, "Are you going to at least go swimming?" you answer, "We have to
leave right away. But I'm coming back, August 16th. The 16th at the
very latest. To stay longer." What you have just said, to them, you've
just announced to me. This sentence, awkwardly constructed, perfectly
depicts the awkward interplay of our eyes; you said that without looking
at me. And I found that touching. As if out of respect for me, a kind of
respect for yourself. Betsy announces, "Well then, August 16th,
there'll be a huge dinner party at my place. At the mill. For Mr. Duck."
John turns towards me and whispers, "The 17th would be a better

idea." Good-bye kisses. We leave.

On our way, I say silly things to you like, "You know, Duck, I'm not fooling myself. I know that time is not on our side. The time we'll spend together will be time gained, but the time without you will not be contrite." I am doing the talking, and this time, you're the one who's quiet. You look preoccupied, sullen, or perhaps it's a resentment? Why ever did I use the word "contrite"? I explain it to you. "Contrition, the worst kind of shame, the most poisonous of moral remedies . . ." I am getting more muddled: poison, moral remedies. You're not even laughing. And yet, it's laughable. Or perhaps you're moved, like me, just as much as me, since you're leaving again, since you're leaving? The summons for the three days service is at seven in the morning, in a suburban barracks, north of Lyons. I try to be cheerful, to tell you everything I plan to do until August 16th, the classes to prepare, the readings to undertake, and then Fontaubes, about which I speak in a guilty manner, almost as if I wanted to earn your esteem, your attention, and an answer, a word, a judgment. But you remain quiet. Under the rocky hill, in the path, as you push back a fig branch to pass through, you rip off some leaves and the embryo of a fruit. I don't like that gesture. That nervousness. Ripped-off leaves which you hold in your hand. I tell myself that the whole village is going to see it. Door closed behind us. The house. You are almost elated, suddenly. "Is there any cake left?" Within three minutes, your bag is ready. In an envelope I placed 300 francs. The envelope is sealed, I hand it to you. "It's not money I'm giving you, but simply a little something to make the last stage easier, on the 14th or the 15th." And I also hand you the duplicate of my house keys, two small keys, "so you'll be able to come in if I am not here." You take it all, looking embarrassed and quite happy.

In the car, heading toward Avignon, this time you're the one who's talking. I have a knot in my throat, I admit it. I'm still sitting on the bridge of Petit-Pont. Gazing down on the river. At the far end of everything. I hear you explaining to me, like a point of pride, that you're leaving "without money," that you won't write to anyone because you will have "no time." Laughter. "It's better that way." You also say, "As for schemes, you're the one who provokes them, we'll talk about that later . . ." You want me to drop you on Nationale 7, but on second thought, you decide to take the train. "I have to have dinner with my psychiatrist friend. He's going to tell me what course to follow tomorrow morning to get myself discharged." You rest a hand on my knee. Avignon, red light. You turn your head to the right. Impossible to meet your eyes.

Parking, the train station. Your duffle bag. I run ahead of you, to buy your ticket. You catch up with me at the ticket window. "Come on, let me . . ."

I give you the ticket. You smile without daring to look at me, and that's fine with me because suddenly I'm afraid of your eyes, there, at that moment. With your head down, you put the ticket in the back pocket of your pants. "Meet you on the 16th of August. Draw a bath, I'll be dirty, and make sure there is something to eat, because I'll be hungry." You turn on your heels, and you disappear without turning around. I almost feel taunted. I'm always waiting for people to turn around to say good-bye. No. Nothing more. You came. You're leaving again.

And I almost feel happy. I say to myself that everything is fine like this. Quite fine. And that everything is over. Even if you come back, even if you have the keys, even if I draw a bath, even if there is something to eat. Seven in the evening. Daylight saving time. It's still broad daylight. The crowd at the station, travelers leaving, and arriving. And only at that moment do I get scared. I pound the steering wheel with my fists, repeating, "no . . ." "no . . ." and "no?" Peyroc. An empty house. The phone's ringing. Ruth: "We're expecting you for dinner. That's an order." On the table there are the fig leaves and the embryo of a fruit.

22

"When I meet an optimist, I look at his shoes: corpses always leave telltale signs, around the edges." John is proud of himself. Betsy turns toward Ruth. "What surprises me about your husband is that he always has a retort, brand-new, saved up. Did you ever hear that one before?" Ruth smiles. Betsy calls on me to corroborate. "What about you, Pierre? I can't really believe that John comes out with things as serious as that without hearing them from others first." John watches me. I say nothing. I simply smile, as does Ruth. There are four of us around the new table, an immense oval of black lacquer, chandeliers, candles, silverware, a cold dinner prepared by Mrs. Vérini. The others, the young men, including Oswyn, have gone off "to visit friends." And the four of us, points of a compass, we observe each other. John, always amused by silences, seems to be making fun of us. He says, "I first heard this retort from my father, who was very fond of France."

Ruth: "It's not nice for Pierre." Betsy: "Only the French like the French." John: "I find you really very optimistic!" And we laugh for laughter's sake. To dispel the silence. Perhaps also because we love each other. We like each other. Ruth announces to John that the Debrukes have arrived. They have called up. They are expecting "the Fontaubes gang" around their swimming pool, name the day. "Mrs. Debruke even told me, almost reproachfully, that we never got together." John looks at the three of us. " With them, never is already too often." And we laugh again. It's ridiculous: we need to stand up to pass each other the dishes. Betsy: "But the table is beautiful!" Ruth: "What are you thinking about, Pierre?" John: "No, who?"

The dining-room windows are opened onto the garden. The swimming pool is lit from the inside. Betsy glances at John: "Did you check to see if those pool lanterns are waterproofed? I read in a newspaper, there was an accident, someone who dove and who was electrocuted." Silence. Betsy adds, "I adore tragedies. I would love to be the one to announce them. Like you, Pierre. Admit that I'm just a tiny bit right." Betsy says *vous* and *tu* to me, like a flea hopping about, Fontaubes' silences and comforts. Ruth looks at me. "Tell us about Duck. You're dying to do it." John: "Leave Pierre alone, I was worse than Duck at his age." Ruth: "When you met me?" "Yes, precisely so. I was worse and I met you!" Betsy: "Perhaps we might be able to change the subject." Ruth: "Perhaps . . ." John: "Impossible!"

In the kitchen, we put everything away. Ruth pulls me aside. "Duck is too young for you, much too young. I'm very fond of him. And you're much too fond. I hardly know him. And you'll never know him well enough. It's not a judgment. But . . .but I would like to see you happy with someone, someday, and yet you'll never be. You realize this, you keep going on. We've all kept going on." She turns toward me, clings to my neck like a small insect. "Only misunderstandings can last. Quick, jump out of the circle!" Betsy breaks in: "I know what you just told him. But in the state he is in he can't listen to you. I wonder if he can hear you." I put on a cheerful expression. "I understand perfectly. Thanks." Every time I say thanks, I think of Duck. We go into the living room. Right behind me, Betsy exclaims loudly, "He is really in love. How about pushing him into the pool? To see what happens!" Laughter. I step out into the garden. "Let's go for a walk."

Picturesque, or destruction? "What were you thinking about, at the train station, right after he left?" John walks beside me. Betsy and Ruth are following us. I answer, "The way it was before. I wondered how it was before him, and I had already forgotten, forgotten everything.

Before him, there was nothing else, nothing, with one shake of the magic writing screen. He erased everything. And then it lasted only a second. Time enough to pound the steering wheel with my fists a few times, repeating, no, no!" Betsy whispers, "Yes, yes, and yes!" Ruth: "Shut up." We're walking in the darkness. Without really deciding to, we're heading toward Peyroc. "Will you ask us in?" Betsy grabs my arm. "You will show us your collection of tragic writing screens?"

On my terrace, Betsy and Ruth sit on the deck chairs, John and I are seated on the floor, on cushions. "Hard as nails, is it horsehair?" Four bowls, the herb tea is served. Betsy looks at John. John looks at Ruth, Ruth is watching me. I smile. "I promise you that I won't wait for him. My sentence for suffering began to be reduced on the very day Duck and I met each other." Betsy: "What was reduced?" Ruth: "Let him speak." Betsy: "Then let's talk about something else. Did you know what President Ping-ping-whatever told the Chinese when he resigned from his high post?" Silence. Betsy smiles. "He said that when you've sat on the toilet with no results, you must let someone else take your place." Silence. We haven't laughed. Betsy said, "I did it on purpose. Anything we can say, together, is on that level. And everything that everybody can say to each other, from now on, is not on a greater level. Prove me wrong."

Later, I have just driven them home, they get out of my car, in front of the Fontaubes gate. Ruth kisses me on the lips. "I know you won't be coming tomorrow because of Stéphane and the others. So, see you soon. I'll let you know when they've left." Hopping back and forth from *vous* to *tu*, like Betsy. She glances at John. "Maybe they'll leave with Oswyn!" John pinches my cheek. "Get some color back." He kisses Betsy and shuts the gate, squeaking of the hinges, sound of the latch. Betsy says to me, "You can't even hate us. You need us and we need you. Come to the mill too, whenever you want. I have too many things I want to tell you, too bad!" She slams the car door shut on the "too bad!" Exclamation point. Her performance.

Four miles, the road back, Peyroc, the parking, the plane trees, the washhouse, my house, I left the lights on. For one moment, I got the feeling that Duck was waiting for me. During the time it takes to open the door, I toy with the idea. He's here? No, he's not here! I throw away the fig leaves. I set out the bowl and plate for tomorrow's breakfast. My pouch, my napkin. I look for the pouch marked X. I'll ask Emilienne to embroider the initials D.C. With a pair of scissors, I clip out the X, tiny threads of wool. Music: he won't write. Reading: I won't be able to write him. Reading abandoned: I have trouble concentrating on anything other than him. The Avignon train station. He doesn't turn around. He did not turn around. Ticking of the alarm clock on the night table, middle of the night. In a few hours, Duck will present himself at a barracks north of Dijon. I see him again, on the bed, he's sleeping, his two hands grasping me.

Instinctively, I rub my arm and pick up my book again, reading out loud. I must force myself to concentrate. But I see the table with black lacquer, the dishes, the silverware, their dream, their luxuries, and all these words, like bitterness or disguised screams. We're all afraid of what we haven't been, and of what we will not become, the prisoner's fear. Once again, I abandon the book. I was reading out loud without paying attention to the words. Saint-Mandé, rue Boursault, Fontaubes. Where am I myself, where have I ever been myself, fully? To those questions, the die-hard optimist would answer by hiding his shoes. I get up so as to write down John's remark. To write down what they said. Like Duck, I have just made up my mind "to keep everthing!" It was on that evening that I really began to take notes, by living the story, because it had been lived so badly, because it was already badly lived, as much by him as by me, and everyone else too, even before it had begun. Everything is plundered, plundered beforehand. I feel hunted down. Who will ever understand that what we're dealing with here is a freedom, and not an inventory, an unpacking, a comedy, a trifle, picturesque. Destruction, yes! That evening Duck eats away at me and is already touring around the Mediterranean within me. While stuffing everything into his travel bag, he snatched my pair of sandals. "Can I take them? I doubt very much that I'll be able to buy any." That, the bathing suit, Bernard's medal, and the button of the grey-and-blue checkered shirt that Ruth gave me back before dinner. "Here, look at what I found by the swimming pool!" Fetishes. You don't collect them, they collect themselves. They establish their own collection. Peyroc's bats, and Fontaubes' vultures.

And Betsy: "I have lots to tell you, too bad!" Why "too bad"? Her sense of humor? Or else age, when abruptly, it calculates everything? I hear her joke around, entertain, say about herself that she'll never find a fourth husband and exclaim, "From now on I can only be beautiful with men who don't have the slightest reason for looking at me or keeping me. I am their adornment. Around me, they say: But who is that woman, she must be a princess, an Italian princess, but of course, it's Princess Alibi. I am Princess Alibi!" Ruth says about Betsy, "I love her, because she chases away black butterflies."

John, two days later, drops by in the late morning. "They have gone to the beach. Can I spend the day with you? We will talk about nothing, and nothing!" He stayed. He slept on the terrace. Now and then, he'd get up to drink a glass of water, in the bathroom. I took advantage of it to tidy up the basement, straighten up the woodpile, the bottles, and the old cardboard boxes. In the late afternoon, we have tea. John whispers, "Oswyn is leaving tonight. He's taking advantage of Stéphane's car to get back to London, by way of Paris." Iced tea. John tastes it. "You'll never know how to make it like my mother . . ." He smiles. "Excuse me, but we've all reached that point." He laughs. "I like your house. There's really only room for one person."

Five or six days later. Ruth calls me. "We miss you, come back." The days go by. I live comfortably. I don't get any mail. Emilienne, at her window, tells me, "No news is good news." A large truck in front of Carolon's house. They're taking away the trunk.

23

Three letters on the same day. Emilienne: "Enough is enough. I envy you." First letter.

"Dijon, July 11th.

"A few words. I'm getting back on top of things, after many rotten days. As soon as I got here, I heard that I had been replaced for the survey job. This type of surprise will have annoying repercussions, for my budget is always a masterpiece of balancing. But I'm used to these worries and they can't affect my morale. The three days in the service went well, that is to say, very badly. I think I'll be able to get discharged. I acted crazy. I simply jumped out of a second-floor window. I sprained my foot. Fortunately, I have your sandals. I'll spare you the family squabbles and my brothers' difficulties in crossing over the parental doormat.

"Now, everything is better. But what a contrast with the tranquillity of Peyroc. I'll try writing you before I leave because I have a lot to tell you. I have discussed at length with Louis, my psychiatrist friend (who is my conscience), everything that has been happening to me for the past two months and also what you have lived through up to now. I'll talk to you about it.

"Above all, don't worry about me. My problems are almost resolved and anyway I know how to approach them. I'm rediscovering, as I write you, my lucid optimism.

"My plans haven't changed much. The day after tomorrow, I'm going down to Saint-Raphael with my parents and my brothers. From there, I'll decide. Two solutions: either I go to Marseilles, I try to work on the port for a month to solve my problems, or I'll go off, with my parents' help (which means I'll need to work in September, for Christmas and for Easter), and drift around, to recharge my batteries and preserve what I call my contact with reality and the possible. At any rate, I'll rejoin you toward the end of August, around the 16th.

"You see how everything is falling into place. It will be hard for you not to answer me (you won't know where to find me) but it's better. You know I can overcome quite a few things by only relying on my own resources.

"Think of yourself and don't let insidious demons take hold of you. Work. Take long walks. Be strong, without losing sight of the rules of the game around you (they're only rules) and by only trusting reality.

"I am neither too weak nor too depressed to confront what is to come. I simply need to muster all my energy.

"Don't worry if you don't hear from me too much. Love and see you soon. Only trust what is. Duck.

"P.S. I hesitated to send you this letter, but it's written. And I find it rather reassuring. One of my brothers is probably going to live with me, at my place, when school starts. I don't like to have people in my care, except, in point of fact, my family. Forget what's in this letter. By the same mail, I'm sending a card to Marie, showing a stork."

Second letter.

"Uzès, July 11th.

"My Dear Pierre.

"I am barely coming out, with great trouble, of a horrible shitty situation, a persistent nervous breakdown. Crucifying insomnias against which I struggled with a sleeping pill cocktail, as ineffective as it was harmful. Add to that the tension of this first year of retirement, a "psychological aggression on emotional level" (sensual passion, mad, and with no hope of reciprocity for a Portuguese emigrant who was working not far from my place) and the postoperative shock of an operation on my spine: I cracked up.

"Following my brother Léon and my sister-in-law Eliane's advice, first stay in a neuro-psychiatric clinic of the Marseilles region. I didn't find it very agreeable. It was the kind of sleep cure for ritzy ladies. I came out of it too soon. A frightful relapse with suicidal tendencies, sexual obsessions: I became scared stiff of going insane, purely and simply.

"I was promptly installed in another clinic. Closer to my brother, at one of his colleague's clinics. Artaud spent some time there. When the weather is nice, for three days, on the bench where Antonin perhaps champed at his bit, I have been champing at mine.

"On the intellectual level, everything's back in working order, but as far as graphic expression goes, there's a screw loose somewhere. Do you recognize, here, the tiny but legible script of my notes?

"My address? You'll find included a detailed map printed through the good works of this worthy establishment. Come!

"This unfortunate parenthesis began at the end of February. You'll laugh if I tell you his name is Sévéro. He's the one who came again and again to my place. He's twenty-seven years old. He's married. He has children back home. I haven't touched him. I was ready to have his family come to France. He can only come and see me here every other Sunday. The last two times, I was asleep, naturally. A brotherly kiss. Roussel."

Third letter.

"Rue Boursault, July 11th.

"My Pierrot.

"I dreamed about you last night. You were trying to sneak back home, and I lying in wait for you behind my door. There you were, between the second and third floors, on tiptoe, not daring to pass in front of my door. I didn't know whether I should show my face or not, speak to you or not. I don't like this dream. Does it correspond to our reality, this small amount of time and space which we share together, when we do share? The possibility frightens me so much that I'm writing to you in order to break the spell (?) of the dream in question.

"The insurance company agent came to draw up a report at the fourth floor tenant's apartment. What a fuss for just a little hole! He wants to have the whole room repainted. There were no damages to report at your place, right? I don't know why I remember one of Bécassine's witticisms, my dear reading buddy from Biarritz, I'd spend entire days with her, in the storeroom of my parents' shop and Bécassine would explain, at the slightest pretext, 'Scoldings are like bad-tasting medicine, you must swallow them down in one gulp.' Like the dream; you must put an end to it.

"I had begun to tidy up the room of my future baby-husband. And then I gave up on doing anything. Another memory came to me: my grandmother who never got the beds ready before we arrived, when we were spending our vacations with her. Like her, then, I'll do everything at the last moment, when he arrives. A matter of superstition. Or emotion.

"Tadzio left for his vacation, at the company's expense, with his wife and children. The last days, at the studio, he looked at me in an amused and worried way. At last, he understood. By way of a farewell kiss I simply whispered into his ear, "But it's not yours." And I saw the dear man blush with relief. No comment, like a self-explanatory cartoon. And not to be continued, like a comic strip without any real plot. It's fine like this. Men are courageous, don't you think?

"I'm in the process of finishing the printer's layout for a brochure on 'Back to School.' I could already tell you everything about the price of book bags and uniforms. I'm doing some drawing, also, for myself. Sometimes the night hours are long. And I miss you. This letter is on the verge of becoming a love letter. I'm still lying in wait for you, in my dream, and wondering why you don't dare pass in front of my door, why you want to get into your apartment without me finding out?

"I told you I didn't intend to come down to Peyroc this summer. Yet I'm toying with the idea of acting like everybody else and leaving Paris August 16th. Coming to your place would be a nice break. A word you're not fond of, I know. I'll arrive on the 13th, and I'll leave on the 15th. Possible?

"Mariette is tired. She hurt her finger while slicing a capeline molding. I brought her to the clinic. Her whole hand is bandaged up, but she keeps on working. Boubou got away. I found him in the square. It's unbelievable. He's begun to walk again. Ordinary news, ordinary lives. What about you? Is Ruth still as charming as ever? What about her friend? And her husband (sic)? I am sure that the water of their swimming pool is as pure as ever. I neither envy nor ridicule them: we all live where we live. As for me, I feel really good, almost two.

"No mail to forward. Nothing interesting. I tell myself that this way you'll sleep later in the morning. If Mrs. Emilienne doesn't talk too much at her window. You ought to take a long trip.

"What a letter! I hadn't written such a long one since Sam, Jacques & Bertrand. A good or bad sign? See you tonight perhaps, a new dream, but knock at my door, make your presence known. No need to hide. A whole life playing hide-and-seek? Love. Marie.

"P.S. Included is the gas and electric bill. Sorry. I received the card from Sète. Thanks."

24

Where do bats live during the day? Is it possible that vultures prefer lying-in-wait to seizing their prey? As the reader of my own text, I worry, I scrutinize it, and reject it in order to come back to it, all the better, day chapter or night chapter, is this all that we are and is this all that I lived? The spider's stratagem: the threads of the web are taut. One says, "I'll be back," the other, "Come!" and the third, "I'd love to come." The text watches, observes and lies in wait for the person who is lying in wait for it. We are all here hunting each other, as much in what we are as in and through what we create. We seek out the exceptional, power or death, power and death, to the ultimate degree, together, if it's possible. And finally, we, all characters of this text, are still living at the moment when I write. We have conquered nothing and we are alive. "Drifting about," as Duck said, speaking about our lives as though about vacations. Letters read. Envelopes ripped open hastily. Dijon, Uzès, Paris. Mariette repeats, "Everything always comes in threes, without fail." The text is listening. I smile about myself, images. These things which grip me, these memories which tear me apart, these origins which order me about and hold me in their grasp, these facts which I narrate as precisely as possible so as to question thoroughly, all of this is what carries me away. I am not in the process of writing a novel: it is writing itself. The more it writes itself, the quicker it goes along, the more I must pace myself, pace the words and pay attention. One of life's facades is going to crumble. I have given up with Duck. Given up being entirely myself in another. Given up carrying the other in his entirety within me. We'll never speak together. Each one has his role to play in the comedy.

That 12th of July, I have just finished reading the letters. I clear the breakfast table, the bread, the paper I haven't even opened. I wash the bowl, the plate and the silverware. I put away the butter and jam in the refrigerator. These gestures are important because everything, in my house, must be neat. A neatness in view of an expectation, when you forbid yourself from waiting any longer.

Betsy phones me. "Why don't you come over? Robert and Gérard are in Saint-Tropez. Ruth is spending the day at the Debrukes', John left this morning for London. A round trip. Oswyn really isn't worth the trouble. More trouble. That's the only word on our lips these days. And we spend our whole time criticizing each other. Each of us believes himself to be better than the other, asserts himself as different. We are birds of a feather insofar as we will never flock together. You are listening, are you there?" For a second, I think she is crying. But I hear her laughter at the other end of the line. "I am alone by the swimming pool. I am terribly afraid of drowning. Come and be the lifeguard. Stop going around in circles at your place." I reply, "I am going around in circles because that's how I learned how to walk." "It's nothing, only a figure of speech. So, are you coming?" I look at the letters, on the table. The butcher's van passes in front of the house. On the washhouse square, three honks. The neighbors' voices. "And now, he's arriving early . . ." Betsy sighs. "You're not saying anything?" "No, I'm staying here. I feel good. Come if you like . . ." The sound of a kiss on the receiver. "Too bad!" She hangs up. I hang up.

I suddenly remember one day, before the Nikko Hotel: instead of dialing Marie's number, I had just, absent-minded, dialed my own and out of curiosity I waited for the busy signal. But to my great surprise, the recording—"the number you have just dialed is not in service, please call information"—had been activated. It had amused me, puzzled me, then scared me. I had hung up brusquely. And Marie, a few minutes later, when I had told her of that little incident, had said, "It's normal," then, "We were all born marked by silences, sped along by others, those very people who brought us into this world are in the lead. I give you Biarritz and I take Saint-Mandé. What would that change? We'll never be happy, considering our births, social fuss, and bother, and conventions. It may be better that the number you called was out of service. Maybe that is the only real answer. The truth. You're not even smiling. You're on my path, I'd like to reach out to you. I am on yours, and you're not reaching out. We get along fine, simply because we each believe we're still capable of reaching it. Are you smiling now?"

Behind the scenes, the silences. Here, I am repeating things as at a show rehearsal. One of life's shows that I haven't lived yet, held back as I am by so many strings and preconceived ideas. I accept the task of representation. I present myself, I make presentations. The part is written in advance. I am still rehearsing, but I'll play only once: too late to astonish. Mariette, talking about her hats, always quotes this show business witticism, this artist's witticism, Diaghilev, she pronounces Diaghlev, saying to Cocteau, "Astonish me!" As for me, I'll only astonish once in my life, and it will be too late to congratulate myself over the others' astonishment. And it's not blackmail. When death takes me away, I'll still be in the process of rehearsing, repeating myself. Behind the scenes, the silences. I have no show to put on. The spectacle and its preparation, its development in a hope of getting at the truth of the character, are enough. Life assigns roles for a show which some of us, either too sensitive or too strong-willed, will never be able to play. With the money he received for the trunk, Carolon is going to take the waters at Gréoux-les-Bains. He has just informed me, "I am only doing it for my pleasure. Twice a day, clean towels." He is leaving his sister behind "in Emilienne's care," who will only have to "get her out of bed, and put her back, and feed her if she's hungry." Carolon notices the three letters on my table. "Do as I do, don't answer. For me it's easy, I have forgotten to know how to write. I used to know how, I even had a certain style of my own, a trifle bureaucratic, but nothing ever came of it."

Ten in the morning. I leave the house. I wore the same things as when I went to Séte. I am going to Uzés. Unannounced. I have the map directing me to the clinic. I hold it in my hand like a pass. Emilienne asks me if I am going "to the shore." I speak of "a friend who's very sick." I correct myself. "No, he's tired." I get myself in deeper. Once the front door is closed behind me, the telephone rings. It's Betsy again. Too bad for her. Emilienne says to me, "Aren't you going to answer it?" I smile and I go on my way.

At the steering wheel, I take stock of the three letters. First, Duck's. My name, cut off. An oversight. Or perhaps a reticence, like a fear. Not even "Pierre," "Dear Pierre," or "My Dear Pierre." Nothing. And his psychiatrist friend, Louis, who is "his conscience." What does that mean? I remember some expressions: "lucid optimism," "contact with reality and the possible," "only relying on my own resources," "only trust what is," that "I don't like to have people in my care except, in point of fact, my family." And this August 16th, which has become "around the 16th." Perhaps Carolon is right. One shouldn't reply. One shouldn't write. You always do damage when you write, especially when you want to be nice, to love, to brings things to life a little. On a street corner Duck is waiting for us, me and Marie, springs out in front of us and pretends to scare us. We saw him take his hiding place. It's a game. And yet Marie screams and calls Duck an idiot. Words are also always lying in ambush. They attack, especially when they are predictable. I am going to Uzès because Roussel wrote me. "I was asleep obviously." I will phone Marie to ask her not to come between the 13th and the 18th of August. I'll have to tell her why.

There he is, in the clinic garden, sitting on a bench, his hands resting on his knees. He's looking at his feet. And I don't like the sound of my footsteps on the gravel. I pause. I take a deep breath. Sometimes, sobbing is a mark of courage. Like an outburst, the violence of presence, a clash. I could be far from here, go away, play, make a pest of myself, relax, only lend importance to short-lived ecstasies, read, throw away, forget, seek out extremes of pleasure, satisfy myself with judging what others undertake, accept to never be myself, and play my role in the show, living-dead, put up a good front, yet here I am. I have arrived. As if by instinct, Roussel raises his head and spots me. He gets up, totters a little, takes a couple of steps, I rush towards him. He falls into my arms, a small, heavy old man that I will be someday. I hold him. I have never held anyone in my arms in this way: I am holding him up, and he's standing only because I am here. Small, all shriveled, his hands gripping my shirt, his face glued to my chest, he bangs the top of his head several times against my chin, repeating, "It's you, but it's you . . ." We sit down on a bench. He takes my hands and kisses them like a child. A way of hiding his tears from me if he has begun to cry, then he looks at me, smiles and whispers, "Make me laugh!" He gestures towards the clinic. "All of this is quite laughable. But they take good care of me. And I really can't say if I feel like leaving." He falls silent, replaces his hands on his lap, looks at his shoes, then closes his eyes. "Talk, talk, say anything."

And I speak to him of Barbaroux, d'Arondelle, the tar-written graffiti on the school walls, the directress's nervous tics, the reshuffling of syllabuses, the number of my students who received their diplomas. "Keep on talking . . ."

I tell him that I don't like the gravel surrounding this clinic, the smell of the balatum in the hallways, that old disheveled woman in slippers, who tried to grasp me by the arm at the top of the stairs heading to the garden. "You're mistaken, she's amazing. I speak to her, I do. She lived in the Far East for fifty years, I travel with her. I had forgotten how to travel. But keep on talking . . ."

Peyroc, petty lives, Fontaubes, schemes, and Paris once again, the chimney fire, Marie's baby. What else? Roussel turns toward me. "You're hiding someone from me." I smile. There is a gust of wind. The sky is brilliant. "It's noon, my dear Pierre. There is a cafeteria here. The only modern section of this establishment and I am allowed to invite you. We'll do as at the Balto, but this time you're going to tell me everything." He gets up, reaches out his hand. He needs me to walk. He motions to a nurse in the distance not to come for him. He squeezes my arm. "I feel like a sweet young fiancée. And after you've told me everything, I too will try to tell you everything. They won't change us. That's exactly why I am here and why you've come . . ."

After the meal, we return to the same place. Roussel says to me, as he sits down, "It's my bench. They have assured me that, during my sleep cure, no one had come to sit there. Out of respect for me. Everybody here knows me already. It's my bench. And when I tell them that it was also Artaud's, or Antonin's, they don't understand. I am the only one who understands myself. And it's the unique reason that helps me to understand how things came to this. Once again Roussel grabs my hands, but this time he squeezes them so hard that he starts shaking a little. "I don't like your Duck, your Daniel, because he's too charming. Or rather, yes I do, I envy you, give it all you've got and capture him. But dictate, do dictations, and rap him with a ruler if he needs it. By listening to them too much, they very quickly blame us for only thinking of ourselves. It's the only way they have of defending themselves from sharing their lives, something they'll try to do in time when they're no longer the age they are. And so on and so forth. What if I were to tell you I waited forty years before taking a man in my arms, without being ashamed? What if I were to tell you that I'm still hiding within myself, because I hid much too long? What if I were to tell you that I was the first to tell on myself, to point an accusing finger at myself, to ridicule myself? It's horrible how we ridicule ourselves, especially when we take ourselves seriously. Why is that?"

"Let him be. Let him travel around, but don't wait for him. And for once, listen to what I have never been able to listen to: don't wait for this young man. Don't wait for him anymore. Do you have a picture of him? I am sure that you have his letter in your pants' pocket. You don't? Not even in the car? Then, you left him at home, so as to come back to it more surely, this evening, to read it over again. What if I were to tell you that last month, before the accident, I had started washing Sévéro's laundry with mine, and ironing it, like mine? I was doing him a favor. I could do him at least that small favor. When I woke up, a week ago, a forced awakening, like my sleep, my sister-in-law Eliane was in the room and the first thing that I said out loud was "but, who's taking care of him?" Eliane made me repeat what I had just said. For twenty-one days, I had ironed, in my dreams, my dear Sévéro's intimate articles, but he's never come by to pick them up. I'm not sick you know. I feel heavy-hearted, crushed, and very good this way. Protected. Eliane couldn't possibly understand that. Neither could Sévéro. And Duck, your Duck, will only understand later when it's too late, when it will be too late. The bench will be in the shade around a quarter after four. We

have time. And willpower. Speak to me about him, when he laughs . . ."
I look at him. "Before the accident? What accident?"

With the tip of his foot, Roussel pushes the gravel away, clears off two
small oval surfaces, bare ground on which he rests his feet as well as his
hands in his lap. He tries to sit up straight. He can't anymore. He
winces, he has a stabbing pain in his back. "I am all warped by forty
years behind a desk. No matter how much I leaned towards them, the
students wouldn't listen. Or so little. Or less and less. What about you?
Do they listen to you? That's the accident, Pierre. At first I had something rare to offer them. They still listened to me. I was the only one
conveying a message. My subject. Belles lettres. They respected me.
Then, they became more and more deaf, and I got out of the habit of recog-
nizing them, of putting a name on each face. Then I often forbade myself
from confessing this to you, when we would go to the Balto, or when you'd
invite me to your place, another rarity which I knew how to savor. I was
afraid of frightening you and having you hunch over prematurely. And
what's more, those moments that you gave to me, I didn't want to spoil
them. Now I can tell you: don't lean over the desk too far, you'd get
dizzy. They are learning French the way we learned Latin. The language is dead. And the last year I spent with them, their deafness was
only equalled by my indifference. I had become grey, completely grey,
like the sky of Paris in the winter or the sidewalks in the spring when you
lower your eyes when someone too handsome walks by." A nurse
draws near with a glass and pills on a saucer. One by one, Roussel
places them on his lips and swallows them with a sip of water. After
each pill, he glances at me. For the last one he winks at me. The nurse
tells him, "Don't stay here, when it gets shady, otherwise you'll catch
cold." Roussel looks at her. "But, I am leaving with this gentleman."
The nurse smiles. "Your sister-in-law called to say that she wouldn't be
able to come today. But Dr. Roussel will come tomorrow before he sees
his patients." The nurse places the saucer on top of the glass and goes
away. "Look," Roussel whispers, "it's like the end of a mass."

"This is the accident I'm talking about: when I came back to my village,
with my books and my memories of Paris, I wasn't expecting anything
more from faces. But all it took was for Sévéro passing in front of my

house twice a day, glancing at me, flashing me a smile, an emigrant's smile, therefore a brotherly smile, for me to start lying in wait for him and waiting for him again, but so late in a lifetime, waiting for each of his daily appearances, morning and evening. Until the evening when he came into my house for a drink. Then other evenings, I taught him French, the simplest words. After a month, I realized he didn't even know how to write. I had him practice in penmanship notebooks. I started from scratch, for him and with him, beginning with the alphabet. My house had become school again. I had vaguely considered buying a TV set. But Sévéro had just stepped into my life. He alone represented all the decisions I had to make. He made lightning progress in a few months. And this is the accident I was talking about: the only kind of people who meet each other are those who can do nothing for each other, those who are separated beforehand. On some very cold evenings, he would sleep at my home, downstairs, there was a sofa bed near the fireplace. He slept naked. I saw him. But I didn't touch him. This father was a child, and I'd laugh like a little brother, next to him, at my desk, filling whole pages with a, e, i, o and u. Therein lies the poem, believe me . . ."

"Perhaps we should relearn everything, redo everything from top to bottom, with the other, in order to discover a common ground. But age forbids it. There is always a discrepancy of attention and knowledge. One surrender doesn't mean the other will follow. It makes him run away. And if he doesn't take flight, everything else around you works together, to drive him away. One evening Sévéro and I were copying the following sentence: 'We are going to take a nice trip to the seashore, and on the beach we'll build sand castles.' It's a sentence from a second-grade penmanship book. We'd known each other for four months. Sévéro was applying himself. I was, too, because I didn't want to get ahead of him. Outside, it was black as pitch. We heard laughter, then very quickly, shouts and insults. Sévéro looked at me with surprise. He was about to get up, when a rock smashed a windowpane near the fireplace. You can guess what came next. The next day Sévéro was fired from the farm where he was getting paid under the table. Illegally. How was it possible to defend him? And we got into the habit of seeing each other on the sly, outside of my house. Yet again on the sly! So, I told my brother and Eliane about everything. I asked them to step in.

They were speechless. The family, in cases such as ours, always prefers to have a fuzzy view of us. This time, however, they shook hands with Sévéro. They saw him. They helped him out the way one helps to save someone from the family. To save! And then it got much worse. All that because of a rock, a village, and because of coming home to that village. 'We're going to take a nice trip to the seashore and on the beach we'll build sand castles.' To conjugate the future! Forty-first lesson. I said this sentence over and over again to myself the whole time I was sleeping, ironing my friend's intimate articles. There are so many ways of touching someone. I lost all my hair. I feel older than ever. And yet. I repeated that sentence in order to maintain a link with Sévéro. And whenever I close my eyes, I find myself washing and ironing. The shutters of my house are closed. Overnight, people stopped greeting me in the village, they smiled as I walked by. My back pains became more and more unbearable. They had to operate. It was the beginning of February. The merciless round of clinics. Now, the house is up for sale. My brother Léon says that he's going to find me a little place, nearby. It's a real town. You can go by unnoticed, if you still bother to hide. But when I see this clinic, this terrace, these pergolas, I tell myself that I'll never get out of here. It's like a mother's womb: the original water. You feel good there. And this little space that I'm clearing under my feet by pushing away the gravel makes me feel as if I'm in my stocking feet. And so in this garden I'm gently resting in the very heart of life. Our bench is in the shade now. It's a quarter after four. Tell me about Duck, when he laughs . . ."

He clutches my arm. We head toward the clinic. He greets the disheveled lady who is still waiting at the top of the stairs. "Actually, she's always there, she's afraid of going down." And at the end of the hallway, a smell of balatum, administrative offices, nurses, we take leave of each other. He kisses me. "Get away while there's still time, it's a matter of will power. And one day, if you pass by Tulle, remember that Séréro lives there, from now on. He works in a garage, at one of Léon's friends, the Alfa-Romeo garage. Phone Eliane, if you want to see how I'm doing. Here, apart from letters, messages are not passed on. I'll be thinking about you on August 16th. Have a better life." He kisses me again. And I leave him, without turning around. "Thanks again for coming. I know you won't come back . . ."

25

I stroll around the streets of Uzès. On a copper plaque, to the left of an oak-wood door, I read, "Dr. Léon Roussel. Hospital Resident. Pulmonary Diseases. Appointments Only." I don't know why, but this makes me smile. A breeze begins to blow, but it's not the Mistral, a sluggish and deceptive gust rising from the west. The sky clouding up. Tomorrow it will rain.

At an outdoor café, I am waiting for night to fall. I watch the people who are passing by, those who live here, tourists and children too. I try to read summer on their faces, in their eyes, in their clothing, gestures, shouts or laughter. I listen to what is being said at neighboring tables. If someone unfolds a newspaper, I read the headlines from afar. But all I see is Roussel, in profile, his head down, staring at his hands, on his lap. He is speaking. He is still speaking. There is something rich and happy in his voice when he pronounces the name Sévéro. He is fighting. He has his reason for living. His complete reason. Why, free as we are, proud of our freedom, have we grown used to no longer knowing how to listen to confessions for what they are, everything except laments? Café customers coming and going. There are the regular patrons, the handsome playboys, the old men playing cards inside, a Dutch family, girls sitting in pairs, a jukebox, the shelves of liquor and cigarettes, off-track betting, daily lottery, and a waiter who, every time he passes in front of me, nervously wipes my table. The formica is a curious mirror. I waited for the night to come there because I hadn't known how to talk to Roussel. And I am only really listening to him now, and afterwards.

Around nine in the evening, I am standing in front of Dr. Roussel's house. There is a light on, upstairs. It's probably Eliane I make out at the window, intermittently. She's watching for her husband to come home. And I dare not ring the bell, introduce myself, pay a visit, ask questions. I remember Roussel, after school, tossing off one of those bitter-sweet expressions for which he had a gift: "Helping others adds to the troubles of all concerned."

On the way home, the headlights blind me. I drive slowly, at the edge of the road, the illuminated road markers guiding me, a white line unrolling and leading me on. I tell myself there is no such thing as a passing mood, a short-lived anguish, or a passion which becomes, suddenly, all-consuming. All aspects of a being are interrelated and we present ourselves to other people as strong, worn and weighted by everything we have become in order to undertake the ever more impossible exploit of meeting someone, the absurd hope of at last being what we are, of being born in a strange land, skin, skill, wit, and presence identical to an identity, the other person, nothing less than the other. To read oneself and to listen to oneself in the other, to even forget your very own image. Within the present of every event, we are fiercely attached to the context, text of each one of our lives. And the other renders us helpless. All he need do is play the game a little in order to disarm us. Everything becomes a farce. And if the other yields, if he too has hopes, then the villagers throw rocks and city people avoid us, no difference. Where did I read, "By frequenting the society of men I lost the innocence of my neuroses," where, when, and who thought it, wrote it? How heavy he was, my dear Roussel, when he threw himself into my arms! And his story? Always the same story!

I don't like to drive at night. I don't like to drive at all. At the steering wheel of my car, alone, I feel like a target. I am frightened by the kind of statements you come across in daily newspapers under the "news brief" section: "Two bodies were removed from the tangled mass," or else, "Suffering serious injuries, the driver of the car died on his way to the hospital." And what if there was no white line anymore, on the right, at the edge of the road? It would mean plunging off, a fit of dizziness, blacking out. You are always leaning forward, as at a desk before your class. Roussel is right, you shouldn't lean too far. For once you do, life holds no more surprises. The sensitive individual is forced to play the role of a beggar. And with each line, here, I feel accused. This life, which is mine, will be held in contempt the way one holds in contempt a fundamental truth, heard too often, no longer listened to. What happened in the world today?

Today, I received three letters, I paid a visit to Roussel, he spoke to me about himself, I spoke to him about myself, we took leave of each other, and now I'm running away from him. Turning my steering wheel to the left, I myself would become that "tangled mass." No, I stick to the white line. Panic turns us into night birds, blinded by light. And Duck writes to tell me to trust only what is. On this very same road, we are driving back from Sète, I've just spoken to him about a possible trip to Italy, together, and he doesn't answer. He rests his head on my shoulder, he holds my forearm with both hands, and I switch gears slowly, when necessary, I don't want to awaken or startle him. Let him sleep, he hasn't learned to read, like me. Panos, Jean-Pierre, Loïc, so many others, and now Duck: passion is inevitable, it urges me on, and I have no right either to denounce the games, the pretexts, nor to denounce myself, I, Forgue, Pierre, Henri, Emmanuel, son of, and of, offspring of a couple. And I myself nothing. But what happened in the world today which is so important as to challenge me to fight for, and to justify in my own eyes, the importance of my story? Only matters of love are truly serious. Everything else is merely entertainment. A story which gets more and more entangled. Roussel, nothing is more beautiful than a little bit of love for Sévéro. Mariette, nothing is more true than one of your hats. Those in the highest balcony can applaud. Nothing is more sensual, mysterious or true than everything which is happening in your womb, Marie. Here's Peyroc. The plane trees as you enter the village. Parking my car. I believe, at the very instant that I yank up the handbrake, that Duck is here, beside me, and that every-thing is starting over. Everything is always starting over. My head is spinning. I get out of the car. It's raining. The onset of a storm. July 12th. Evening. Last year.

Slipped under the door, a message. I recognize Betsy's handwriting. "Open if you're not afraid." Inside the envelope, six color snapshots, six different poses, Duck and I. Duck is looking into the lens and I am looking at Duck. I don't recognize myself. I recognize him all too well. He is young. I am less so. He has a sober air about him. I am smiling. He lets himself be kissed. I kiss him. These pictures serve as proof: once again I am inventing a story and yet I am living it. I thought I was holding, and I am held, I thought I wanted to share and I am torn up, the suffering is real, I derive no pleasure from it whatsoever. A pain, perhaps, the pain of these lines. I place the pictures on my desk, side by side; like pawns I arrange them in the order they were taken. I hear Betsy telling us, "A little affection!" And I played that game. I kiss. Duck lets himself be kissed, and, in the last of the six photographs, theoretically the most perfect, I am making a face. I am smiling on command. I am happy on their command. And Duck has his eyes almost closed. He's already somewhere else. In the envelope, a letter from Betsy. I read it.

Transcription. Word for word. I also keep everything, from now on, in order to defend myself. Solitude is a slaughter which one would want to discuss and let drop once and for all. "The Mill. Late afternoon. I waited for you by the swimming pool. I thought you'd drop by anyway. But the very fact of waiting for you kept me company and I almost feel like thanking you. One day, in Munich, I had dragged my second husband to a performance of *The Woman without a Shadow*. I was beautiful, he was proud of me, and he loved me only insofar as the image which others communicated to us about ourselves flattered him. He was sad, ugly, and he didn't like opera. I loved him for the jealous fits we would instigate and for everything he gave me, since he gave me everything. But, sooner or later, everything is no longer enough, and the image reflected back to you by your social circle will no longer do. Then you see yourself as you are, each one of you, separately. You tell yourself that the farce has gone on long enough and you split up. That evening, during the first intermission, we strolled through the foyer.

Everybody was on display, friendly greetings, the typical black-tie crowd, the extravagance which especially fascinates those who pretend not to dream about it, the elegance which sometimes goes hand in hand with money. Yes indeed, that night Heinz and I could no longer stand each other. But we were wonderfully paired and we were still the darlings of society. He had the power of money and I had the beauty of death. Beauty when it begins to sag, like my breasts. I know, from this observation, that you'll recognize the author of these late-afternoon lines. A matter of being frank. Only those who have kneaded my breasts and had eyes only for them are truly vulgar. As for Heinz, during the intermission, he observed all these people with an air of irritation, those known, unknown, on show. I hear him telling me, almost reproachfully, 'We're still better than those people!' And I reply, 'Yes, the only thing is, each person is telling himself the same thing.' And the game is over, always the same game. There is nothing earthshaking about this remark. Yet it defines us and catches us all more or less red-handed. I apologize for the snapshots: here you are as you are and here he is as you desire him. You blew it. It's the most precious gift that Princess Alibi could offer you. A gift so very useful that you probably won't know how to use it. Since you started visiting us ten years ago, I have never really dared tell you what I think about you. These revealing, almost heart-breaking pictures, since they were my doing, finally provide me with a chance to do so. I too know how to write and to express myself. So here goes: you'll never be loved in the broad sense that you desire because you impose solitude as the prerequisite for all relationships, because you are alone, but we all are alone, because your mere presence speaks of solitude and we can't tolerate it. No one will ever tolerate it. We love you a little, in small doses, because you force us to flirt with the evidence of what we have not been and what we will never be. And we reject you, rather quickly, too quickly, as much for our benefit as for yours, because you fling all sorts of photos into our faces. That way you have, for example, of looking at me when I smooth myself with tanning cream, or when, in the evening, I get dressed up to make an impression. Yes, I still have a right to doll myself up, and to amuse myself if everything is falling apart, when everything falls apart. Since everything does fall apart. Everyone will reject you, always. All you have to do is play the game, like everybody else. Talk about everything, except us, and yourself. Half-way from everything, lost, you observe us too much. And the intricacies of your love life are touching only insofar as they concern the failure which permeates them from the very start. I know by experience. My own experience. So please understand that I did not wait for you today to keep me company. Once again, you were even more present by not coming. I called you simply because I wanted to tell you what I've just written. Your friend, Betsy."

The storm rages. Rain is crackling on the roof. I forgot the deck chairs out on the terrace. I take them in. They'll dry out, against the wall, in the vestibule. I take a bath. I wash my hair. I file my nails. I brush my teeth. I take out clean towels. I drop the white shirt I wore in Sète and Uzès into the hamper. I arrange. I put away. I clean up. I put on some music. I am hungry. I eat. I feel chilly. I slip on two pairs of socks. I light a fire. The house is smoky. I open the windows. Fires don't catch well, in the summer, when it rains. I toss the snapshots one by one into the fireplace. Let him sleep! Let him go away! Let him stay away! It's over, over with him, and with the Fontaubes crowd. They don't understand, or is it rather that they understand all too well! They want to understand everything, argue things out. It's over with Roussel, Saint-Mandé, Jeanne, Françoise, over with Barbaroux and the faculty lounge, they won't see me there anymore, over with the West Side Club to which I'll return, defiantly, to make conquests for a night, for nothing. The snapshots are blazing. Midnight. What the hell, I'll phone Marie anyway.

"You sound strange." "No, on the contrary, I feel very good." "Then, everything's going very badly." Marie bursts out laughing at the other end of the line. "Why are you calling me so late?" "Because it's raining . . ." "Because what?" "I was kidding. I got your letter. I'll be expecting you on August 13th. Try to get in on the seven o'clock train. We'll have time to have dinner together. It's as though the table were already set." Silence. "But what's wrong, Pierre?" I don't answer. I throw a log into the fireplace. The charred photos vanish into the embers. Marie insists, "But talk, talk to me!" I smile and whisper, "You remind me of Roussel. I went up to see him today. I didn't know how to listen to him. And I . . . I tell myself that I'll come pick you up on August 13th at seven. You'll sleep upstairs, and I in the study. We'll take long hikes." "Are you sure you don't want to tell me anything else?" "I'm sure, Marie, sure. How's Mariette?" "Very well." "And rue Boursault?" "All the stores are closing one after the other. I got a card from Duck this morning. And I immediately threw it away. It showed a stork carrying a baby and . . ." Silence. I hear Marie lighting a cigarette. ". . . and I didn't like that. Are you seeing him again?" "No." "Will you be seeing him again?" "I don't think so." "Then everything's getting better?" "Everything's getting better." "You're lying a little." "Yes, I'm lying. But I'll be there on the 13th, at seven. A month from now." Marie bursts out laughing, exclaims, "A month from now, a century from now . . ."

I can't remember what we said to each other after that. I wander through the house. I bump into the walls. He is here, sitting at the table. I've already asked Emilienne to embroider the initials D.C. onto the napkin pouch. What the hell. He is here, in my study, rustling my papers, picking out a record. He is here, in the bathroom, I hand him a towel, he's just shampooed his hair. He tells me with a laugh, "I'll get a friend of mine to give me a haircut on September 11th, the day before classes start, not till then." He is here, on the bed, naked, he is asleep, I fixed breakfast, he fell back to sleep, I have to awaken him. He is here, everywhere, in the house, already here, still here. He's even in the fireplace, reduced to ashes. I repeat "Go away" so loudly that Emilienne could hear me. And I know that nothing will come of it. Nothing. But I repeat "Go away." I lie down, on my stomach, diving headlong into the pillows, burying my face. The face from the snapshots. I'll be forty on September 2nd. He'll be twenty-two on August 27th. I can hear him telling me, "We'll celebrate our birthdays on the same day, just as if . . ."

I am dreaming. He's back. I kneel down, behind the door. I slip off the sandals I gave him and kiss his feet. No. I am dreaming. A completely different opening scene. I come home. He arrived while I was gone. He's taking a bath. From the bathroom, he shouts, "I'm here." And I pick up a knife. No. I am dreaming. I'm sitting at my desk. I hear the sound of the keys in the lock. He's coming in. Concerned. "Are you here?" I don't answer. He sets down his bag, climbs the few steps, draws close and stands behind me, without saying a word. He places his hands on my shoulders, grabs my neck. No. I am dreaming. He arrives in the middle of the night. He wakes me up when he slips into bed. His skin tastes of salt and sweat. I kiss him without opening my eyes. He takes my face in his hands, and, pressing, his fingertips against my eyelids, forces me to look at him. Suddenly, I grab his throat. No. It's not possible. Dreams are naive and logical. Marie will be here: so, well before August 13th, he'll come back in broad daylight. He's hungry. He wants to take a bath right away. I strangle him in the bathtub with Bernard's chain. I yank off the medal. I wait for night to come. I dig a hole in the basement and throw him in. I cover his body with dirt. I rearrange the pile of logs. Emilienne saw me. The police are already questioning me. No. I meet up with him at Saint-Raphael. We're going to the beach. There are waves, a breeze. He's proud of his bathing suit which he snaps with his thumbs at the tops of his thighs. We go swimming together, far from shore, where we can't touch bottom. I grab his hands, place them around my throat, and I ask him to drown me. He does it. Held down, under water, I feel good, horribly good, carried away. I've rediscovered the original envelope and water, a deafness. Thank you, Duck. No. I had the lock changed. He knocks at the door and I don't open. No. I press him down against the bed, I hold his wrists above his head and I lick him under his arms. And he laughs, "Hee-hee." And he lets himself be taken, a strange surface in which I plunge and lose myself. Scent. No.

I get up. Five in the morning. July 13th. My stomach is wet. I go wipe myself off in the bathroom. I see my reflection in the mirror, above the sink, the face in the snapshot. I am alone, I had an orgasm. He's not here anymore. I lie down and fall asleep instantly. Unchanging dream, one image, one alone: Roussel, a prisoner of my home in Saint-Mandé. He is stationed at my bedroom window, on the third floor, and I stand, immobile, near the bench, in the Uzès garden, the same gravel, a rake in my hands. Behind the garden gate, neither Saint-Mandé's nor the clinic's, just a gate, a man, youthful, is waiting, with his back turned. He dare not look at us, but I have the impression that it's because of us that he is there. Roussel would like to be able to call him. The stranger is wearing blue linen trousers and a woolen jacket. Suddenly he grabs one of the bars of the gate and clings to it. I don't move. Yet I am being paid to do the raking. Roussel is looking at me. He would like me to open the gate. But I don't move. I don't move. Move out of the dream.

Awakening with a start. Six o'clock in the morning. I need some fresh air. I slip on the two pairs of socks like slippers, I throw the patchwork blanket over my shoulders, and I climb out onto the terrace. Wet flagstones. Shreds of mist over the vines, below, and like the train of a gown, tattered clouds, creeping above the Rhône, another river, the scent of dew and waking. To the east, on the Mount Ventoux side, the sun is already burning brightly. A frozen sun. The morning air is swirling. The storm has gone on its way. Everything is washed clean. Everything is brimming over. I would like to be able to thank Duck for having drowned me, far from shore.

A scream. "Come quickly! Madame Beylac! Madame Vérini!" It's Emilienne, on Carolon's terrace. So early in the morning. A scream.

26

Carolon came back just in time for his sister's funeral. An opportunity for each of the village's inhabitants to see everybody else, assembled together, and especially not to speak to anyone they haven't spoken to in many generations. In the course of their daily routine, the widows gossip among themselves, thrown upon each other on the main street, but they don't really confide in each other. As for the farmers and the grape growers, they have inherited too many rivalries or else a primitive kind of pride. At the cemetery, I stand off to the side. In fact, everyone steps aside. And yet we're all together. Only Olaya stands a little closer to me. She prays, in Spanish, mechanically, her lips slightly moving, as if quivering. As for Carolon, he is neither grief-stricken nor unmoved. He glances at one, the other, assumes a polite smile, a smile of respectable sorrow, but his eyes twinkle ironically when he is greeted, sympathy extended. He tells me, on the way back from the cemetery, "I'm sure she died a virgin at eighty-three. Imagine all that space she took up for nothing. So then, she will only have lived for this funeral. Look at them, Pierre, they're all caught up in settling their irrigation problems or property lines. For those people, each new death is a blessing." In front of my house he pinches my arm. "When I come back, for good, from Gréoux-les-Bains, I want to see some color in your cheeks, and everywhere else. You're in mourning for someone, inside. And you ought not to let it show anymore."

I receive a letter from Marie, hastily scrawled. "July 13th. My sunny Pierrot. It's too easy to accuse oneself of self-pity when one finds oneself in the state that you're in. I sense that you are all gnawed away within, possibly eaten away if things are really that serious. And there's no remedy to prescribe, not even the remedy of will power, so often called upon by cynics, the weakest among us, those with delicate palates and sharp tongues. But don't let it get the better of you. The reduction of your love-sentence is possible. However, I know there's a world of difference between the time you spend with the other and the efforts to achieve this reduction. You are harpooned. And what of it? Hang on to Peyroc's rock. Every day, decide to do something you've never done before, to go where you've never been before. Leave your home and your self open to welcome a little disorder. A month from now, to the very day, you'll come pick me up at the Avignon train station. I already have the ticket. You see, everything's falling into place. I'm not asking you to be dishonest, but I know that on that day your eyes will look like the sky swept clean by the Mistral. Let it go. I'm not telling you to let him go, because I respect him too much. He's charming and is under his own charm. He's adorable, and he can only speak freely when he feels that he is adored. He thinks he can still count his age on the fingers of both hands, without having to start over again, afraid he might have made a mistake. Let it go. With a big kiss. Love, Marie."

Emilienne brings back the pouch with the initials D.C. I thank her. "when is it your friend is coming back? He seems so nice!" I smile. The same smile as Carolon's in the cemetery. The smile is enough. Emilienne tells me about the night of the storm, as though it were an historic occasion, her restless sleep, a dream, a premonition. Quickly she goes off to Carolon's and finds "mademoiselle, dead, at the foot of her bed. She must have tried to get up to call for help. She didn't talk much anymore, but she was cheerful, when she was young..." Emilienne never sits down when she visits me. I kiss her. She leaves me. I hide the pouch with Duck's initials under the pile of sheets, with the stolen snapshot. Fetishes. Trophies. What you throw away, when you're in such a state, is worse than what you keep. As I write these lines, if I close my eyes, I can still see Betsy's snapshots, Duck's eyes, his curls, my face and my frown. I am posing.

Splitting up in every direction. John did not come back from London. Ruth left for Maroc without even telling Madame Vérini. "Those people think they can do anything. I'd never trade places with them." Betsy asked Justin to inform me that she was going back to Zurich at once. "She's instructed me to return the Waterfields' pool keys to the Roberts! And do you have any idea who they are, the Roberts? Well, they're two men who live together and who can't even muster up a hello or a thank you when I wipe their windshields. So, as far as the keys go, they can come and get them themselves. I'm telling you all this, Mr. Forgue, because they don't like you, they say so themselves, and you repay them in kind, without saying a word. Sometimes it's honorable to keep quiet."

And the days go by. I receive a card from La Baule signed by my mother, and my sisters, and the oldest among my nieces and nephews. I answer by return mail, in the same affected and affectionate way, saying that here, too, "I'm living under blue skies." How complicated our life is, and these white lies, how precious.

I spend my days by the Rhône, or else I take drives in the morning, early, up to the Nesque gorges, or else to the Vanesque forest preserve. I wander about. But I never go very far. Quickly, the fear of not being within speaking distance of anyone seizes me. Twice, I stop in Avignon. There's the festival and the crowds. I've barely passed through the walls when, hit by a dizzy spell, I turn back. I am alone. With him. He is here. There is nothing I can do about it. And if I think about his sandals, his bathing suit, his crooked smile, his fake departure from Paris, his sunburnt back, his dives into the Fontaubes swimming pool, if I think about his skin, his chest, his eyes or his laughter, my heart beats faster in spite of myself. The will has no power over these things. At moments like these, I take a deep breath and tell myself pain is cured by pain, but I don't believe it.

All of a sudden, a vacuum opened up around me. John, Betsy, Ruth, the Roberts, Carolon, Mariette so far away, Roussel at Uzès, Marie won't write me before the 13th, they've all left, or are elsewhere, tied to their routine or seeking adventure. It's too easy to say that this sort of vacuum is of our own creation. Neither hypocrites nor cowards, we all too easily come to mean nothing to others when the game is over. And, when in love, surrendered, we mean everything to another, unique, bound. To the very end this text will possess the innocence of the facts as they unfolded, and the fragility of feelings, such as they possessed me. Sharing is only possible anonymously. I am writing.

I go swimming at lunchtime, in the Sauvenargues public pool. I have my place, by the diving board. You quickly create ridiculous habits for yourself when you forbid yourself to wait for or to love someone. And if I didn't find that same place, every day, I would get quite upset. It became *my* place, my observation post. I watch the children swimming, I hear them shouting. To my right, there is always the same couple. A young couple. She, slender, pale, long brown hair in a ponytail held in place by a rubber band which she is continually readjusting without realizing it. She plays *Master Mind*, tirelessly. He, athletic-looking, a small suntanned animal, glasses at the tip of his nose giving him the air of a bank clerk with a bright future, or an executive on his way to becoming a vice-president. He is reading *Historia* magazine, doggedly. Once in a while, I look over at him. He knows it. But I never meet his eyes. But she senses it, and stares at me. I turn my head. They are married. They wear the same wedding band, wide and flat. He has a red bathing suit. She has a black suit, one-piece. They never go into the water. They are there. They take in the sun. I find it touching to imagine how they embrace, how they live their lives, their conversations, their ambitions. I would have liked to be able to speak to them. A ritual, every day, twice, I swim a lap. I go into the pool by the ladder in the shallow section, slowly. The water is icy cold. At first, I can't catch my breath. The water is green, the smell of chlorine goes to my head, memories of Lutetia. The children are playing ball, they're diving, laughing, yelling. And I force myself to swim, up to the ladder in the deep end. I get out of the water. I am dripping. He is still reading *Historia*, she is laboring over her *Master Mind*. They have their heads down. I stretch out on my towel. I wait for the sun to dry me and warm me up.

Around three in the afternoon, the mob starts to arrive. The background hum becomes a racket. Jumping from the high diving board the children try to outdo each other in their attempts to make the biggest explosion, splash the farthest, *Historia, Master Mind,* or the book I brought along, which I open only to pretend to read. Where is Duck? I decide to leave. How is he making out with his trip? I walk away from the pool, its green water, its toddlers, its shivering kids, and the lifeguard who strolls around the pool, his feet in wooden clogs click-clacking relentlessly. This scene whirls in my head, and yet I need to come back to it every day, before or after my outings, in order to see other people. The water and the sunshine of others. The vacation spot of others.

An air-gram. Duck's handwriting is practically illegible. "Sibenik. July 21st. Dear Pierre. A person should never write in a fit of depression, and I'm sorry I talked to you about my problems so rashly. Now, everything is resolved. My military duty will apparently only last for a trial month and the forty-eight hours I spent with my family in Saint-Raphael did wonders for me. Unity has been restored and each of us knows he can count on the others. It also gave me the time to get my head together again, after three days of army duty and Valium and coffee which my friend Louis had advised me to take. (I faked a suicide attempt by jumping from the second floor, but the chain of events set into motion as a result proved too much for me to handle. Terrifying.) Eventually I was able to get away to hit the road. I wanted to do it. It's a way of running headlong into the world, especially after the soft life in Aix. The time I spent with you did me a lot of good, and at any rate, I'm coming back in mid-August for "our" birthday. It's very likely I'll be back in France around the 16th and I'll call you sometime during the end of the trip to tell you where I am and possibly request your help to get up to Peyroc. But let me tell you about my itinerary. I've decided to hitchhike, at the start, so I'd have enough money to come home. I wasn't sure that my cargo-boat strategy would work out to get me back. I spent the first night in Genoa, in a public garden, second day, crossed through northern Italy as far as Trieste where I slept (on the beach). The Yugoslavian border gave me a lot of trouble since I took a whole day to reach Riga (which the Italians persist in calling Fiume). Stowed away on a boat to Zador, then, today, I'm staying in the mountains, near the Slapovikrke waterfalls. There's a campground. I was able to take a shower, illegally. I'll stay for the night because I'm already weak and tired. Tomorrow, I head for Dubrovnik, then the part that scares me: crossing Yugoslavia to get around Albania, and reaching Sofia and Istanbul, the goal of this trip. It's a town where all kinds of deals are possible. I hope to find something to eat there and maybe a good opportunity for getting back. It's a strange sensation, for my pockets are almost empty, already, but I feel at peace, my sleeping bag under my arm. I look at what's around me. I don't feel empty, merely a spectator. And anyway, I want to get to know Istanbul. I hope I'll be able to write you from there. So then, don't worry. I'm used to being on the road and I know very well how to get out of tight spots. The Yugoslavian police don't look very cooperative, but my combination of French-Italian-English will do. I hope you stayed in Peyroc. What more would you find anyplace else, or in Paris? More space? Places all too familiar? Are you busy preparing your courses? I'll be in Peyroc with you (how about going to the shore?), then in Dijon (two days) and in Paris, at your place. I'm going to finish my report and I'd like to get a part-time job. We'll talk about it. Take care of yourself, and soon, all that time together. With all my love. Thinking about you. Duck."

A postcard showing the Boiana church, 11th-12th century. "Sofia, July 24th. Dear Pierre. Saved at the last minute by a French woman, a tourist (no money for the visa). Damned fountain pen of this public writing room in the Sofia post office. Borne up by the hum of the city, I am floating, on the outskirts of the Orient. Last stop before Istanbul. Tired and starving, but out there, everything is possible. Thinking of you. Love. Insatiable Duck."

A postcard showing the Galata bridge and the new mosque. "August 1st. The air is thick with spices. Dear Pierre. Quick deals in Istanbul. I'm surviving here. The city is fascinating, on the outskirts of the Orient. Fabulous treasures. I'm leaving for Izmir, in two days, hitchhiking. The trip back is very much up in the air. I'm going to try to return by way of Greece, but I'm starting to get tired. Once past Athens, hitchhiking is easy, but very long. Thinking of you. Love, Duck. PS. You'll be getting my mail in Peyroc. Hold onto it. I'll telephone in two weeks, from Athens."

He doesn't feel empty, merely a spectator. He's on his way back. He's hitchhiking. He's hungry. Damned Sofia fountain pen. I read this letter and these two postcards, I reread them, in order to detach myself. But the only thing is, the air grew thick with spices. And the outskirts of the Orient are right here. He wants us to go to the seashore. And soon all that time together. You believe you're detaching yourself when, in reality, you're growing attached. This letter and these two postcards, from Duck, how many times I must have stolen away to kiss them. But stolen away from whom?

Mrs. Vérini brings me a small chocolate cake "because I just know you'll never finish a big one." I invite her to sit down, she accepts, she's in no hurry, she has, most certainly, serious things to tell me in confidence. "I told Mr. Robert and Mr. Gérard that I won't go back to Fontaubes before Mr. and Mrs. Vaterfild return. There are so many of them around the pool that every time I finished counting, somebody new would show up." I serve iced verbena. We clink glasses. She looks at me and utters this short polished sentence, touching, that she must have repeated to herself before she came by, nothing in Peyroc surprises me anymore. "You know, Mr. Pierre, in order to be happy, a person needs to take stock of his life before he lives it." She smiles. "As for myself, I allow myself to be of use to others when I am sure that I can make myself useful without them needing to order me about, for whatever reason." She puts down her glass, strokes it, and murmurs, "In life, everything is paid for in cash." She falls silent. We look at each other. We smile at each other. "At Fontaubes, they go swimming, naked, exactly as if I wasn't there. And that's not natural . . ."

27

From July 12th to August 13th, one letter and two postcards, a snapshot hidden with a napkin pouch under a pile of sheets, a patchwork quilt in which I wrap myself naked, at night, a mother's work, it's hot, it's cold. I go into the municipal swimming pool of Sauvenargues at the shallow end, more and more slowly and reluctantly, every day, a necessity to wake myself up, when everything carries me away and lays hold of me: I don't belong to myself anymore. I forbid myself to watch for the mailman. And yet everything about this forbidden action amounts to keeping watch. I really don't get much sleep anymore. During the day, as well as during the night, I lie in wait, neither day nor night, floating: Duck has a duplicate set of keys.

So I try to put myself in other people's shoes. I try to understand like other people, the why and the how of all this, when attention, once absorbed, can no longer be distracted, when the being, riveted, is completely at the mercy of the absence, the most subtle and poisoned of presences. I know Duck, so little, hardly at all, and I'm beginning to wonder if this suffering has not been brought into being by myself alone, if the loved person is nothing but the pretext of the text and the author of the turmoil, his own victim. But this is other people's reasoning, when they believe themselves to be stronger. The only true strength is love's capacity for catastrophe when you still believe in it, for meeting someone when you wish it, for failure when you want to avoid it, even when the proof of the failure is under your nose. Only in lies have I seen love affairs succeed, and only in death have I seen passion consummated.

Only in hypocrisy have I seen social success, only in exhaustion, tenacity and annihilation of the artist have I seen the creative task—if only seemingly—consummated. The censors may well smile. They will not have the first word: that of love. Everything may happen. Everything does happen in the world. The most preposterous fictions become realities. The most respectable values, fundamental values, are scorned, burlesque skits, sideshow farce. It's the age of contempt and sneers. Everything is fit for consumption. Everything is consumed. What remains is the attachment, the escape attempt, the absurd hope of forming a couple or of finding a companion. And when all is said and done, that's all there is. Even if paths don't cross, even if a rift opens within the couple, inevitably, jealousies about others, each person's illusions.

From July 12th to August 13th, night and day, all I remember is the blue or starry sky. In the village, when I go to the grocer's, I don't let my feelings show. But no one is fooled. Their eyes grow concerned. But nothing goes beyond this concern. Everyone remains in their place, a stranger to others. Mrs. Vérini, feeling guilty about confiding in me, is cooler. Olaya always manages to pick up and bring back the laundry when I'm not there. The presence of my car, under the plane trees, lets her know. The conversations with Emilienne restrict themselves to one subject: watering the flowers at the windows and on my terrace. I have taken only one deck chair out. The bees, wasps and yellow jackets have made their appearance. And at night, mosquitoes. At dusk, the swallows are beginning to rehearse their big departure, lined up in a row, on the electric wires. There are ten of them, then twenty, then fifty. The days go by.

Everything was written in advance. I willed nothing into being. The organization of turmoil is not voluntary. Neither is the reduction of my sentence to suffer. Gradually, isolated, I regain the territory of my solitude. At times a gust of wind intoxicates me, the scent of the fig tree, the hum of the ivy, a face, or even the scenery. I speak to myself, out loud, I make up stories, homecomings, other murders, other deaths, I dream of embraces or gazing eyes, I burst into laughter at the wheel of my car, I imagine journeys. But these are short-lived visions. And everything, inevitably, leads back to Duck. He reenters the scene, he is this character who walks by in the background, who says nothing and who attracts all the attention towards himself, within himself, captures it and does not return it. Confronting him, you have no choice but to gesticulate and ramble on in the vacuum which he creates as he passes by. He is the person made of water, of salt and of fluidity whose geography I am barely familiar with, his manner of walking, the curve of the back, the jutting hips, folds and valleys, craters, tensions, unbroken nature of glances and smiles, virgin lands, skin. Sometimes, at night, I hear him laugh. And I pummel the pillow with my fists. Cold sweats. Or else I see him running on a beach, near Izmir. He beckons for me to follow him, pointing towards the waves and the open sea. He takes off *his* sandals and *his* bathing suit. Others join him, others with whom he would be happy. The heat is suffocating. I have trouble breathing. I get up to drink a glass of water.

From July 12th to August 13th, I undertake the task of copying Roussel's notes, second thoughts, additions, deletions, a legacy which I work back into shape. I erase my elder. In the hallway of the clinic, he tells me, "I know you won't come back." And it's true, I am afraid of visiting him a second time. I tell myself that he'll pull through all by himself. "Uzès, August 9th. My Dear Pierre. As you can see, my handwriting is more and more shaky. Each capital letter has become a genuine adventure for me. I resisted, until today, the desire to write to you because I don't want to bother you. I felt you to be both so happy and tortured. But how can I thank you for your visit? I can't tell you what state I'm in. Anxiety, insomnia, and all of it brought on by myself. Through my cowardice, I allowed myself to be locked into a vicious circle and in the grip of fear, I could not find it in myself to muster up some courage. How can one muster courage in the grip of fear? And here, my flight ended, my back to the wall, I'm going to rebel and I'm going to howl, howl that I am a worthy being, that I have a talent for life and that this talent should be exploited. And the hell with my fear, with my kindness, with my pity, with my cowardice. I'm someone who can't be counted on but if someone counts a little for me, I come back to life. Sévéro has left for Portugal. He did not have a residence visa. They were not able to keep him at Tulles. Léon and Eliane paid for his trip back. He didn't even have time to come and visit me, or perhaps my brother advised him against it. And here I am, again, compelled to live off dreams and imaginary presences. If you're preparing your classes, tell me that life is what you're writing. Pass unnoticed behind each line and each word. That's how I managed to survive. Let the schemers scheme. And take care of yourself. Don't write to me. Writing to you does me good. Reading you would hurt me. I won't write to you again until the day I get out of here. Your friend, Jean-Claude Roussel."

First novel, my novel, this novel. There is no hoax within these pages. Everything grows sharp. And I can't help but ask myself probing questions. The text is unfolding and at times you must turn around and assess the path you've traveled. The past lies ahead of you, goes, comes, carries away, inspires. It carries with it the only possible driving purpose, a known for the unknown, a future indicative. At each sentence ending, at each period, there lies an entire future. At each comma, a pause for breath. I don't see life through black-colored glasses. I see it in its true colors. I am not dictating failure. I am bearing witness to it. It is: the couple doesn't exist. Confronted with the text, innocent, able to make an uncompromising effort, I'll always be writing the first line of the first novel. Why should we want, no matter what the cost, to express a political or social reality, forgetting in the process, the text's spontaneity, its fundamental nature, bringing to life feelings, attitudes, embodying them in characters who by definition are irreducible to any political or social label? I feel myself to be painfully judged before the fact. And I find myself unable to stop to proclaim it. How is it possible to speak of the river without going up to its source, and without mentioning its bed? Each page is a towpath. Yes, it's a metaphor. The metaphor versus the theory. Hardly set down on paper, the theoretical text is already all burned out, worn out, spelled out. Ideas pass away but feelings and attitudes remain. The determination to convey a message is the scourge of everything which identifies itself as political, social and French. I have only one message to get across in passing. And all I can offer to share is its passing sense. And my life, which is folding up, unfolds, only to fold up once again. I leave these schemers whom Roussel mentioned in his last letter to idle behind their wheels. What I am seeking is the final idyll of the consummation and the beginning.

From July 12th to August 13th, between Fontaubes and the Rhône, between Uzès and Mount Ventoux, under Peyroc's rocky hill, main street, the house with flowers at the windows, behind the white door, I conduct myself the way a person conducts himself when he is expecting someone while at the same time forbidding himself from waiting. Duck is traveling around within me, wearing out his sandals, a complete tour of the Mediterranean in order to bind me. And why him? Him, of all people? Him, by chance, the end of a hallway in the Nikko Hotel, he is hiding, is waiting for me to give me a fright, "boo," and burst into laughter. Passion is the interlining of a sadness. Only sadness remains to be seen. Such a trifling sadness, and yet.

You dash along, you gallop, you're knocked all around. You're no longer touching your stirrups. You let go of the reins. A metaphor, another one. The afternoon of August 12th, the day before Marie comes, I have had it with fondling the naked sheet and soar away from my bed, our bed. It's rocking in my head, too. To go across nights and to go across days. I leave home and head towards the car. I need to meet someone else. Chapter twenty-eight, the high-heeled Turkish slippers.

The morning of August 13th, Carolon is back. He invites himself to have dinner with me. I don't even have time to tell him that Marie arrives this very evening and that there will be three of us. He pinches my cheek. "I don't like how you look. Take a look at me, perky, at Gréoux they treated me like I was a pasha. There, now, I am going to visit our divine neighbors. A courtesy call. They were so very fond of my sister." He looks like he is in a hurry. He tells me, at the door, Emilienne is watching us from behind her window. "See you this evening, I'll bring the wine!"

28

After dinner, sitting around the table. Carolon spoke to us about Gréoux-les-Bains with his usual gusto. We laughed wholeheartedly. Marie, in turn, described Paris deserted, the Paris of vacation time, and the Batignolles, "a small village that died suddenly." Carolon retorted, "A village cannot die. Now there's a really city-rat idea. When I was a teller at the Savings Bank of Dulon de Provence . . ." He pauses, his words hanging in midair. "I . . ." He hesitates, then he smiles and glances at me. "Let's not play games anymore. It's your turn to speak, Pierre. You promised to tell us a good story. A real-life story, which happened last night, isn't that right?" Marie crosses her hands over her belly, takes a deep breath, looks at Carolon quizzically and turns toward me. "We are waiting for your 'Turkish slippers with the heels.' And we insist upon each and every detail."

At this table, the fourth chair is empty. It's to this chair that I tell my story of the night before, the fine for a month of waiting. And what's more, I am surely afraid of meeting Marie's glance, or Carolon's. Sometimes a glance stills the tongue.

"Yesterday, the end of the day, I saw myself alone, already, like a jerk, with my classical music, my slice of ham, and what was left of Mrs. Vérini's chocolate cake. So I took off in my car. I'm going to tell all.

Everything up front. With just the right words. Words which will not deceive. Concealed love is not love. We are all unmasked members of an underground. Yes, Mr. Carolon, I am crazy about the young man who passed through here, at the beginning of July. I didn't introduce him to you, but I know you have seen him and you didn't agree. Your eyes cried out for me to watch my step. It's one of your expressions. And you, Marie, I didn't have time to tell you a little while ago, in the car, but you sensed it. I am all bound up in love. I wanted to give Duck what was best within myself. And from the best within to the beast within, yesterday, I broke out. I needed to meet someone, anyone, a guy, young, old, handsome, ugly, hairy, dolled up, smelly, I didn't care. Anything, except a Robert, a Gérard, or a scented handkerchief from Fontaubes. I needed arms to throw myself into, legs to spread apart, backs to lift up. Take, I had to take, in the mud of the other's mouth, lick and be licked, moan and then good-bye. And come back here, appeased. To wait, wait again, with black butterflies, and Duck, in my head. Duck plays with me. You always play with people. You create objects, and properties for yourself, in order to play with them. He is roaming about in my sandals. But his sandals, which I lend so much importance to, are nothing in the light of what I discovered yesterday . . .

"At the wheel of my car, Avignon, Cavaillon, Aix, when I arrived, it was dark. Cruising and darkness. No one. Everywhere, it was too early. In Saint-Elzéar, I drove around the village three times. Sometimes, at the urinal of a bowling ground, there is a kamikaze, a farmer's son, a good farmer and family man, or a tourist. There, again, nothing. No one. So I took the road to Carou. 30,000 inhabitants. A plastics factory. Usually, around the closed-down train station, there is a little action. Nothing. No one either. I had already driven over 120 miles. I headed back toward the valley. Uzanges. Near the BNP, there is an underground urinal. The gate was pulled shut. I had a hard-on. All alone. And full speed ahead toward the highway. Trucks. Vacationers with their campers. Too crowded. The freeway to the sun in the opposite direction, directly north, the Luzerches rest area, the air of Velpré, the Arbonne rest area. At each stop, I would pull up. In the trucks, drawn curtains, they were all sleeping. In the men's rooms, I looked for graffiti, invitations, drawings. Nothing: everything had just been repainted. Last night, I got the impression that there was not anyone for anyone anymore. No message. And my waiting. I was spilling over. I needed arms. That's all. And a mouth to crush up against or insert myself, standing up, holding another head than mine in my hands. To shut out the world, for just one moment. To come for nothing, but not to come for Duck. Are you listening? I am telling you everything.

"Midnight. Two-hundred-forty miles on the mile gauge. Headache. Since six o'clock, like a flash, I only saw the road, the plane trees, the intersections, the stop signs, and the places, all deserted. I exit from the freeway. At last a town. A real one. Big. Hollow. Montélimar, Orange, Valence? I don't remember. At night, cities don't have names anymore. You look for the stone enclosures. The cold. You lie in wait for the other person's footsteps. No, Carolon, don't make me drink. I don't need it." Carolon turns toward Marie. Marie glances down. Silence. I can't stop anymore.

"In this town, outskirts, where the guys usually hang out, nothing. Not even a parked car. Once around, twice around, at a street corner, a dark-haired guy, scarred, blue jeans, motions to me with his hand. A smile. The hitman. The killer-gigolo. To be avoided. I plunge back into the city, find the boulevard, and park at the special place, our place. I am in shock, jostled. The black butterflies have multiplied. They can't even fly in my head anymore. Duck, on a beach, near Epheses, must have taken off his sandals, my sandals, to take a midnight swim. Who's waiting for him, in the waves? Migraine. I'm not hard anymore. I pound the steering wheel and slam the door as I get out. The hitman is there, all smiles, a cigarette in his hand. He asks if I have a light. At that instant, behind the plane trees, a shadow, white pants, tight-fitting around the ass, T-shirt, a small muscular guy. I leave the hitman with his unlit cigarette and position myself behind the car. White pants walks in front of me. I say hello to him. He ignores me. Ten after midnight. He takes a few steps. After all, at this time, in this town, he might have trouble finding someone better than me. So then he retraces his steps. He comes up to me and whispers. 'Hi. Where is your place?' 'Far away.' 'Then, let's go to my place. There are two of us, any problem?' 'What's the other guy look like?' 'If I'm living with him, then he's like me. Just follow us. It's the Peugeot 404, over there.' That's all. The hitman throws his cigarette away and crushes it out with the tip of his cowboy boot. That's all I saw, while starting my car. The boot. And the unlit cigarette, nervously crushed out." Carolon says nothing. Marie would like to interrupt me. Too late. Carolon almost knocks over a glass while pouring drinks.

"Ahead of me, the Peugeot 404, and the two of them. I only see the backs of their necks. White Pants, who is not driving, and the other one, who is. A bad sign. He's the one who makes the decisions. The train station, a large intersection, then the highway, due north, Mammoth, the gas stations, housing projects, secondhand car dealers, the suburbs, the new developments, left-turn signal: I turn left. New buildings. I picture them living together as a couple, in a quiet, comfortable two-bedroom apartment. Suddenly, a wall lined with trees, an open gate, they go in, a steep path, and on the right, on the left, walls of freshly sawn logs. Are they taking me to a saw mill? A maze. No more city, no more darkness, no more shadows, nothing but chopped wood and the smell of chopped wood.

"In the middle of these mountains of boards, a house, tall and narrow, which was beautiful in 1900. White Pants gestures to me to park along the wall. I get out. The other one has stayed in his car. White Pants reaches out toward me. 'Don't worry, he's going to catch up with us.' The smell of wood, of resin and of sawdust, a fresh smell, a shot in the arm. Zero hour thirty minutes. All those miles to reach this point. Back entrance, a steep stairway, grey, one flight, two flights, second landing, catastrophe: on a lamp table knickknacks, cups, plates, chocolate pots, a quaint clutter of antiques. I say to myself, 'Shit, I've met up with a pair of bag ladies.' Fourth floor, White Pants opens the door. A large hallway, under the roof beams, drapes, rugs, a collection of kinglets, cookies, lithographs. The lights were left on in the living room, low easy chairs, low tables, seashells, pink and lilac lamp shades. I look at White Pants, a little guy, a little dippy, the beginning of autumn in him too. 'I'd like to take a piss. Which way is it?' 'First wait for Roger to arrive. You want a drink?' I shake my head no. I wait. White Pants takes out some glasses, bottles. Zero hour how many minutes? Why, but why have I traveled all this way for this, for them, for nothing? A sound of keys in the lock. The door opens. At the far end of the hallway, Roger, the end of autumn, pasty complexion, the first signs of baldness, thin lips, thin pointed hands. He sets down the keys on another side lamp table, carefully takes off his jacket and hangs it up. I'm fed up. I say, 'I'm going.' White Pants holds me back. 'No, everything'll go very smoothly.' He winks at me. Roger approaches me, his head down. I introduce myself. 'Pierre . . .' He hardly shakes my hand, doesn't answer and heads into the kitchen. White Pants sits down on the sofa. 'You having a drink?' 'No, really, no.' In the kitchen, the sound of the refrigerator being opened, being closed. White Pants motions for me to be patient. Roger comes back, a glass of whisky in his hand, and glances at us, with a look of surprise. He says, 'Oh! Fine,' and he disappears into the bathroom. The sound of water in the basin. Shall I go on?" Marie looks at Carolon. Carolon empties his glass in one gulp and turns it upside down on the table, his way of refusing any more drinks, twenty, thirty times a day. Silence.

"White Pants sits down next to me. I want to kiss him. 'No, wait.' I get up, I'm fed up. White Pants holds me back. 'Then, get undressed.' He gets undressed. I get undressed. Thirty seconds. Not more. Suddenly, everything is going very quickly. I tell myself: Roger inherited the sawmill, White Pants was only an employee, they've been living together for nine, eleven, fifteen years, objects with other objects, where are the windows? Silence in the bathroom. Roger is watching for us. White Pants, naked, walks into the bedroom and gestures for me to follow him. Drapes, night-light, everything had been made ready. Ten of one. Above the bed, an Algerian tapestry, glistening, of Arab horsemen. Kneeling, on the bed, I grab White Pants's head and press it against my belly. White Pants pulls himself loose and leans over, facing the door. He shouts, 'Roger, are you coming?' The bathroom door slamming. The sound of footsteps in the living room, in the kitchen. White Pants draws near to me, takes my face in both his hands and kisses me on the lips, closing his eyes. A kiss which is too wet, right away. Too quickly. End of kiss. Again he leans over, hanging onto me. 'Roger' twice. I want to leave. White Pants clings to me. He smiles feebly. Then, in the half-open doorway, as pale as I am pale when I utter Duck's name, Roger appears, his arms folded, his chin held high and without moving his lips, in a high-pitched voice, he says to us, 'Oh, excuse me, am I disturbing you?' And he disappears. Shall I go on?" Carolon wipes his lips. A dog barks, then two, then three. A car passes by on the street. Emilienne closes her bedroom shutters. The television broadcasts are over for the evening. Marie smiles.

"I jumped out of bed. I got dressed in a flash. White Pants stayed behind in the bedroom. Roger shut himself up in the kitchen. I checked to see if I had my wallet, my keys, everything: you never know. One o'clock in the morning. More than 200 miles without counting the trip back. And to leave just like that, without a word? No. I knock at the kitchen door. I go in. Roger turns his back to me. I tap him gently on the shoulder. He turns around. Then, I saw myself, jealous, broken, tortured, worn-out. I was Roger. And I told him, 'Sorry!' while shaking his hand, a bit too firmly. I even whispered 'thanks' unawares, but as I left, in the hallway, White Pants was there, standing up, naked in a black and yellow kimono, hastily slipped on, his feet in Turkish slippers with heels. Yes! Real Turkish slippers, pointy-toed, in thick bright leather. Slippers which he nailed onto heels! High heels! To perch himself up!" Marie is nodding off. Carolon shrugs his shoulders like a child.

"I rushed down the stairs. No sooner had I reached the bottom than the light went out. I found the darkness again, the walls of sawn wood, and the smell, the smell, this powerful scent, violent. When I got back here, it was three in the morning. I was drunk. Drunk with nothing. Drunk with them and with us. I wanted for day to come, clinging to my penis as to a mast. I was on my way back to Duck. But Duck or someone else, why?" Carolon whispers, "One slipper more or less, it's always the same story." He turns his glass around and pours himself another drink. "Why this need to count to three when people don't even know how to count to two anymore? And what's more, all those miles . . ."

Marie looks at me. "What was his name, this White Pants?" "I don't know. When I saw his heeled slippers, I couldn't say another word."

29

We have just walked Carolon back home. Marie takes my arm. "I don't like you pink, lilac, and mauve." I tell her about Betsy, her second husband, the Munich Opera, the confessions during intermission. Marie murmurs, "People always give themselves, or give reasons to themselves, after the fact. They can never give them beforehand." Marie rests her head on my shoulder, we stroll up the main street, like two lovers. Marie adds, softly, "Harmony is not found in opposites and in passions. To find it, there has to be someone who deserves you." In front of the house, she admires the ivy, the window lights, the starry sky. She looks at me. "I don't like the verb *to deserve*. But . . ." She laughs and holds out both hands for me to kiss.

In years past, I would go back to Paris some time during the first days of August, because I wasn't expecting anyone. Last year, I stayed in Peyroc because I was expecting someone who, so I tried to convince myself, would not be coming back. As soon as the door was closed behind us, Marie asked, "When is he coming?" "In three days, on the 16th, perhaps." "You're expecting him, yet you don't want him to come back anymore?" We do the dishes. I wash, she wipes. I can still picture her, rue Boursault, that evening she announced she was pregnant, the evening Bernard confided in me. Four months have just gone by. Procession of days. Marie folds her napkin and wants to put it away.

"Where is my pouch marked X?" I don't answer. I run water to rinse out the sink. Marie puts the glasses and plates back into the cabinet. With a hint of sharpness in her voice, she softly lets slip, "I don't believe you did that?" I whisper, "Yes, I did . . ." She laughs. "Say it louder!" "Yes!" And we laugh, good-heartedly, as if Carolon were still here.

She only took along a small traveling bag, very few things. "Otherwise, Olaya is going to scent everything with lavender again, and that's Tadzio's eau de toilette. By the way, he's back from his vacation. He resigned. He's going to work in another studio. He wanted to have lunch with me to explain *everything* to me, but I refused. I pecked him, just like this, with my fingertip, on the tip of his nose." And with her finger on my nose, Marie breaks into laughter. "A mere trifle makes him cross his eyes!"

Marie takes a bath. "My first midnight bath, in a long time . . ." I make the bed, in the study. She calls me. "You can come in, you know!" I stand awkwardly, at the bathroom door, a furtive glance. And it amuses her. In the water, she caresses her belly. "Everything looks good. You can hold out your hand and touch me there, like that, here, do you feel him? Don't be afraid. You're going to forget everything . . ."

The next day, at the Sauvenargues swimming pool, we take our places next to red-swimsuit and his wife, *Historia* and *Master Mind*. Marie whispers into my ear, "She plays alone? But you need two people to play that game." After a moment of thought, she adds, "I've just said something stupid." Red-swimsuit, White Pants? I shouldn't have told my story to Carolon. Marie stretches out right up against me. I am sitting with my legs crossed on my towel. She grabs my hand. "You're thinking about Carolon, and you shouldn't be." Marie is wearing a maternity blouse, "so I won't shock the children." Stretched out, she closes her eyes, in the sunshine. "Do like me, let yourself be caressed." Red-swimsuit observes us, furtively, as he readjusts his glasses and turns a page. In fact, he only looked at Marie. Later, they get up, both of them. Without exchanging a word, they put away their things in a basket. Marie watches them, blinking. "You're right, they're very beautiful, both of them." They glance at us, a slight nod, a faint good-bye, and they are off. August 14th: the end of their vacation. Marie smiles. "They look very good together, both of them, perhaps because they're not speaking to each other." I get up, run a few steps, and dive headlong into the deep end. Two or three laps. I want to regain my strength. To forget? When I come back to Marie's side, she rubs my back with her towel, as in the old days, at Blue Skies, when I'd come back from the beach, all wet. Marie laughs at me. "I'm sure you're thinking about your sisters, and you're wrong, once again!" We laugh.

In the village, Marie causes quite a stir. Madame Beylac congratulates her while looking at me. Mrs. Vérini promises a set of baby clothes. Olaya has taken away Marie's bag to clean it. "It's not right to come here without taking anything along!" Justin asks me for permission to kiss Marie on both cheeks: "That way, if it's a girl, I'll have been the first to have titillated her." Emilienne, looking kind and concerned, asks Marie, "When's it due?" Marie answers, "The beginning of November." Emilienne looks at us. "Why don't you wait to have it here? It would be a birth in the village." The grocer's wife tells us, "I'm warning you, about next year, I have everything but diapers."

Evening of August 14th. Last day of the Avignon Festival. We attend the ballet performance in the courtyard of the Palace of the Popes. Marie made me climb over the city walls, like a great adventure. In the Place de l'Horloge, a crowd, festive mood, greasy papers, bursts of music, Marie makes fun. "It's not even quaint anymore . . ." She walks very close to me, as if she wanted to guide me. "You're being eyed, you know. You should have come more often."

Back home, I go to bed. Marie sits down at the edge of the small bed, leaning her elbows on the desk armchair. In this room, everything fits together. She tries to fold up her legs. She looks at me, amused. Several times she puffs on her fingers, as if she wanted to blow away the chill, gold dust or a haze, a gentle action, a repeated gesture. Marie is beautiful like this, keeping me company. For a long time, she stays where she is, without saying a word, with an open gaze. She's waiting for me to fall asleep. But I want to look at her in the same way that she's looking at me. And once again, she puffs on her fingers. Then she leans forward and closes my eyes. I kiss her hand. She gets up, turns off the light. I hear her, barefooted, on the stairs. She goes to bed. You hear the sheets, at night, sometimes, when someone else slips into bed. And from the upstairs bedroom she says, "Good night!" I answer, "Sweet dreams." It's what my mother used to say to me, when I still believed total sharing was possible.

For breakfast, Mrs. Vérini brings us eggs "fresh from this morning," a cake "still warm," and fresh milk: "You need it, Madame Marie . . ." Marie says to me, "Now this, on the other hand, is a real feast." She drinks a large glass of milk, murmurs, "And it's too beautiful to be false." Mrs. Vérini doesn't understand. Marie wipes her lips. After breakfast, she puts her napkin into my pouch.

Generous feelings provoke suspicion, painful feelings even more so. Happiness lies only in the instant, intimate clash of beings, of gestures, and attentions. Marie says to me, "Duck will be two days late . . ." I want to answer. She places a finger on my lips. "No, don't say anything. Everything has to end up very badly, that's to say, quickly and very well." She's laughing at me, or else at herself, I can't tell anymore. Out of the blue she adds, "I don't know anything contemptible, except contempt itself," or else, "Death is only the privilege of those who die." Her brand of humor. After a pause, she goes on: "If we talk about this ten years from now, my son will be ten years old, it'll be too early. And if we talk about it now, it's already much too late. The state you're in eludes all generalizations." Then, laughing, "I don't know anyone who's more an inhibitionist than you are. We all are. We admit it in different degrees. Without any doubt whatsoever, therein lies the mystery of our meetings and attachments."

We spend the day of August 15th in the cedar-tree forest, on the crest of the Lubecon. Marie dozes on the ground, upon a blanket, curled up on her stomach, one arm stretched out in front of her, the palm of one hand turned up toward the sky. In the clearing, far from the road, away from everyone and everything, we brought along nothing besides the blanket and, since morning, Marie hasn't said a word to me. I can still see her, in the car, she glances at me with a smile, pinches my arm, helps me shift gears, looks at the countryside or else points out a beautiful house. She also rests her head on my shoulder. I drive along, but she doesn't fall asleep nor does she grasp my forearm. There, no sooner has she stretched out on the blanket than she falls asleep. And I, standing up, barechested, barefooted, in my swimsuit, I circle around the clearing, but I don't dare wander off. I must keep an eye on her, or perhaps protect her. This feeling seems new to me, unsettling. I am not telling myself the story of an imaginary father. But Marie is here, self-absorbed, her arm outstretched. If I observed her carefully enough, I could modulate the pace of my breathing with hers. Within herself she bears a messenger who, I hope, will not forget the message. How can one express truth at every moment? One being, inevitably called to meet another, or other beings, can do nothing but doubt, and doubt means forgetting quickly, splitting apart, nothing is permanent. Here I am, in the clearing. I circle around my friend, so close, so far away, so familiar and, in the final analysis, so very much a stranger. But here I am, and a fear overcomes me, little by little, for we have left the roads and the paths, we have abandoned the trail, and in the depths of the forest, on the very peak of a mountain, we have become isolated. What is overcoming me is the fear of a prowler. I must not wander off. I must watch over her because she's asleep, because she's no longer one and not quite two, because she's going to be delivered of a child. And everything's going to begin here, suffering, all this suffering. And joy, in fitful bursts. Marie wakes up, stretches out, holds out her hand toward me.

Late afternoon. The sky is clouding over. Emilienne declares, "It's normal, this is summer's turning point!" On Carolon's terrace we are having pastis. Carolon, too, is not going to make a habit of this, he says nothing. He looks at us, proudly, and stares at me with a touch of concern, the very beginnings of a defensive smile. Ruth is back at Fontaubes. She kicked out Robert, Gérard, and their whole gang. On the phone she told me, "I lose my temper because I need to lose my temper. I hold it against you, you as much as the others, because you let them carry on the way they did by not coming. I'm not inviting you, but do tell Marie that I would have liked to see her again, perhaps the day after tomorrow. . . . Can you tell Mrs. Vérini that I'm back? I absolutely need her." Silence. I want to speak, Ruth interrupts me. "Don't get the idea that I'm calling you up only so you can give her the message. I'm perfectly capable of visiting her myself." Another pause. "And on second thought, yes, I am only calling you up so you can tell her it's an emergency. Have you heard from Betsy?" "No, nothing." "And from John?" I remain silent. She repeats, "John hasn't written to you?" I answer, "No, sorry." She sighs. "I really don't understand what's going on this summer. Don't hold it against me. I'll call you back when everything takes a turn for the better." When I drop by Mrs. Vérini's to inform her, even before I tell her the news, she says, "I already know. But Mrs. Vateurfield can come by herself. Treating others kindly means treating yourself kindly."

The evening of August 15th, Marie and I go out to eat. An inn, along the road to Orange. Very formal. The Maître d' addresses us as sir and madam. Marie says to me, "We've forgotten our wedding rings." At night, on the way back, it's raining. The road is slippery. In the opposite direction, a steady stream of cars. Our highway, right bank of the Rhône, is used as a "holiday detour route." Yellow headlights, white headlights, Marie asks me several times not to drive so fast. Peyroc, the house. The sound of rain on the roof. Marie says to me, "Very well, we'll stay here tomorrow. To make a point about coming back."

The day of August 16th. Marie is taking a bath. She decides to make a fire. Marie fixes breakfast. Marie goes up the stairs, goes down, opens the closets, looks for magazines, fixes tea. "Where are the clean dish towels?" Outside it's raining, continuously. I am sitting at the desk. I am preparing a course on Montesquieu. Now and then, Marie comes up to me, kisses me on the head, or on the neck, without saying a word, and she goes away. I hear her about the house. She's entertaining herself, touching everything, she probably needs to make a little noise to signal her presence to me, a continuity, for want of permanence. We'll never be a couple except for other people. And I tell myself that she's expecting Duck just as much as I am.

Around six in the evening, the phone rings. Marie waits for me to answer. I pick up the receiver, she takes a step backwards and turns her face away, looking very much present. A voice, far away, a woman's voice with a husky accent, asks if I'll accept a collect call from Athens, from Daniel Carbon. How many times, during that month, did I fantasize about answering no? And I say yes. "One moment, please." And Duck's voice, cheery, buoyant, "Pierre? Hello, Pierre?" "Yes." "It's me!" "Yes . . ." "Well, I'm on my way back. With a little bit of luck, I'll be there in two or three days. Is that too late for you?" Marie is looking at me. I offer to let her listen in. She declines and goes upstairs. "Pierre, are you there?" "Yes . . ." "I thought we'd been cut off. In three days, how's that?" "Listen, Duck, why do you assume it would be too late? You do what you want, you show up when you want. Or you don't show up. I'll be here, or I won't be here. Too bad, or all for the best. I wonder, in the end, if you're not the one who's carrying on." "Who's doing what?" "Carrying on . . ." Pause. Duck says, cautiously, "So I'm on my way, OK?" I don't answer. Duck, his voice lively once more, "Good! I have to go because we've got to take the boat, and I can't be late." I smile. "Who *we*?" Duck sighs, "So long. I'm on my way!" He hangs up. I hang up. Marie comes down into the study, puts on some music, opens the window and says to me, "It's not raining anymore. How about going outside?"

The scent of wet vines, the sky thick with clouds, and tatters of mist, a sunset in the foothills of the Alps. "I . . ." Marie takes me by the arm. "No, don't say a word. Take a deep breath." A long stroll, until night falls and catches us by surprise. We head back along the main highway. Marie says to me, "What about Roussel?"

August 17th and 18th. Marie and I dedicate ourselves to living an uneventful life, as if we had always lived this way, a life as a couple, silences, tender attentions, some questions, but never the incidental kind which trigger confessions, arouse or awaken warm or hard feelings. Sauvenargues, the Rhône, Mount Ventoux, la Nesque, in the house as well as driving around, or facing a beautiful site, now and then Marie repeats, "I feel good, what about you?" I answer, "Me, too." And we're both happy, happy with each other. Olaya returns Marie's bag, all clean, sparkling new. "What with the rain the other day, I had some trouble drying it out. But look at it now, for what it's worth. I've sewn up the bottom, and the handles, you're going to be able to use it for big trips!" Marie is happy. "Oh, you know, Mrs. Olaya, with the baby coming along, my itinerary is all planned out."

August 18th, three o'clock in the afternoon, Marie is ready for the trip back. She starts work again at the studio tomorrow and prefers to travel during the day, rather than spend a night on the train. "You never know. In the daytime you can call for help. And I feel like I'm waiting for someone who's in a terrible hurry." She opens the trunk. "I'm taking one of Mrs. Vérini's jars of jam, for Mariette. OK?" She places it in her bag. At the last minute, I go up to the bathroom to take an aspirin. From upstairs I hear a brisk knock on the door. Marie opens it. Duck's voice. "It's me!" And I double up over the sink, a fit of cramps, a sensation of drowning. I had forgotten. Athens, his voice, he hangs up. And yet it was over.

I go down. The door has remained open. Marie is standing, with her bag. Duck and I kiss each other on both cheeks, awkwardly, without looking at each other. In a dazed voice I say, "Marie's train leaves in forty-five minutes and there's no time to lose." I take Marie's bag. Marie kisses Duck. We go out into the street. I turn around. "I'll be right back. There's something to eat in the refrigerator." Duck doesn't move. We leave him in the house, the door open.

I start up the car. Marie murmurs, "Why did he knock on the door since he had duplicates of the keys?" Mrs. Vérini is on her way back from Fontaubes and sees us. She kisses Marie at the car door. "I'll give the baby clothes to Mr. Pierre. Pink or blue?" "Blue. And thank you." "Oh, it'll only be some knitted things!" A little farther down, we run across Olaya who is heading toward the house. Waving good-bye. Marie says to me, "I forgot Carolon," and then, "I'll send him a card." And huddling against me, "That's a stupid thing I said to you. Duck had no choice but to knock the way he did. He looked really happy about his trip and proud to see us again . . ."

On the platform, Marie kisses me. "So, understood? Very badly, quickly, and very well." She lowers her eyes, gets on the train. I hand her her bag, she smiles. "Or else, try to pretend like you were meeting him for the first time . . ."

So, Duck and I made love the way I like to make love: from Avignon to Peyroc, nothing more than the road back, I was heading back toward him. How sweet the road was. And how bracing, the air. This after-August-15th air, this after-the-storm, turning point of a season. You begin to feel that the days are growing shorter. You sniff, breathe in the summer already slipping away. Crouched on the small landing between the few steps which lead to the study and the stairs which lead up to the bedroom, Duck is waiting for me and faces me when I open the door. He smiles, lowers his eyes, raises his head, smiles again. On the table he has unfolded a map of the Mediterranean with his itinerary marked in red pencil, stage by stage, a large circle, a rope to hang myself with. It's exactly what I thought when I saw the marking. Leaning up against the closed door, I have a dizzy spell, slight trembling, cramps, and this feeling I am drowning. The road was so sweet on the way back. It had a meaning. But now Duck is here. He says in a hushed voice, "Mrs. Vérini brought me something to eat." Still lower, "Mrs. Olaya came to pick up my underwear." I look at him. He wets his lips. "I waited for you before taking a bath . . ." Silence. "Can I take a bath? Or else . . ." He holds out his hand. "Come . . ." Meet him for the first time? Orgasm or grief, the tears are the same. Burst into laughter, nothing but outbursts. On the bed, we are drunk and defeated. Duck closes his eyes. If I move away from him, he reaches out his hands, gropes for me. I am alone. And I am here all the same, throwing my body against his. He closes his eyes. He moans. I get out of bed, he catches me. And we roll around on top of each other, the blanket yanked off. Patchwork.

Night has fallen. So quickly. Duck whispers, "Now, I'm going to take my summer bath. Do you have any Marseille soap?" At the foot of the bed, the sandals. Worn out.

30

Petit Navire Hotel, two stars NN, a scenic restaurant with a view of the seashore boulevard. In the daytime, it's a parking lot. And at night, a desert. On the other side of the boulevard the beach is grey, and after that, there is the sea. On the horizon, islands. We arrive on August 20th, in the late afternoon. I'm the one who made the decision to leave right after lunch. I felt Duck was unhappy, too constricted, in the house at Peyroc. Perhaps I was afraid, too, to hear him announce that he wanted to go back to Dijon, to go back home. He said nothing. Or rather, from time to time, "But believe me, I feel very good." Why this "but," and those staring eyes whenever I asked him to tell me about his trip? Olaya brings back the laundry. Duck is cheerful, with her. He kisses her on both cheeks. He offers her a silver-coated belt buckle. "I bought it in Istanbul for my mother but I'd rather give it to you." Olaya refuses, he insists. Almost a tussle. Olaya has coffee with us. When she leaves, I close the door after her. Once again Duck lowers his eyes and falls silent. I say to him, "We're leaving. Right away. I need a vacation."

The house suddenly appeared empty to me because Duck was there. And I didn't want to admit it. Just as I could not understand Duck's silence, a sullen silence, happy silence, or was it due to exhaustion after his trip, how could I tell?

In Avignon, we stop at the bank. I withdraw the maximum amount, 1500 francs. When the check is drawn from my account, in Paris, it will bounce. Too bad. At the steering wheel of my car on the freeway, Duck fell asleep, his head on my shoulder, clinging to my arm. I make a few calculations. If the hotel is not too expensive, we'll be able to stay five or six days. As far as Duck is concerned, I'm loaded with money, because I'm older. Or rather, from his point of view, I don't have to worry about such matters, because at my age, everything is a matter of course. I have never really known how to manage my affairs. I imagine the house in Saint-Mandé as a safe from which I've crawled like a hoodlum, an outcast, leaving his loot behind. All I ever have behind me is that little bit of money I need to keep myself out of debt. And the money that I earn, franc by franc, is always too little. Marie calls this "a rich man's rags." Barbaroux, one day while we were talking about our teacher salaries, said to me, with a broad and cordial smile, "But you're not married, you have no children, and your parents are rich!" My parents are rich? At the wheel of the car, I calculate. August 27th is also Duck's birthday. I want to give him a nice present. As we enter Toulon, Duck wakes up. "Where are we going?" I don't even know myself. A little later, in the opposite direction, the cars are on their way back from the beach. A sign. "Salins, the Port." I turn left. Villas, set back in pine trees. Small villas. Nothing in common with Blue Skies. And a sign. "Petit Navire Hotel" with three capital letters. It was the name that attracted me.

The proprietress is wearing a blond wig, almost twice as high as her head. "We have a room facing the sea, but it only has one double bed." The woman stares at us, unruffled. I murmur, "That's not a problem, it's only for a few days."

The room, flowered wallpaper, plastic lamp shades, green bedspreads, I don't like green, a leaking toilet, which Duck tries to fix right away by banging on it, nothing works, it's running, a shower with a cheerful curtain, tulips and roses, and out on the tiny balcony, a table and two camping chairs. We're on the second floor. On the third floor, the scenic restaurant. Duck says to me, "The proprietress is a real Madame Beehive." And laughing, he tussles his hair, pushes me onto the bed, throws himself on me. One laugh for so many silences. His head in the pillow, he murmurs, "I'll have to get a haircut. The Turks called me a playful puppy." That's practically all he told me about the trip. And here we are, the Petit Navire Hotel, room 103, second floor, two stars NN. What does NN mean?

A direct contact with reality. Where does the relationship end, and where does the emotion begin? Once you start to tell the story of your life, you won't be able to stop. Sentences are gestures. Therein lies the embrace. Words caress or scratch. What was that "quaintness" Marie was talking about, what "feast"? All you have to do is cross the boulevard to be on the beach. Duck took nothing with him. The grey-and-blue checkered shirt, that's all, and a pair of pants because mine don't fit him. He's wearing my clothes. "The lavender-scented clothes are for Dijon." For a short sentence like that, you could go around the world, you could lock yourself up forever. Here is a vacation, our vacation. And the Petit Navire, little sailboat, is rocking. Around Duck's neck, Bernard's medal. "Let no one force me, nor prevent me." He puts it into his mouth every time I get the feeling he's going to speak to me. And he's not even aware of it. Stretched out, leaning with my elbows on the towel, I look at the sea, the islands, I listen to the children shouting, the sound of the balls, the "oh!," the "ah!" and the "good job: you bastard, you got what you deserved!" Volleyball players. On his towel, sitting with his legs crossed, Duck does not dare glance at who is coming, who's going, who's passing back and forth in front of us. Neither staring out at sea nor into the clouds, he's contemplating another horizon. On his tanned feet, there is the outline of the sandals. Like a brand, a tattoo.

And everything really begins when everything draws to a close. If only our eyes had met, at that moment, we might have been able to speak to each other and begin to know each other. But I felt Duck was tormented by the stories he had not yet lived, and was stubbornly resisting the one, the unique one, which he could have lived. Together.

On the evening of the second day, I come back from the beach before he does. On a scrap of paper, a dialogue of the deaf, I scribble him a message, as if far away from me. I had no choice but to write him. "I don't particularly enjoy the role that you're making me play. Who do you think you are? All this is not very spontaneous on your part, or is less and less so. Your silence is composed of so many petty lies, petty complaints, petty ironies. This is what I call scheming. It's a shoddy comedy which is beginning all over again. Go to it! Beside me, on the beach, you act as if I was holding you on a leash . . ." Duck walks into the room. I hide the message. He would really like to know who I was writing to, but he understood, and asks no quesions. At times, silence is a sure sign. Duck takes off his swimsuit, goes into the bathroom and takes a shower. This time, I write to him, "Dear Duck. One gesture or one glance is worth more than a sullen conversation. But as for gestures, not a one. As for glances, even less. This morning, at breakfast, our eyes didn't even meet, not a shadow of a smile. A gesture, a touch, getting in touch, this slight effort would have been enough. And the tone you take, when you talk only to force words to my lips, reduces me to a state of confusion which, in reality, has its roots within you. You haven't been here since you've gotten back from your trip. So then, what else can I say to you, except that I'm cold and that, under any circumstances, I don't want to play the role you are thrusting upon me with your (affected?) taciturnity and with your (youthful?) evasions. In reality, between the two of us, you're the one who is calculating the most. Calculation, need it be said, has nothing to do with money. It's a question of behavior. It measures out glances, gestures, words. It reduces conversation to the point of being no more than an empty silence, the point of no return. And it assaults the other person with everything that he is, sequestering him in a state of isolation wherein everything is calculated, measured out beforehand. Togetherness, when it is desired, does not lend itself to calculation. Pierre."

Duck comes out of the shower. He dries himself off, wraps himself in his towel, and stretches out. I read him this letter, in an emotionless voice, enunciating clearly. When I finish reading, Duck holds out his hand. But I fold up the letter and slip it into my pants' pocket. Duck smiles out of the side of his mouth, looks at the sea and murmurs, "At any rate, Paris is in your blood and you'll never understand." He motions for me to join him. As soon as I sit down on the edge of the bed,

he closes his eyes. Stubbornness. My rage. I get up and go out, closing
the door behind me, calmly. "We'll meet upstairs for dinner. I'm going
to take a little walk." Room and one meal, 97 francs a day, per person.
Duck is the one who, by keeping quiet, is forcing me to calculate. It's
true, I'm not familiar with the suburbs. I'm going to be forty years old,
I'm not familiar with the newly constructed towns, nor the new
inhabitants of these new towns. Another generation. When I was nine, I
was afraid of death. I had read in a newspaper that a lady (photo:
evening dress, her eyes blindfolded, Salle Pleyel) had announced the
end of the world for the coming year. It was the end of the forties. I was
afraid because I was going to be ten. When I was nineteen, I was afraid,
because I was going to be twenty. It was too late. But too late, for what?
I didn't want to admit, in my relationships with my family, my teachers,
my friends or the others, that when all is said and done, there are only
two types of people: those who beg for charity and those who grant it.
When I was twenty-nine, I nearly quit my job in order to raise goats.
What Marie calls "National Pompidolian Ecology," the "euphoria of
the sixties." I was afraid of turning thirty. When I was thirty-nine, last
summer, room 103, second floor, green bedspread, the first two nights,
I slept at the very edge of the bed, as if above a precipice. Duck took up
all the room, clinging to my arm. If I tried to stroke him, with my
fingertips, the fingertips which are holding this pen today, he let me
understand by a sound in his throat, a sigh, or a heavier breathing,
playing at sleeping beauty, or a genuine sleeping beauty, that he did not
want me to touch him. And he squeezed my arm all the tighter, with
both hands, clutching tightly. The older I get, the younger I become,
and too watchful. Does the capacity for love really grow in inverse
proportion to age?

Third message. "3:30 A.M. I think that enough is enough. I waited for
you to come to dinner until the restaurant closed. Stupid scenery. Are
you going to come back with your lips still soft? All the better. We can
always go someplace else to lie to each other, and pretend, for a little
while longer. I am exhausted. When you slip into bed, don't wake me
up, please, and leave me half the bed. I do believe in Duck, but Duck is
pretending that he doesn't understand my drive and my demands. Not
what I am imposing, but proposing. Listening is a kind of embrace, and

so are gazing eyes. And step by step, without one person dragging the other along, two friends can sink their teeth into life. Why this withdrawal, your withdrawal, and your sealed lips? Your youth? But what kind of youth? So, *basta*. I have no use for stubborn people. Not that it makes me sad, but rather, at its worst, furious. An urge to beat you up. You're beating me up. And don't accuse me of not extending my hand and of not welcoming you. Friendliness, in a word, does exist. And spontaneity, freely offered. Tomorrow, first thing, good-bye, you split. You have the duplicate of the keys in Peyroc for your belongings. Work things out somehow. Go get listened to someplace else, admired or pitied, but not loved. Pierre." I place this letter on Duck's pillow. I get the feeling that I haven't slept for months. And I fall asleep. Instantly. Duck: the space of an instant.

The next morning the letter is still there. Duck did not come back. His wallet is on the night table. I order breakfast. For two.

The tea is cold. I have been waiting for an hour. On the beach, the first bathers. And observed from the balcony, the morning scenery, the islands, at the horizon, in a luminous mist. Duck comes in. He sees the letter, picks it up, unfolds it, reads it, refolds it, places it next to his wallet. He gets undressed, walks into the bathroom. Sound of water in the sink: a cat bath. Then he joins me on the balcony, sits down, drinks his cold tea. I look at his lips, they are not untouched. His chest, and under the table, his knees and his thighs: the body does not lie. Duck brings the small pitcher of milk to his lips and empties it in one gulp. Croissants, bread, butter, jam, orange juice, he doesn't leave anything on the tray. He wipes his lips with a paper napkin, which he crumples up with a smile, looking happy, almost beaming. "We're going to play volleyball this morning. I'm going. Are you coming with me?" He slips into his swimsuit and leaves the room. A minute later, he's crossing the boulevard, barefooted, his towel in his hand. I take the letter back and hide it with the two other messages in an inner compartment of my toilet case. Also in this compartment is the bottle of 10 mg. Kerela pills that I have to take in case of an attack.

When I join him on the beach, Duck seems worried. He asks me, in a mechanical voice, "Did you see those pictures Betsy took?" "Yes, I threw them away." "Who gave you the right?" Silence. He glances at the volleyball court. The players haven't arrived yet. He shrugs. "And you've really gotten no mail for me?" "No. And who was that *we* in Athens?" He jumps up, clenches his hands, as if he was going to strike me. "Myself, the girls I was traveling with. On second thought, no, it was us. Us!" And he dashes toward the sea, dives in headfirst, hurts his knees. On this beach, you would need to walk out for a few miles before your feet don't touch bottom anymore. As in Sète. The water is murky. All you need do is turn your head around to see towns and concrete. The Riviera.

Duck comes back, belly flops on his towel, grabs one of my hands, presses it against the sand and kisses it with a moan, or is it the very beginning of a laugh? "Let's stop this, please." At last, he looks at me, his lips parted, slightly quivering, wet all over, he's shivering. "I make an effort, in spite of myself, but it all gets the best of me." He gets up. The volleyball players are here. Duck winks at me. "Are you coming?"

We play with the others, one or two hours. I lose track of the passing time. During these moments, I am living a real hollow day. Dazed. On the platform at the Avignon train station, Marie repeats to me to pretend that I am meeting Duck for the first time. And as chance would have it, Duck and I have been picked for opposing teams, I see him head-on, slapping the ball and sending it preferably toward me, so I can play a little, we exchange the true glances of those meeting for the first time. There is Bob, Paul, Martin, Luc, all of them very handsome, but I see only my Duck. Yes, I say, "my Duck," because he's acting like an owner, because he's held me a whole summer long on the string of his graffiti, a marionette.

After five or six games, we go into the water. Both of us swim far from shore, without ever losing our footing. Now and then, Duck dives into the water to catch one of my legs and to bite it. A playful puppy? We kiss furtively. "What's your name, mister?" "Pierre, and yours?" "I'm Daniel, Duck to my friends . . ." We burst into laughter and as we go back, we splash each other and push each other into the waves, like children. Lazy waves, noon, a rediscovered happiness.

Each of us picks up his towel. We dry ourselves off. Out of breath, I feel like I'm breathing for the first time in months. Bob, eighteen or nineteen years old, long hair, blond, small build, athletic, approaches Duck. Around Bob's neck, Bernard's medal. Bob takes it off and hands it to Duck. "Here, thanks, I'm going to get the same thing made for myself." Duck accepts it, without the slightest embarrassment. Nothing in all this is done on purpose. A simple goof-up. That's all. Bob turns toward me. "If you play more often, you'll make progress!" Duck squeezes the medal and chain in his fist. He smiles at Bob, his teeth clenched. Bob seems surprised. He says to Duck, "Could you lend me your towel? I forgot mine." An intimacy.

I don't say a word. Duck keeps quiet. He doesn't want to have lunch. He's not hungry. Bob and the others have gone. We're supposed to meet in the late afternoon "for the return match!" Duck murmurs, slightly pouting, a heartbreaker, furious with me, mad about himself, "I don't know what's going through your mind. I met them yesterday, with some girls, at the port. He simply asked me to lend him the medal." "And you agreed?" "Yeah, I agreed." I murmur, "So then, I don't see what the big deal is?" Duck looks at me, a small boxer, ready to pounce. "Yes, it is a big deal. And you're the one who's turning it into one. After all, I'm free." He gets up, violently tosses the medal onto the towel, murmurs, "It was too good to be true." And he goes off. Voltaire. *My mother's crucifix.* I smile. Sometimes sheer terror inspires a smile.

At dinner time, he meets me at our table. The maître d' takes his order and hopes that we'll "enjoy our meal." Duck doesn't say a word. I keep quiet. We eat. From time to time, he looks at the scenery, in the darkness, the necklace of lights along the coast, the blackness of the evening and the ink of the sea. After the meal, we go back to room 103. He takes off one of my sweaters that he was wearing against his bare skin, slips into the blue-and-grey checkered shirt, his shirt. In the bathroom, he combs his hair, checks himself in the mirror. Standing, by the bed, I don't know where to put myself. He comes out of the bathroom and says in a blank voice, "I'm going out for some air, five minutes." I smile. Breathing very heavily, he clenches his fists, as if his heart had suddenly begun to palpitate. I look straight into his eyes. "Which one of us is fooling the other? I'm asking you, calmly: when people go out for some air, they don't change shirts and they don't comb their hair." He answers, "You asshole!" and he leaves the room, slamming the door behind him. Then in the same movement he comes back in, rushes toward me. I grab his shoulder, roughly, the same attack, his shirt sleeve rips right off in my hand, shredded cloth, loved, worn out, tired out, and with the same swing, clockwards, Duck hits me in the face, my left eye, cheekbone, eyebrow, I am sent flying onto the bed. If I hit him back, I'll kill him. I look at him and he knows it. I repeat, "Get out!" and he doesn't move. His mouth open, panting, he takes off the shirt, yanks off the other sleeve. He puts the shirt back on, short sleeves, and he goes out. Leaving the door open behind him.

My head in the bathroom sink, cold water, my temple aching. Jealousy, a stabbing thrust, Bob's eyes and Duck's eyes, Bob's lips and Duck's lips, the body of one and of the other. And Duck's penis, glimpsed this very morning, under the breakfast table, his legs spread apart, a jewel, tenderly fondled. These things cannot be put into words. Love, for a whole population of cultivated people, the love that I talk about in school, must resemble love. Similarities, simulacrums, mind games. The raw material of the imagination is what is seen and heard, what is, and only what is. True harmony exists in the sharpness of the facts. Under the faucet water, I get spasms. It's the recess yard. The nurse drops by to see my mother once more. Why always bring up our families, and our childhoods? That kind of thing holds onto us, from a distance, and inevitably anticipates our moves. We no doubt need to recreate the paradises that we no longer find lying in our future. We explain this emptiness to ourselves by thinking that perhaps we have already experienced them. Two 10 mg. Kerela pills. The dosage to take in case of an attack. I shut the door and collapse onto the bed. I can't open my left eye anymore. To speak the love which, sometimes, makes us intimate, and not the kind which makes us simulate. Word by word. Blow by blow.

11:00 P.M., midnight, three times I take the dosage of pills. But I feel my fingers grow numb, this pain along my arms, my chest as if caught in a vice, my neck arched, mouth wide open, I can't even bend my knees anymore. I feel a quivering deep within me. I have to find Duck. For help.

A robot, on the boulevard and at the port, I look for him. One, two o'clock in the morning. There he is, with Bob and the others at the Navy sidewalk café. When he spots me, he says good-bye to everyone and heads for the hotel, avoiding me. Bob wants to tag along, but the others burst out laughing. Duck disappears ahead of me. Can't keep up with him. I don't feel my legs anymore, nor my body, nor my feet. I am as cold as a corpse, one eye closed, another ache, and I hear Marie repeating, "Death is the privilege of those who die." And applied to my life, that is utterly meaningless. That doesn't simulate love, but it is love, joy, and what is left of harmony. When I arrive in front of the hotel, the light in our room goes out. I crawl up the stairs. The knob on room 103 is round, I can no longer make a fist, I can't open it all by myself, I call out softly, then more loudly. Then I begin to push with my shoulders. I can't breathe. Too late, I'm drooling. And there I am, on the stairs, tumbling down to get to the fresh air outside. I have to hide. Duck did not open the door! I cross the boulevard, and on the beach, near the volleyball courts, behind the sailboat shell, headfirst in the sand, the quivering intensifies, then explodes. It comes from far away, from the deepest place within my body and from Saint-Mandé, it comes from family dinners and reproaches, silences, and expectations. It possesses me. I don't have a head anymore, just an enormous empty room in its place. A child's room. And a child, imprisoned, within, very small, not yet born. It's myself. Permanent image of this seizure. And my mouth is full of sand. Spittle everywhere. My pants wet, soiled.

When I come to, a truck is collecting the hotel trash. Dawn is breaking. I'm afraid. I lift myself up against the shell of the boat. I breathe with difficulty. Little by little, I get my strength back. My pants have dried off, behind and in front, strange trappings, stains. Here too, with my back to the sea, I feel that I've reached the very end, but I'm no longer ready for everything, it will be the last time. And they all clamor for the kind of love which simulates love!

That idea, that morning, kept me on my feet. I met no one on my way back to the hotel. I was ashamed, yes ashamed, and shame, once again, is Saint-Mandé, Paris in my blood, or the hypocrites. I open the room door, a gesture, like a cramp. There's a note on the bed: "You scare the hell out of me, I'm going to sleep somewhere else." I pick up the bottle of Kerela. Two more pills. A little water. I am trembling, the bottle spills onto the floor. I don't have the strength to pick everything up. I partially collapse onto the bed, buckled over. Fitful sleep, taste of grey sand, with my clothes on, filthy, slobbering. A mess.

Shaking me, Duck rouses me. I only see him out of one eye. He drags me into the bathroom, sticks my head into the toilet bowl. He thinks I've tried to kill myself. He wants me to throw up. But I repeat, "No . . . no . . ." He undresses me, sits me down in the shower. He cleans me off, soaps me up, with a washcloth. Everything is starting over again. Jeanne, Françoise, Lutetia, the entire film of a lifetime. Then Duck dries me off, picks me up. I lean against the wall, I want to walk by myself. Eight o'clock in the morning. Duck stretches out against me, on the bed. He says to me, "Sorry . . ." But his voice is slick.

We have to be out of the room before noon. Duck murmurs, "Let's go to one of the islands, and this evening we'll go back to Peyroc." I open my left eye. He smiles feebly. I've just heard him speak in the same voice of that first day, over the phone. The same voice. He orders breakfast. For two.

31

Nine in the morning. I pay the hotel bill. Mrs. Beehive hands me the hotel calling card. "Next year, if you write us in advance, we'll reserve a room with twin beds." Overdrawn check. I had not planned for the meals and the extra charge for breakfast. Duck stands off to the side, in the hallway, he picks up brochures, chooses two postcards, puts them back in the rack.

Next year? Mrs. Beehive looks at me funny. I tell her I got a ball smashed right into my face, during a volleyball game. And without even being aware of it, as she takes the check I hand her, she smiles. "I'm not surprised. All games are dangerous." Duck has gone outside.

Before leaving the room, I picked up the bottle of Kerela and what was left of the pills in the bathroom wastebasket. Duck had thrown everything away. Why did he believe that it was an act? Why didn't he answer my plea? Who's really playing? The person who is played with or the person who denounces the game and controls the situation by escaping? Or neither? I picked up the bottle of Kerela and slipped it in the inside pocket of my toilet case, with the two messages, the letter and Bernard's medal. Duck then leaned over to throw the grey-and-blue checkered shirt sleeves into the wastebasket. Opposite gestures: a question and an answer. Nine in the morning. We leave the hotel parking lot. Duck looks at me. "Will you be able to drive?" Then, "This boat ride will do you good." He sits beside me, his hands on his knees. It's going to be a beautiful day.

In Salins, a pharmacy. I buy some cotton and a disinfectant. Duck dabs my eye, my cheekbone and my eyebrow. I buy a pair of sunglasses. When I take out the bills from the wallet, Duck turns his head away.

At the Salins exit, a stop-off in a gas station, full tank, check of the oil and tires. I pay. More bills. Duck is putting on his sandals. He is whistling faintly. In the car trunk in a plastic bag, on the side, rolled in a ball, are the pants, shirt and sweater I was wearing the night before. Dirty laundry for Olaya. But I tell myself that I won't dare give it to her. I'll wash it myself. Or else, I'll throw away those pants, the way one thinks, sometimes, he can throw away bad memories. Duck says nothing. When he turns towards me, he looks at my left eye. A black eye.

At the landing stage parking lot, we lock the car. Duck doesn't want to take a sweater with him. The sun's already hitting hard, dim light in a heat haze, the last breath of a summer. Porquerolles, Port-Cros, or the Levant Island? Duck says to me, "As you wish." I insist. He gently shrugs his shoulders, almost a voluntary tenderness, aborting. "No, wherever you like, you choose." On a poster, "Port-Cros, National Park." I choose Port-Cros. We'll get there around eleven. There'll be a boat for the return trip at four-thirty. Gift shop, fear of the sun, I buy a cap, with a visor, ridiculous. When I pay, Duck goes outside.

Twenty minutes later, on the boat, Duck sat down all the way up front, leaning over rails, his face like a prow. He turns his back to me, grey-and-blue checkered shirt, short sleeves, and his heels stretching up from his sandals. The new glasses hurt me a little behind the ears. The cap is a little tight on my forehead. The boat is moving away from the coast. I try to breathe. Like a dizzy spell, I feel like the entire earth is nothing but a sailboat overturned on a beach. An image. A frozen image. Why this one-day trip? And the peacefulness of the sea? The air is stagnant.

With the boat, moving forward, I can breathe a little. Seated on the bridge of Petit-Pont, that morning in Sète, dangling legs, I am still astonished, Mr. Pertuis, villa Toula, plopped in his armchair, facing the pond, can no longer hear what is being said to him. He reads last Sunday's paper over and over again. So many, many Sundays in order to reach this point. Nothing is difficult really. Everything's beautiful when you don't cheat. It's a very beautiful story, if one wishes it so. It's a very beautiful story, if you wish it so. And I think I'm smiling, seated in the rear, near the pilot's booth, facing the open sea, even if I know and I feel that I have no desire to talk anymore. Petit-Pont and Petit-Navire, Sète and Salins, a whole summer long. I have a lump on my cheek, and my eyebrow is swollen. Once again, I close my left eye. From the night before, there remains this ache and this stiffness, like a spinal sword, in the back. In the fore of the boat, Duck is not moving. I won't be able to say another word.

A few minutes of stopover in Porquerolles, then we sail off again. An impression of open sea and of a trip that would never end, eternal return of feelings, cross fire of silences. On the front deck, in the sun, the passengers stand together in families, or in couples. I am the only one, alone. With Duck. And Duck, still up front, his hair wild, his whole weight on one leg, leaning out. He doesn't turn around until the boat enters the northern creek of Port-Cros. He passes in front of me, without saying anything. I lower my eyes behind my glasses. Two restaurants, a café-terrace, a few houses and the ruins of an overhanging fort, the rest is nothing but vegetation. A sign reads "National Park," another, "No Smoking," a third, "Respect Nature and Silence." At the end of the pier, Duck is waiting for me. We are lost. Where shall we go? We have five hours ahead of us. What a big trip, what a feat! No sadness in this, but rather the cutting edge of lucid awareness. Near the café, a souvenir stand. I buy a map of the island. Damned 100 franc bill. The cashier woman doesn't have any change. She looks for it in her bag. Duck is waiting. And then, without saying anything to each other, the map unfolded, Paradise Path, Solitude Dale, Mount Vinegar, Crest Path, Pirate Creek, the hiking times are marked down, we choose our paths, another loop, with the tip of our fingers, another graffiti. Duck starts off, ahead of me. I follow him. I have kept the map. He takes off the grey-and-blue checkered shirt and knots it around his waist. We come across an island guard, military outfit, German shepherd on the end of a leash. And everywhere: "No Smoking," "Respect Silence and Nature," and arrows to indicate the paths. This kind of silence scares me. This kind of nature scares me. They let everything grow, trees, bushes, everything. Soon, it's nothing but a tunnel of dry and raw vegetation, trails too neatly outlined, narrowly cleared to permit passage. The path is steep. Duck walks ahead of me without turning around. This kind of silence, thick, oppressive, is becoming a burden. We must climb over the island mountain. Only the prospect of a panoramic view, up from the top, on the other side of the crest path, urges me on. But inside me I bear the weight of a night, the contraction of a seizure. Attached to a younger man, I feel that I am hanging upon the mystery of his trip without me, a lone voyager. I try to pace myself and stop listening to the gushing of my heart. But I can't take it anymore: here is the brother I didn't have and the family I still have. Here's the silence of a childhood, shadow and unjustified reproach, and this dry smell, resinous, the sound of footfalls on the bed of pine needles. I must reach the top, I must see the other side, the view, the Mediterranean noon and the south. I must. And I tell myself that that night in Salins, room 103, boat shell on the beach, is a night from my fortieth year soon. The night of those who continually chase after the light of others and who only meet those who haven't played the game long enough yet in order to know when to come to a rest at one being. Duck would like me to go faster. He turns around. "OK?" But it's only the expression of his haste. On the map, it says that the path we took will lead us to the crest in only one hour and forty-five minutes. We don't run across anyone else. A tunnel, sheltered from the sun, and without any air to breathe but the violent scent of a glutted nature left to itself, covering itself in layer after layer, carefully supervised, sequestered, without anything wild or sacred to bring it to life. Duck disappears ahead of me.

He's waiting for me, all the way up on the top, at the crossing of the Crest Path. Up here too, trees and tunnel, we still see nothing, on the other side. We try to guess, that's all. My whole life trying to guess, to delight, to listen and to share. And I don't have to judge myself or judge

Duck here, as I speak about myself, about him, about us, that day. It's the way it is. I don't have to tear him apart, or tear myself apart. What we lived through was intense. We are still living this story and this is how we lived it. To the very last word. Sometimes the text creates an illusion, and the novel lies. There is only true greatness within the scope of what is human, harmonious, tragic, and joy only in the most precise expression of a sensibility. That morning, at that crossing, I waited for a gesture from Duck, a word, a glance. I couldn't say anything anymore. I'm waiting for him.

I take off my cap to wipe off my brow and my sunglasses to wipe off not a tear, but what's running from my left eye. Duck takes the map, unfolds it, folds it up again, and hands it back to me. "I'm going up to the top of Mount Vinegar. It's marked twenty minutes, will you wait for me?" The Petit-Navire, Mrs. Beehive, Mount Vinegar, I smile: all of this is true, inexpressible and true. Duck takes my smile for a sign of tenderness and runs off, like a child who has just been given permission.

I wait for him, a few minutes, seated on a rock, at this path crossing. But my heart is beginning to pound so hard that I hear nothing but that noise, a metronome, my sisters are taking their piano lessons in the living room, they are quite bad pupils; one day, at her wit's end, the teacher won't come back. And I, I'll always be "too young to begin." I have learned to decipher, interpret, on the sly. I have learned and lived everything on the sly, even when I thought myself to be out in the open, my face unmasked. And a prisoner of this crest, I'm still in hiding. What prompted me to think, at that instant, about the floor of the Saint-Mandé living room, about the carpets which you had to fit back into place, about this mirror of our childhood wanderings, we never leave any footprints? And the first time I was given my identity card, when I had to press down my fingerprint, I suddenly became afraid of leaving only a spot of ink, no real fingerprint. What prompted me to think about that incident of my life, trivial, at that instant? And today, this text, like an identification mark and a quest. I want to find my identity. It's a joy. And if the known being, absent, escapes by ridiculing, let the unknown being, present, here, welcome and share. I give everything. The swindlers may well laugh and demolish, find this to be generous, ideal.

The others, sincere, friends of both sexes, lovers, will perhaps make allowances for the text, for human nature, and not for circumstances. Like an echo.

Within a few minutes, the silence unsettles me to such a point that I stand up, shaking. I can't wait for Duck any longer and I must go back by the shortest way, go back to the port and the sea as quickly as possible, to see, to see houses, people, who can call for help in case of another mishap. I remember a seizure, in Evolène, when I was six. I remember a seizure in Cuelga, south of Spain, on my thirteenth birthday. A girl, kneeling by me, wipes off my mouth. She's nicknamed the Loca. I remember a seizure in Oxford, at the Parson's Pleasure, on the lawn. I am dragged away in the coatroom. Michael Watts watches over me. I am a sorry sight. I remember a seizure in Clos-Monet the day after my parents sold that weekend house, near Paris. In front of the door, there was a moving truck. I was twenty-four. I remember a seizure, in the hallways of a clinic, Sutton Place, in New York. I was visiting my friend Rasky. I was thirty. I remember Loïc, all bloody, I had just struck him because he didn't want to leave my house. He was hanging on to the furniture, the walls. And I see white, I fall. I am thirty-two. I remember Patmos, on vacation. Jean-Pierre is packing and spits on me because I'm drooling, and, he says, it's disgusting. I remember a seizure, at the West Side. Taking shelter in the restrooms, I fall under the sink. They waited till closing time to slip me out the door. There were no taxis that morning. Every time I have fallen, there was no one. And every time I got to my feet, it was to wait, more intensely than ever, for someone. A kiss would have been enough, or a glance. One single sincere glance. I must get back to the port.

I look at the map with my right eye. My left eye is oozing, tears in spite of myself, and my cheekbone is burning. A blow. A repeated blow, wildly struck. The shortest path for the way back is precisely that of Solitude Dale. I can't rename it here. It's on the map. It's written. And it makes me smile, as if restored to health. I am finding a new strength to climb down this mountain and head back to the port.

At the souvenir booth, I buy writing paper, an envelope, a stamp and a pen. I write: "Port-Cros, August 26th. Mid-afternoon. Dearest Roussel. I am thinking about you and I'm writing it down. Ever since my visit I have been thinking about you. I'm thinking about you, released and without fear. I'm thinking about you because confusion is so human that it's nothing but love. I won't find the proper words to comfort you. Words are not pills. Even when I think them to be new and effective, they are nothing in regards to the help one would like to extend. Come back, come back quickly. And don't be afraid. It's the fear of recess. You must, then, know how to ask your buddies to defend you. I never knew how to do it. Do it. Love is binding. We must bind ourselves together. I beg you, as simply as I possibly can, to regain a certain stability and to come back. I'm thinking about you. I am here. Your brother, Pierre. I can't do without you and there are many of us in this position. Are you so very far away, really?"

And I recopy this letter to have a duplicate of it. You always write to yourself, and at a certain point of happiness, of conflict, or of unhappiness, everyone saves himself as best he can. I recopy. It's our duplicate set of keys, Roussel, and I know you won't hold it against me. I write your name and temporary address on the envelope. It feels good to realize that I know this address of the clinic by heart. I have found the sun again, the air and the view of the sea. The atmosphere of this island is strangling, a German shepherd at the end of a leash. I stick the stamp on the envelope, I fold the copy of the letter and slip it into the rear pocket of my pants. A Cyclops, I throw the letter into a mailbox, beside the souvenir stand. It will bear the postmark of this cursed island. And I'll be the only one to know it. At Guérande or Saint-Nazaire, I used to go to dances to meet people different from my usual company, beings who were unusual and far away to catch me unawares, to teach me how to spread my arms and squeeze against me, who one day would perhaps love, as much as myself, just like me. At those dances, they would stamp my hand too. It was marked "paid" like a tattoo. Duck appears suddenly, out of breath. He's found me. He keeps at a distance. My left eye is sealed shut.

2:45 P.M. At the terrace of one of the two restaurants, we are the last customers. Lunch is served to us hastily, as if we were guilty of being late. "Tourist" menu, "fixed price": appetizer, fish, meat, cheese, dessert. No substitutions. Duck wasn't hungry and he devours everything. I'm terribly hungry, but, a lump in my throat, I can't swallow anything. Duck wipes his plate with a piece of bread, wipes his lips with his napkin, wipes the crumbs on the tablecloth with the back of his hand, and his eyes glide over mine, he doesn't even dare look at me. If I took off my glasses, he would accuse me of flaunting my eye. I keep my glasses on, and, with his tenacious silence, he accuses me of hiding. Who, when, how, why? You only know later. I smile, and he wonders, gets annoyed. He drinks his coffee in one gulp. The waitress puts the check on the table. I pay. The noise of bills. An extravagant price and a ridiculous noise. 3:25. I look at Duck. "You're not saying anything?" He turns his head toward the creek and the pier. A sailboat has just docked. I insist, my voice too soft or too calm, a voice I don't recognize, "You really can't say anything?" He crosses his arms on the table, stares at me for a long while, his mouth slightly pouting, the answer is negative. Then I say to him, my exact words, "But what keeps you from expressing your desires?" And he answers me, tit for tat, with great self-confidence, "I can't express my desires because you have the economic power." Like Solitude Dale, which I didn't call by another name, I don't have here to rephrase the answer Duck gave me. He will be twenty-two tomorrow, and I forty in six days. 3:30. We head toward the pier. We'll wait for the boat to arrive.

The trip back does me good. A breeze has risen, blowing from the coast and the land. We are coming full circle. I only feel inclined to the true long journeys when they are imaginary. I squeeze myself in my own arms, seated, inside the boat. I have slipped on my pullover, but I'm cold, very cold. And outside, up in front, grey-and-blue checkered shirt, Duck rubs his arms, gesticulates, shakes his head. Then, seated, he bends over, takes off one of his sandals, looks at it up close. It is coming apart, a strap has snapped off. He inspects the sole, takes off the other sandal, places them side by side and tosses them into the sea. 5:10. We land. We go straight to the car. Duck is barefooted.

Sitting at the wheel, before starting the car, I dab my left eye with a cotton ball and the disinfectant. It stings, but it's cleaned. I see better.

Then we leave. As we cross Toulon, a jewelry store, I stop, leaving my right-turn signal on, no parking. Duck stays in the car. And with the greatest part of what's left of my cash, I buy the Seiko Quartz electronic alarm clock which Duck had looked at several times, in several windows, in Paris, in front of me, on the first day of our relationship. "Only that one could wake me up in the morning. But it costs a fortune." And Marie, when we talked about it, had said, "Only those who have nothing left but insomnia can afford to buy it." The salesman asks me if I want it gift wrapped. "No thanks. I'll take it as it is." And when I hand over the box to Duck, in the car, Duck opens it, looks, caresses the object like a beach pebble, places the warranty in his shirt pocket and says nothing. I would have wished so much, at least at that instant, for him to get excited. Six o'clock. We get on the freeway. Duck whispers, "At any rate, I don't thank you on purpose."

Aix, Salon-de-Provence, Cavaillon, Avignon-South, toll. I pay. I start the car again and without even being aware of it, I say under my breath, "And what were those little deals, in Istanbul, anyway?" Duck turns his head away as he answers. "It was to scare you."

8:00 P.M. Peyroc. I am forced to hold my chin up in order to open my left eye a little. The grocery store is closed. Emilienne is watching television. No one on the terrace, at Carolon's. We enter the house like robbers. Duck goes to open the mailbox right away and brings back the mail. There's nothing for him. He goes upstairs. I hear the water running into the sink. Then, from the second floor, Duck says to me, "I'm going back to Dijon tonight." Sound of closet doors. He's packing. All the clean clothes in his bag. I fix tea, set out cookies. I open one of Mrs. Vérini's jars of jam. On the table, all my mail, sealed. Duck comes back down, socks, shoes, pullover. He got dressed. He places the alarm clock in the bag, on the top, carefully wrapped. He checks to see if the warranty is still in his shirt pocket. When a person is leaving, everything becomes symbolic.

Then he goes into the study to get a sheet of paper, a pencil, and without a word, leaning on the table, he sketches the layout of his apartment in Dijon. Scalding tea. Without milk. Bitter. Under his breath, he explains, "As I'm leaving sooner than expected, I'm going to take advantage of it, in the days to come, to rearrange everything. I'm going to put my bed here, and in this corner, near the window, a work space. I'm going to make myself a bookcase, with bricks and boards. I know how to go about it. I also have to find a bed, a really big bed. And I have to buy myself a warm blanket." And, without saying a word, I go up to my bedroom, I fold the patchwork blanket, I refold it, an enormous ball of wool, and I come back down. I throw the whole thing into a plastic bag which I knot at the top. I put the package down on the floor, near the bag. Duck smiles, but the nature of his smile eludes me. A crooked smile, warped, a refusal, comma or apostrophe, I'll never know.

9:00 P.M. We are driving toward Avignon. Duck whispers, "You'll forward my mail if there is any?" Then, "My mother will be happy. She's been wanting to have me home for my birthday for a long time . . ." Then nothing else. Not another word. Clenched teeth. 9:20 P.M. In front of the station, a parking place. Duck grabs his bag and the package in the back of the car. And I, once again, I hurry toward the ticket window to buy the ticket. And it's not in order to suffer, and to relish it, but in order to heal. To be decent till the very end. The Saint-Mandé decency, identifying sign, indelible mark. It's a question of following the herd. Duck takes the ticket. I take off my glasses. Duck looks at me, his lips parted, his head slightly lowered. A voice, in the loudspeaker, announces the arrival on track number one of the train from Perpignan, to Valence, Lyon, Dijon, Paris. Duck takes on the look of one in a hurry, two steps backward, then, without saying a word, he leaves.

32

I saw the Fontaubes crowd again. They always make up at the end of the summer, and it's most certainly due to an instinct for self-preservation. I heard Betsy say, after a dinner, God how beautiful the table was, "How could we get along without our sharp tongues and our open minds? It's our way of hibernating." Oswyn was also there and he kept very close to John, as if on a leash. Robert and Gérard seemed in love and discrete, like newlyweds. "We'll drop in to see you in Paris, this winter. When I think that we've never seen your apartment." John invites me to come to London "for weekend trips, it'll cheer you up." Ruth clung to my arm and pressed herself up against me, without saying a word, in the same way people at a show, struck with fear, will grab hold of the hand of the person sitting next to them. No one among them made any comment about my black eye. Duck's name was not uttered. The last evening, Betsy said to me, "We should really plan our summers differently. But it's a little too late." And then, in a confidential tone which was a bit too glib, "It's the beginning of autumn, a beautiful season if you want it to be." Farewell.

I received no mail for Duck. The night before I left, I put the napkin pouch initialed D.C. into an envelope, without any note, and I addressed the whole thing to Daniel Carbon, 5 rue Jean-Jaurès, Bat. C., 21100 Dijon. My first and last letter. Mrs. Vérini brings me over a set of blue baby clothes and some jam "for Paris." I pay Olaya for the summer laundry. Emilienne promises she'll water the window flowers. "They'll still be beautiful for your November break." Carolon makes me drink a third pastis, eyeing me shrewdly. "The boxer-type, K.O., it really doesn't suit you, Mr. Forgue, my dear Pierre. You'll have to buy yourself some gloves." I leave Peyroc September 2nd, the day of my fortieth birthday. My mother phones me from La Baule. "You know that we're thinking about you . . ." I know.

The day I arrived, the white Ford Capri is in front of the Lizard bar, and there's a lively crowd. Everyone has returned to Paris. Facing the street, the shutters of Mariette's apartment seemed to be closed, in a different way. And facing the courtyard, too. I did not dare knock at her door, it was nearly midnight. On the fourth floor landing, I set down my luggage. I ring Marie's doorbell, but she doesn't answer. I hear a faint noise behind the door: Boubou is in her apartment. At my place, on my desk, a hastily written note: "6:00 P.M. My Pierrot. It's about time you got back. We need you. Mariette broke her hip. She's in a clinic in Vésinet. Address below. I'm taking care of Boubou, but frankly, I don't feel well. It's the baby, seventh month, a little too soon, but there's nothing I can do about it. I've just called a taxi. I'm going all by myself like a big girl. The address of the maternity clinic: 13, rue Frochot. See you soon or tomorrow. Love. Marie"

13 rue Frochot. One in the morning. "Oh! you know, she's sleeping. Are you a member of the family?" The intern on duty explains to me that everything went very well. It's a "viable" boy. Then, "We needed to rush him to boulevard Brunot, the best facility in Paris. Here we're not equipped to handle premature births. But are you a member of the family?"

I go back to rue Boursault. I take Boubou to my place. I open my bedroom window to freshen the air. He jumps up on the sill, loses his balance and falls. I tried to catch him, a fistful of fur in my hand. Gare St. Lazare, three in the morning, I would dearly like to find a guard, a railway worker, someone. "But sir, you're not permitted to walk on the tracks. Do you realize, it's at least as far as Cardinet bridge, one mile, and anyway, it's very dangerous." Eventually someone accompanies me. There I was at the very bottom of the trench. The guy murmurs, "It's really a lot of trouble for a dead cat." He looks at me. "But I understand you." And one hour later, Boubou's body in my arms, I walk up rue de Rome, I cross the bridge, here I am on rue Boursault. The owner of the Lizard gets into his car. He sees me passing in front of Mariette's apartment with the cat, stretched full length, hanging heavily, in my arms, and for the first time he speaks to me. "Oh, well, that fellow has been trying to get away for so long, he finally got what he deserved." In the building trash can I lay Boubou down and I replace the lid.

Rue Frochot, ten in the morning. I am sitting by her bedside. Marie wakes up, smiles and murmurs, "But what happened to your eye?" I answer mechanically, "You have a boy. They're taking good care of him. What are you going to name him?" "I don't know. I'll decide when I hold him in my arms." She smiles weakly. "Like my grandmother when . . ." I stroke her on her forehead.

Boubou. A cat's death always seems trivial or too cruel. Yet, human beings create better victims for themselves out of animals, a new kind of offertory. We had lost track of Boubou's age and he couldn't see anymore. Where did he draw the strength which enabled him to get around again those last months? Boubou fell, thinking he was escaping. You always believe you're on the ground floor, with sure footing for an escape. Blaise Cendrars. And I know I'm taking a very big risk by offering these explanations here. But when all is said and done, animals are the only real victims. Marie says to me, "Don't tell Mariette. She'll never come home from Vésinet." Then, "You did right to tell me. But what's wrong with your eye?"

Boulevard Brune, I insist, because Marie told me to insist that I see him, and always the same question: "Are you a member of the family?" I note down all these things, here, as much for the repetition as for the lyrical drama of a cat's death, because there's no final period to anything and life lays its claims, with all its complications, other people's complications, right away. The baby stayed in an intensive care unit for three days. A nurse explains to me, a file in her hands, "The declining curve is normal; the rising curve is satisfactory. He has a great chance of surviving." And in a room, empty, a kind of watchtower, she points out one of the many incubators, on the other side of a glass partition, porthole, control panel. "He's in the second row, the third from the left." Probes, wires, treatment by mechanical sleeves, the room is sterile. The nurses move about, a mask over their mouths. Only their eyes are visible. And in the incubator, second row, third from the left, I only see a little thing, a little being, so many ties and so much care. When I come back to rue Frochot, Marie says to me, "And so?" I answer, "He's beautiful!" "That's all?" "He looks like he's taking things as they come . . ." She smiles. "You know, Pierrot, it's like a kidnapping. But he'll live. They'll give him back to me. And I'll know how to wait."

Vésinet. Mariette is lying down. They've put her hip in a cast and her whole upper leg. She's sewing a cushion in Indian material, and it makes me laugh. "I've been adopted right off by all the needlework ladies. They've already come to ask me for advice. So everything's going very well. Marie has been so nice. Be sure to tell her that when babies arrive too early, they're sturdier. But what's wrong with your eye?" "There's nothing wrong with it." "Yes there is. Come closer." She sticks the needle into the cushion, puts everything down on the night table and pulls herself up a little. Here I am trapped, forced to bend down, and Mariette kisses me on the forehead, murmurs, "And I hope you're not going to start all over again! It's not worth the trouble." She laughs. And then, suddenly, a steady procession of friends appear in her room, each one older than the next. Between two visits. "It makes me feel younger. And anyway, I'm new here. Do you know that they're working on a Christmas pageant?"

At the hairdresser's, Jean-Louis says to me, "But what's wrong with your eye?" He cuts my hair. Sound of the scissors. He looks at me, in the mirror. "Why do you always pick guys like that?" I answer, "You don't choose. And yourself, with girls?" "Me? Oh, I just take them, and throw them away."

Twice a day, I go to rue Frochot. Marie asks me to go back to boulevard Brune, but in the same sentence, she tells me that it's pointless. "He's fine, just where he is, the way he's being treated, and the way I'm being treated here. All the same, I would have liked to be able to cradle him. All he needs to do is bear up, until we meet. Myself as well. Yes, I did say myself as well. Hold my hand, tighter, tighter than that. Thank you." What strikes me about Marie is her determination, this health, temperament, so close, her eyes, gestures, admissions of weakness like a call for help. "I don't like your summer story, because it's mine. You always tell yourself that everything happens too late. And then, when you think about it, when everything is reduced to an image, you understand that it all happens too early. Or too quickly. I want to name my son John, so he won't stand out, so that he'll have the time to perceive other people before they spot him. Pretty words, my dear Pierrot, but it's high time for all of us to be able to express ourselves. The doctor told me I could leave the day after tomorrow. I'll go back to work, at the studio, on Monday. I want to. And since they won't give me back my little John, my Johnny, before a month or two, I'm asking you to put me up at your place, while I'm waiting. You start teaching again on Monday, too, don't you?" She falls silent, kisses my hands. "I'll make up for not cradling John later." Instinctively, as I was leaning down, I ask her, "Do you need anything?" She teases me: "Don't start talking like everybody else, please. It's a very beautiful story that we're living, because we're living it. Will you call the studio, to let them know?"

The Balto terrace is surrounded by boards. Remodeling. A sign announces the opening of a pub, the King's Arms, rue de Sèvres. I walk by the Lutetia pool building. There is an awning in front of the entrance. They're installing green plants as if for a big wedding, it's the opening night, tonight, of the shopping mall, September 10th. I had a locksmith come by to replace my bedroom doorknob and I've put the dictionary back into place. Among my papers, on the desk. I come across the Nikko Hotel bill. So much time, so many hallways, a whole summer ago. I rip up that scrap of paper. Bernard phones me. "I'd like to see you again . . ." I make a date, for dinner, at my place, a week later. "I'll have this friend, a woman, staying with me, and I'll give you your medal back." Bernard seems happy. He says to me, about the medal, "I didn't dare ask you for it back." I throw out the newspaper Bernard left behind, and the doorknob, broken. I also throw away the giant eraser. Order is being reestablished once more in the apartment. Each time I bring down my trash can to empty it into the building's larger one, as I replace the lid, I think of Boubou exactly in the same way as I think of Duck. A twinge in my heart. And cities are even bigger trash cans, which keep us from living, or which suffocate us. An invitation to a play in which Loïc has a part. A postcard from Jean-Pierre postmarked Patmos, what a coincidence. "It's over. I won't even have had the time to introduce him to you, but it's all for the best. Traveling shapes old age. Your friend Jean-Pierre." In the high-school corridors, I'm coming out of the vice-principal's office, my schedule in my hand, I bump into Barbaroux. "You don't look as well-rested as you have in years past. But what's the matter with your eye?"

A black eye fades away. And yet the blow remains. Struck, delivered, the blow is still landing. I've just reread myself, here, the way you reread a letter. It's not him, it's not me, it's no longer what we lived through. We have become someone else's others. Someone else who might be reading this letter. And yet, everything's here, our love, such as it was, hardly a love which resembles love, a clear text. Perhaps a love affair always happens last summer, and writing, in the summer to come. Our love: footfalls on a bed of pine needles.

I'm searching for a title: "The Young Man of Summer Past," "Duplicate Keys," "Middle of the Night," "The Convict's Fear," "Hopes of Coming Home." No, it will be "Our Share of Time." Some might be able to ridicule and allude to greater works. A major work. But I do not share their delusions of grandeur, petty references. I could only refer to my most naked desire, that of simply being myself and of being myself within this eternal first novel. My despair is full of willfulness; my expectations, of sheer endurance. They will never force words to my lips. As an epigraph to "Our Share of Time," I'll write: "A novel is not told, it is lived. To each man his own feelings, footfalls on a bed of pine needles." And that's the way it is, determined. The ending is happy, painful, and sweet.

And now the hope of publication will begin. Nothing is ever to be taken for granted, and it will make another story. And then success or misunderstanding will begin, it's the same thing. Then, perhaps, multiplied in the privacy of separate readings, this story, this novel, this text, will speak just a little the way people no longer speak. Then, barricades will be thrown up. Intellectuals adore ramparts across a vacuum, they want to be able to say this is my right hand, this is my left. I've seized this text with both hands, the way you embrace someone.

One year later, to the day, first anniversary of meeting Duck, I'm finishing up this novel, first novel, my novel, my love and a failure to give birth. Now, I can walk by myself. I leave to those novelists who deal in appearances and simulacrums the joy of being in each others' company. Of praising and congratulating each other. My deepest sympathy.

And I have not made a mockery of Duck. Love is only human, undifferentiated, all of nature.

Little John was given back to us on November 7th. On the day Marie moved back to her place. She walked into her apartment, the baby in her arms, like a bridegroom carrying his bride on their wedding night and I left them together. From now on, I live more comfortably on the floor above. Even if, at times, while opening my bedroom window, I try to catch a falling cat. He alone, really, escapes my story.

November 9th. 8:00 p.m. My doorbell rings. I open the door. It's Duck. "Can I come in?" I don't say a word, dumbstruck, misfit. He walks past me, his fists in the pockets of a jacket I've never seen him in. He stands, in the hallway, looking vaguely embarrassed, or hostile, I can't tell, perhaps it's an overshyness, or the pride of those who still have the greater part of their lives before them? Duck asks if Marie has had her baby. I answer, "A little too soon." I would have liked to have added, "Because of you." But, as far as that goes, there isn't any evidence. The only thing that counts is life, Marie crying for joy, boulevard Brune, when they finally place her baby in her arms. She cradles him. "I was fed up with seeing him in that incubator, hooked up to all those wires . . ." Duck murmurs, "I'd really like to see it, anyway . . ." I repeat, "Anyway?" Duck falls silent. I sit down at my desk, my hands resting flat on a stack of homework to be corrected. Duck remains standing, motionless, opposite me, his head down, looking slighted, stubborn, shocked, no way to tell, I'll never know. A text can only give a single version. It is always biased. As a mirror-image of the couple, it can only be unfair. Duck says nothing, nothing, nothing, for several minutes on end. The telephone rings, I don't answer. It's Marie calling me for dinner. She holds the baby in her arms, and it's her I feed, like a child. For two days she has been saying to me, "I can't let go of him. I'm afraid now. I'm holding onto him. I promise I won't hold him too much, but now, I need to." I proceed with the feeding of the mother.

Duck sighs, turns on his heels, looks at the table, the sofa, the bookshelves, the hallway, the bedroom door, and the closed door, the repaired one, mine. Once again he faces me, raises his head and says very confidently, "So, then, are we going to see each other again or not?" I look straight into his eyes. I have no answer to give, neither yes nor no. I look straight, very straight into his eyes and I read nothing, really nothing in them which might enable me to speak, or simply answer. To continue.

He lowers his head, clenches his fists in his jacket pocket. The black eye has disappeared, but I still have a nervous tic in my left eye. A bothersome detail. Very fortunately, Duck doesn't see it. Those kinds of details to which one lends a great importance. I breathe in, I sniff, I inhale once again the scent of spring and the smell of summer. Roussel makes a little place, in the gravel, for his feet. I must not answer. The new students in my classes have nothing in their eyes either. On the high-school walls, a new slogan, in tar: "Tomorrow, let's wipe them out!" But everything has already been wiped out. I no longer see life as they do. And yet everything is beginning over again. Or perhaps it's only an impression? I watch Duck. I haven't answered. He raises his head, avoids my eyes, pulls his left hand out of his jacket pocket and slaps down, violently, the duplicate set of keys from Peyroc. He leaves. I get up, catch the door that he wants to slam, and go out onto the landing. He's rushing down the stairs. I shout, without planning to,

"The next time open your heart!" He answers from the third-floor landing, "The next time it'll start all over again the same way!" The telephone rings. I go back into my apartment. I pick up the receiver. It's Marie. "You sound like you're out of breath." I answer, "I'm coming!" The building door slams, like an echo in the courtyard. 113 rue Boursault, 75017 Paris. Courtyard stairs, fourth floor on the right. Pierre Forgue. Signed: Pierre Forgue.

Joucas, December '78.
Joucas, April '79.
A Emmanuel.